MW00794953

A REBEL WITHOUT CLAWS

JULIETTE CROSS

**UNION
SQUARE
& CO.**

NEW YORK

UNION SQUARE & CO.

NEW YORK

UNION SQUARE & CO. and the distinctive Union Square & Co. logo are
trademarks of Sterling Publishing Co., Inc.

Union Square & Co., LLC, is a subsidiary of Sterling Publishing Co., Inc.

Text © 2025 Juliette Cross
Cover illustration © 2025 Union Square & Co., LLC

ISBN 978-1-4549-5368-5 (paperback)

For information about custom editions, special sales, and premium purchases,
please contact specialsales@unionsquareandco.com

Printed in Canada

2 4 6 8 10 9 7 5 3 1

unionsquareandco.com

Cover design and illustration by Jenny Zemanek

For my precious princess, Noelle

CHAPTER 1

~RONAN~

"I don't know shit about bodywork."

I watched the vein in my uncle's temple bulge, his jaws clamp tight, and his pulse jump in his throat. His heart rate picked up speed as he glared at me across the kitchen table, eyes flaring bright green with his wolf.

His fury had no effect on me. Nothing had any effect on me. Nothing had for a while.

Since Aunt Sarah had had enough of me in Austin and kicked me out, I figured New Orleans was as good an option as any for my new plans. Thankfully, Uncle Shane had agreed to let me crash at his place till I got on my feet again.

Besides, I'd worn out my welcome in more ways than one in Austin.

"Ronan." Uncle Shane blew out a heavy breath, clasping his hands around his coffee mug on the table. "You don't know shit about shit. Except how to get drunk, get arrested, and get your face beat to hell."

I grinned, the cut on my lip stinging. "Don't worry. No matter how bad I look, I won the fight." I win all of them, the legal and illegal ones.

"That's not what I'm worried about." He growled. "You need to find a place in this world, son. A future. One that doesn't include prison."

I'd heard this speech more than once from many different people—my juvie parole officer, my high school art teacher, my grandfather, my aunt, and now Uncle Shane.

"No offense"—I leaned back in the kitchen chair—"but my dreams never included getting greasy working in a garage."

"You got other options I don't know about?"

Not yet. But I would soon enough. My lengthy pause seemed to answer his question.

"That's what I thought. As long as you're here, you'll work for your room and board." His scowl deepened. "And we do more than fix cars. Our custom paint jobs are the best in all of Louisiana. From what Sarah told me, you're pretty talented."

"I don't do that for customers," I snapped.

That was for me, and me alone. My muscles locked, tension straightening my spine.

I didn't like people knowing or talking about my artwork. It was private. I sure as fuck wasn't going to dance to some rich dude's tune who wanted skulls and flames on his three-hundred-grand Harley.

"Fine." He stood and set his cup in the sink. "You'll work with Ty. He's in charge of the engine work." He grabbed his Blood

Moon Body Shop cap off the counter. "Be there in ten." Then he slammed the door behind him.

Heaving a sigh, I let my new reality sink in. I knew enough about mechanics that I was comfortable with cars, but I'd never done bodywork, and I had no interest in learning a new trade.

What I wanted to do was scout out New Orleans for their ring and find partners for my own team.

Later.

Now, I had to get my ass in gear and make Uncle Shane happy so he didn't kick me out before I had another revenue stream coming in.

I splashed my face and checked out the purple bruise on my eye that was fading to green, then ran wet fingers through my hair.

After pulling on my jeans and a Bad Omens T-shirt, I headed out the door. Uncle Shane had built his house on the property next to his body shop. The rest of the pack lived close by on the Westbank of New Orleans, though Ty had told me yesterday when I met him that he lived in the city.

I strode across the two acres to the shop, a radio playing Puddle of Mudd in one of the open bays. The sun was barely up, but it was already around seventy. Summers in Louisiana weren't much different than in Texas, it seemed.

As soon as I stepped into the first bay, Ty popped up from an open hood. "Morning. I heard you're with me today."

"You'll probably be holding my hand for a while." I headed around the old Camaro he was working on.

Ty smiled, wiping his hands on a rag, wearing the BMBS coveralls with the howling wolf emblem. "You know anything about cars?"

"Enough. I refurbished my Bronco." I gestured toward my uncle's white house where my '71 Ford Bronco was parked.

"Still needs a paint job." He leaned over the engine of the '68 Camaro. "We could do it here."

"Not sure I could afford the shop's prices." I'd seen some of the invoices stacked on Uncle Shane's kitchen counter.

"I'm sure you'd get the family discount."

I wasn't so sure. I peered out the open bay at my Bronco with its worn, rust-brown paint job. "She looks rough, but she rides like a dream."

"Good to know you're good on engines." He walked to the wall of tools that stretched across two bays in the back of the garage. "That's mostly what I handle. A lot of the jobs we get are for bodywork only—interior and exterior finishing. But nine times out of ten, we'll find that they're in need of work under the hood too."

I walked around to the open hood. "What's the issue with the Camaro?"

"The guy swapped out the two-thirty engine for a three-ninety-six, and the radiator can't handle it."

"You'll need to change out the transmission, too, with an engine that size."

"Exactly." He glanced at me appraisingly. "I just got the radiator in and was changing it out. Transmission won't be in for a few days."

"Cool."

I settled in beside him and helped, though he didn't really need me. Still, I was going to do what I was told to make Uncle Shane happy.

Contrary to what my family might think, I didn't enjoy disappointing the people I cared about. Seeing the hurt look on Aunt Sarah's face when she told me I had to leave had gutted me. She didn't want to kick me out, but she had two young pups to raise, and I wasn't exactly the role model her boys needed. I just didn't care enough to change who I was. Moving on was always easier.

"What happened to your face?"

"I ran into a fist or two."

"Do that often?"

"Often enough."

Ty was tall and lean-muscled, built like a welterweight. The deep claw-shaped scars down one side of his throat told me he'd been in a fight before.

In the wolf ring, fighters could unsheathe claws and use teeth. Their opponent just had to be fast enough to get out of the way. The fact that I'd never used either and was the champion of south Texas proved I was the best.

Knowing Louisiana had yet to outlaw wolf cage fighting opened a door when Aunt Sarah kicked me out and Uncle Shane agreed to take me in. After a search on the SuperNet revealed there was an established ring in New Orleans with a statewide undefeated team, I knew what my next goal was.

"Damn, man." Ty glanced up at me, pliers in his hand. "I can hear your wheels turning. Something on your mind?"

"Always."

He didn't push for more. I'd known Ty less than twenty-four hours, but he seemed a trustworthy guy, and I had to trust someone to get the information I needed.

"Hey, so where do the younger wolves hang out? Bars and stuff."

"How young do you mean?"

"Like our age."

He grinned and walked back to the workbench behind us. "I'm forty-one."

That shouldn't have been shocking. Werewolves aged slowly, our lifespans five to seven times longer than humans.

"You don't seem it," I told him.

Ty carried himself like a wolf in his twenties, like me.

"I've been told."

He leaned under the hood again. "I'm not a club scene guy. The Cauldron is a cool place. Live music on weekends. It's owned and run by our local Enforcer."

"It's a bar?"

"A pub and restaurant actually. Lots of our kind frequent there."

"Good to know." Because I would *not* be going to this Cauldron place. I'd rather stay off the radar of the Enforcer of this city.

"Zack and Bowie are always dragging ass when they work early-morning shifts. I've heard them mention a club called Howler's."

"Let me guess. Werewolf-owned."

He laughed under his breath. "Yeah. Bowie has a paint job to finish this afternoon. You could ask him about it then, see if it's what you're looking for."

I helped him replace the radiator on the Camaro and while he was rambling on about a Corvette we had coming in tomorrow, a scent caught my attention, sweet and warm like the desert rose that grew back home.

I peered around the open hood and—*holy fucking shit.* Standing right inside the second bay in the sunshine, talking to Rhett, another shop guy who handled the customers, was the most stunning woman I'd ever seen.

She held a tablet, showing something to Rhett with a stylus in her hand, her brow pinched in concentration. Her heart-shaped face was tipped up, freckles sprinkling her nose and cheeks. A pile of wavy copper hair was twisted in one of those knots, a curly strand blowing across her lips.

Rhett studied her tablet, saying something I didn't give a shit about. All I could do was stare at her. Inhaling a deep breath, I tried to catch her intoxicating scent again. She was a witch, for sure. I detected that particular designation right away. Usually, that would be enough to have me dismissing her. Witches didn't typically give werewolves the time of day.

I closed my eyes, focusing on the way my bones suddenly felt heavy, my skin too tight, my blood thick and pulsing with a dull throb. I'd never had a visceral reaction to meeting a woman where I felt incapable of looking or moving away. I hadn't met her yet, though. Opening my eyes again, my fascination amplified at the way the sun glowed around her like a halo.

What kind of witch was she? Maybe it was her powers that had captured me so completely. She must be an Influencer. A Warper, some called them, witches who used their magic to persuade people to do anything they wanted. But I hadn't even talked to her, so how could she be using her magic to influence me?

She shifted from one foot to another, and my body stiffened, readying itself. But for what?

Then she tucked a curl behind her ear and licked her lips. I groaned.

"Dude, pick up your jaw, stop looking, and don't even fucking think about it."

"I can't stop looking and thinking. God. *Damn.*" I pressed a hand to my sternum, suddenly having heartburn.

Ty huffed and whispered, "You're a dead man if you even try."

"Is she taken?" Something pinched inside my chest at the thought.

"It's not a boyfriend you have to worry about."

"Who then?"

"For starters, her very protective father, who would gut you where you stand if he saw you drooling over her. Then there are her two brothers. Diego would rip you a new asshole. Last but not least, there are her many uncles, who include two old and powerful vampires and two grim reapers, one of whom could turn you into dust. Literally."

Not one thing he said deterred me from my new mission. If anything, it spurred me on. I liked a challenge. I loved the forbidden.

And that goddess glowing in the sunlight in pink cutoffs and a floral tank top was the most bewitching forbidden fruit I'd ever wanted to taste.

"Don't do it," warned Ty under his breath.

I ignored his warning and walked closer, unable to stop my body from moving toward her. Rhett had just stepped away to the workbench on the far wall.

She sensed my approach and turned her head in my direction. Her emerald eyes struck me near dumb. When I was finally within two feet of her, I forced my legs to lock in place, because my natural urge was to step right up to her and wrap her close, then take a deep whiff of her drugging scent. That certainly would not make a good first impression.

She observed me carefully with intelligent eyes, taking me all in. I was at least a foot taller than her, but she didn't step back or look away. I liked that. She didn't intimidate easily, and I was a lot to take.

"You're an Influencer, aren't you?"

"What makes you think that?"

I swallowed hard, tongue-tied, because I couldn't tell her the truth. "You're not?"

"I'm an Aura." She smiled, raising gooseflesh on my arms.

I liked the way her eyes tilted up at the tips when she smiled. I rubbed my sternum. The heartburn was back.

"I'm Ronan," I finally said rather dumbly.

"You're trouble."

I chuckled. "Nothing you can't handle."

"How do you know? Maybe I'm the wilting type."

"No. You're not a type at all."

"What am I then?"

I shook my head, drinking in her beauty. "The kind of woman to make a man's world stop turning."

Her lips parted, pupils dilated, breath quickened, and heartbeat thudded faster. All the signs of attraction. Her reaction curled inside me, tightening my body, ensnaring me even more.

She tilted her head and held out her hand. "I'm Celine."

I reached out, my hand engulfing hers, and brushed my thumb over her soft knuckles. My pulse grew loud in my own ears as it raced faster, my head dizzy with desire. And confusion.

Because something happened then that hadn't since the night in Amarillo when I was twelve.

From the deepest part of me, a sizzle of magic warmed my blood, awakening as I—stunned and spellbound—held this young woman's hand. I didn't understand what was happening at first, but then he made himself known. I'd thought he was gone forever, but there was no mistaking his presence. Out of the dark, my wolf locked on Celine . . . and growled.

CHAPTER 2

~CELINE~

Who was this guy?

He had a bruised face and a cut lip, but it was his subtle Texan drawl in a deep baritone that had caught my attention the most. And there was no way I could've missed his wolf growling when we shook hands.

That was a bit daring and aggressive. I'd met plenty of Diego's werewolf friends, and none would even think about growling around me in that flirty purring sort of way. It was a possessive move for a wolf. Of course, Diego would've beaten the hell out of any of his friends who pulled that sort of crap around me.

I hugged my tablet to my chest, checking out his aura, unable to keep from smiling.

"What's that smile for?" he asked, his piercing blue eyes intent on mine. His voice had a raspy edge that swept goose bumps over my skin.

"Your aura is quite pretty."

"Come again?" His grin widened. "You're saying I'm pretty?"

"No." I laughed. "Your aura is, though. It's kind of a pink-ish purple."

His eyebrows—a darker shade than his sandy blond hair—shot up. "Pink?"

"No one ever told you?"

"You're the first Aura witch I've ever met."

"Stop. That can't be true." My magical ability as an empath read his energy quickly, loving the super-confident vibes emanating from him.

"Scout's honor." He put his hand over his heart.

I laughed again. "You were not a Cub Scout."

"Why would you say that?" His sultry gaze and smirking expression was undeniably flirty. "You shouldn't judge a book by its cover."

He dipped his head and lowered his voice, inching a little closer into my space, his gaze never leaving mine. His attention was intense and electrifying and I couldn't look away if my life depended on it.

"You're right. I shouldn't," I admitted, a little ashamed of myself. Plus, that twinge of old unease crept in for a second. "Just because you're a bit"—my gaze flicked to the bruises and cuts on his face, lingering at the one on his wide mouth—"rough around the edges, doesn't mean you're . . ."

His brows rose again, his expression open, urging me to continue, but I couldn't find the right words. For someone who never lacked them, I suddenly felt tilted, off-center, ever since this werewolf had engulfed my hand with his own.

"I'd love to hear the rest of that sentence," he teased.

"Sorry," I apologized quickly, "I lost my train of thought."

He chuckled, the husky sound warming me inside out. "I know the feeling, Celine. I'm a little lost here myself."

"Celine!" Rhett called from the open office door in the garage. He glared at Ronan with annoyance before saying, "I've got it pulled up on the desktop. Come see."

"Coming," I called back, not quite ready to walk away. "So who are you exactly?"

His confident smile hadn't left his face since he'd first walked up, and I found that extraordinarily attractive. I was born and raised among the most capable, confident, and intelligent men. From my father to my brothers to my many uncles and cousins, they all seemed to have that internal masculine factor that told the world they didn't need to prove that they were clever and cool; it was a simple fact. Even my introverted, shy brother Joaquin could make a weaker man wither beneath his superior air.

This was also probably why my dating life had always been so abysmal. Some of that was my fault, and the rest had been borne of the extremely overprotective men in my life.

"Ronan Reed," he said, giving me his full name this time. "Shane Reed is my uncle."

"Uncle Shane is your uncle?"

He flinched, his smile slipping for once, his expression paling. "You're not his niece." He swallowed hard, his prominent Adam's apple bobbing. "Are you?"

I belted out a laugh at his obvious disappointment that we could somehow be related. "No. He's such a close family friend I call him Uncle Shane."

He spread his palm over his chest. "Thank fuck. I almost had a heart attack."

I laughed harder, which softened his features again. "That would be a bad thing if I was blood-related to him?" I teased.

"It would be a travesty."

His sincerity made me quiet and contemplative, my gaze drawn back to his eyes, so deep blue I felt caught in a drowning pool. And for some reason, I was okay with that.

"So"—I cleared my throat—"what made you move here to New Orleans?"

"A lot of things," he said vaguely.

"Do any of those things happen to be related to the state of your face?"

"Yeah," he answered coolly, still intently watching me. "But it's fine. I plan to make a new start here."

I nodded, liking the sound of that. "That's good." Though I still didn't know exactly why he needed a new start.

"Celine!" Rhett called again.

"I'd better go."

"Wait." He stepped forward as I was about to turn away. "Can I get your number?"

"Um, no, I don't think that's a good idea." Even if my impulse was to give it to him, I wasn't a fool—not anymore anyway. I truly didn't know him well enough to hand over my number just yet.

"Why not?" His smile had returned, which was strange since I was in the middle of turning him down. Or rather, delaying the inevitable.

"I don't know you."

"Of course you do. We just met."

"Meeting and knowing someone are two totally different things."

He dipped his chin like he agreed. "That's fine. I don't mind a chase, Celine. But I sure hope you let me catch you."

My heart sped at that imagery. I remained still as he gently pried one of my arms free from where I'd crossed them over my tablet against my chest and took my hand in both of his.

"Very nice meeting you," he crooned softly, intimately.

He held my hand in a semblance of shaking it in departure, but what he was actually doing was cradling it gently and brushing one thumb across the back of my hand, his other thumb caressing the middle of my palm. It was a strangely sensual sensation.

"Till we meet again," he said, finally dropping my hand, which I tucked back to my chest like he'd injured it somehow.

Of course, he hadn't. Not at all, but I was a little dumbstruck over the entire encounter.

"How are you so sure we'll meet again?" I asked.

Ronan simply laughed as he backed away. He winked before he turned and strode back to Ty, working on a car in bay one.

Finally, I was able to move my legs, forcing them to walk away from him and into the office where Rhett was waiting.

"Here's how your design will look on the cover plate and panel," said Rhett. "I just need to know if you have a smaller design for the ribs and frame before I present it to the customer."

Over Rhett's shoulder, I stared at my latest design on the monitor. This kind of work was far from what I did as my day job, but it was also fun as well as being good supplemental income.

"Sure, I can have that to you by Friday."

Rhett was one of the Blood Moon pack who worked and operated the Body Shop. He also treated me the same as all the other men in my life—with profound overprotective instincts. So I wasn't surprised when he said, "Best not get too close to Ronan."

"Why's that?"

"He's been in a lot of trouble. It always tends to find him."

I already knew that. My magic had told me so the second I laid eyes on him. Unfortunately, I've always been drawn to the broken, wanting to fix things if I could. Not that I saw him as someone to fix, only that I couldn't keep my empathic heart from reaching out to him, wanting to know him, help him.

"He mentioned wanting a new start."

Rhett nodded his head, running a grease-smudged hand through his auburn hair. "True, true. I just wouldn't want to— I mean, I don't know that your dad would be happy about you two keeping company."

That made me laugh. "Oh, you're one hundred percent right about that." But there was no one good enough for me in my dad's eyes. I couldn't choose men to date based on what my father would want.

If it were up to him, I'd only date future preachers who said "yes, sir" and "no, sir" and believed in sex only after marriage and maybe not even then.

"Good," said Rhett on a sigh of obvious relief, assuming I had agreed to not talk to Ronan. "I'll hear from you on Friday then. You can just send the new designs through our Google folder."

In other words, no need to come into the shop and bump into Shane's naughty nephew.

"Sure thing. Thanks, Rhett."

I wasn't sure if I was on the right track with this design, which is why I'd stopped by today. Interestingly, I rarely came to the shop, but for some reason I had decided I should pop in and go over this one with Rhett in person.

Smiling at the thought that the Goddess who guided our witch magic might be playing matchmaker, I swished back out of his office and through the garage. And if I swayed my hips a little more than usual, I couldn't be blamed. The wolf leaning over the hood, his hands braced on the frame of the car, his hypnotic blue eyes solely on me, already had me under his spell.

I sure hoped he planned to chase me soon.

CHAPTER 3

~CELINE~

"How long before you know if you passed?" I asked.

My college roommate Lauren had recently taken the bar. She currently lived in Baton Rouge where she'd just graduated from LSU Law and had called to catch me up on how the exam went. We tried to video chat as often as we could.

"One to three months." She snorted in that unladylike way that always made me smile. For someone who came from old New Orleans money, she acted the opposite. Sometimes I wondered if her laissez-faire, often crude demeanor was her own way of trying to separate herself from her upbringing.

"Like it wasn't torture enough having to study for months for the damn thing," she added while putting on eyeliner in the bathroom mirror, "we now have to wait months for results. It's fucking ridiculous. But guess what?" She paused to grin at me in that mischievous way of hers.

"What?" I was laying on my bed, petting my cat Petunia and holding the phone with my other hand.

"I'm moving back home!"

"*Finally*," I exclaimed excitedly and sat up.

She belted out one of her infectious laughs. "I thought you'd be happy."

"When? Have you found a new place yet?"

"Next week and no new place yet." She curled her lip in distaste, now applying mascara. "I'm going to live with my dad for now."

"I'm sure that'll make him happy."

"Yes, but I don't want to have to witness his revolving door of women."

"Your dad lives in like a ten-thousand-square-foot house. I'm sure you can avoid seeing him and his lady friends."

"It's only nine thousand," she countered cheekily. "But I plan to land a good law firm as soon as I get the results telling me I've passed with amazing, flying colors."

"You will. You're like the poster child of manifesting your own success."

"It works." She screwed her mascara top tight. "And I'm not even a witch."

"You should've been."

While most humans didn't know about the existence of supernaturals, there were always some we allowed into our world. Not counting the humans who frequented vampire dens as blood-hosts to get the high from vampire toxin, there were genuine human friends and even family who knew about us but kept our secrets. Most people would think they were crazy anyway if they started spouting about the supernaturals living among us.

Lauren turned to face me fully, propping her hands on her voluptuous hips. "No need for magic when I've got all this." She gestured to her fabulous figure in the cutest blue jumpsuit.

"Got a hot date?"

"No. Just drinks with my study group. Though there is this one guy who's been eyeing me for a while. I think tonight's his lucky night. What about you? Any new men in your life?"

I couldn't suppress the smile spreading across my face. "Well, actually . . ."

"Omigod, Celine. Tell me now!"

"Keep your panties on." I laughed and picked up the phone. "His name is Ronan Reed. He's a werewolf."

"Shut *up*. Sounds delicious already. What else?"

"He's extremely . . ." I paused, trying to find the right words.

"Hot?"

"Yes." I laughed.

"Sweeeet. Tell me more, please."

"He's"—I put my hand in the air, quite a bit higher than my head—"about this tall, has blond hair, blue eyes, and the sexiest voice I've ever heard. And he's extraordinarily alluring. Even with his bruised-up face."

"He was beaten up?"

I nodded, frowning. "He'd been in a fight with someone, but I didn't find out why. He said he moved out here for a fresh start."

Lauren arched a brow, now walking with me through her apartment. "He doesn't sound like the kind of guy your dad would approve of."

I huffed out a laugh. "My dad would *not* approve."

"Fabulous. Now I really like him."

I started walking with my phone downstairs, craving a snack. "Nope."

"I one hundred percent applaud your rebellion, but that's going to be a bit tricky still living at home."

My parents were out together at the park. Otherwise, I wouldn't have even mentioned Ronan within the walls of the house. My dad had supersonic hearing. Literally. But Mom and Dad took walks in the afternoons after the sun had dipped lower. The summer was waning, but the heat index was still unbearable this time of year.

"Don't I know it," I said as I walked downstairs. "I'm close to having enough money to move out, but not just yet."

My parents offered to give me the money to rent my own apartment, but I'd moved back home after grad school two years ago while I built up my counseling practice and saved for a house. I didn't want to waste money, sinking it into rent. Rates were high enough in the Lower Garden District where I wanted to live close to family and my practice. Dad offered to give me the down payment, but it was important to me to save the money myself. I wanted complete independence when I bought my own place.

The truth is, I was spoiled rotten. I was fortunate to be raised in an extremely loving—if not sometimes overbearing—family. I wanted for nothing, truly, except a space of my own that I bought *on* my own. Dad didn't understand, but Mom did.

My brother Joaquin already lived on his own above his restaurant, the Silver Moon Café, a few blocks down Magazine Street.

He'd had no problem borrowing money from our parents, but his investment in the café had already turned a profit well enough to pay most of it back. My income was modest since I was still building up clientele. I didn't want to be in debt to my parents or anyone. It was difficult enough exerting any independence in a family this size with so many overprotective and opinionated relatives telling me what was best for me.

Thankfully, I was close to moving out. I figured I'd be ready to do serious house shopping by the end of the year.

"Well, I'm proud of you. It's about time you go against the grain and get yourself a bad boy."

She said that last part as I rounded into the kitchen.

"What bad boy?" asked my brother Diego roughly.

"Shit," I mumbled, stopping at the entryway.

Diego stood shirtless and barefoot in a pair of jeans in the open refrigerator door, holding a carton of milk and wiping away the milk mustache with the back of his hand, his longish black wavy hair a total mess, making him look even more like a rock star.

"Diego's there?" asked Lauren. "Let me talk to him."

I faced my phone to my brother, mostly to distract Diego from what he'd just overheard.

"Speaking of bad boys," said Lauren, "it's good to see you're keeping nice and fit, Diego."

My brother grinned shamelessly, running his free hand down his washboard abs. "I've always told you that you're welcome to sample the goods, Lauren." Then he put the carton of milk back in the fridge.

I faced the phone toward me again. "Don't encourage him. His ego is already entirely too big."

Diego stopped as he passed me and grabbed my wrist to turn the phone toward him. "That's not all that's big."

"Ew! Gross!" I jerked my phone back and shoved him away.

He laughed as he walked out of the back door and toward the carriage house apartment where he lived. Diego had no problem living with Mom and Dad forever if they let him. He had free meals, groceries, and rent while he tried to make it big with his band. Granted, they were really good, but so far they were only doing small gigs around New Orleans.

"Thank you for that," I told Lauren. Though they'd never hooked up, thank goodness, they flirted shamelessly. But I knew exactly what she was doing just now. Lauren was my ride or die girlfriend and always got me out of a fix. She was well aware that Diego was like my father when it came to the guys I dated, sticking his nose into my business where it didn't belong.

"Always happy to help. Okay, I've gotta go or I'll be late. But I'll see you next week."

"Have fun tonight, and text me when you're back in town."

I ended the call and opened the cabinet, finding the tortilla chips, and then grabbed the salsa from the fridge. I found that crunchy snacks somehow helped when I was anxious.

The back door opened and closed again, and my other brother Joaquin walked in with a covered dish in hand. Though Diego, Joaquin, and I were triplets, I had two totally different relationships with them. While Diego was more of the protective brother, Joaquin was more my friend. We'd always been pretty close. So I wasn't surprised when he immediately picked up on some of my anxious vibes.

"Hey. What's wrong?"

"Why would anything be wrong?" I asked even though I knew he could always read me so well.

He rolled his eyes and set the platter covered with tinfoil onto the kitchen counter. He often brought us leftovers from the café. Then he walked to the counter where we kept the wine and liquor. "Is this a wine conversation or a bourbon one?"

Heaving a sigh, I said, "I don't know if I want to tell you."

He lifted the bottle of Dao with a questioning look.

"Yes," was all I said.

I waited while he uncorked and poured two glasses. He was dressed in his black slacks and white button-down, his regular uniform he wore under his chef's apron every day at the café. His dark auburn hair was beginning to hang down too far in the front.

"You need a haircut," I observed as he sat next to me.

He didn't bother to respond to that and instead went for the jugular as usual. "Who is he?"

"How do you know it's about a guy?"

He took a sip of wine and didn't answer. I was wondering if he had inherited psychic abilities along with his Enforcer designation as a warlock. He was both warlock and werewolf and possibly the smartest, most intuitive man I knew.

"Yes, I met someone, and I'm fairly positive Dad won't like him."

"Why not?"

"Mainly because he doesn't fit the mold of the kind of guy Dad wants me to date."

"You mean, he's not a eunuch?"

I nearly choked on my wine. "Exactly. He's not a eunuch. He's very much a . . . virile male. From what I can tell."

He smiled. "He's a werewolf, isn't he?"

"How'd you know?"

"Because of the way your face is all lit up right now."

I pressed my palms to my cheeks, like I could feel the blush there. "Why would that mean he's a werewolf?"

He shrugged one shoulder. "Just a hunch. I had a feeling you'd finally get around to dating one seeing as all the men you love the most in your life are also werewolves."

He was right. It did make sense, and yet, I had never dated one.

"I think that could be good for you," he added.

"Really?" I was surprised to hear him say that.

"Celine." Then he sighed heavily. "You need to follow your heart. And stop trying to make the wrong guys fit into who you *think* you should be dating. Who you *think* are safe."

We'd had this conversation before. I always went for the super *safe* kind of guy, not one who might be too intimidating or dominant or who might remind me of a certain someone in my past. Because of that, I'd been very unlucky in my dating life so far.

"When do I get to meet him?" he asked.

"I'm not ready for that. We aren't even dating. We just met, but I"—I twisted the stem of my wineglass between my fingers—"I want to date him. Very much."

"That's a start. When will you see him again?"

"I'm not sure. I didn't give him my number when he asked for it."

"Why not?"

"I wanted to, but it seemed kind of nuts. I didn't really know him, and . . ." I exhaled a deep breath. "I wasn't absolutely sure I should."

My old anxiety reared its ugly head, reminding me not to trust too easily. Once, I had trusted someone and had almost come to harm. Thank the Goddess, Aunt Violet had seen what would happen before it did.

He reached out a hand and squeezed my arm on the table. "I get it. But not every guy is like him. You have to trust yourself."

"Wish I'd sensed it that last time," I said softly.

"You were young and still growing into your magic."

Joaquin knew I didn't like to talk or think about that part of my life from high school. It was enough to trigger my anxiety even after I'd learned to move past it all. I closed my eyes, breathed deep, and pictured a clear, blue sky, leaves rustling in the wind, a cool breeze on my face. My mom's trick always worked. I opened my eyes and felt calm again.

"Tell me this," he said. "Is his aura positive? Is it good energy?"

"Yes."

"Would you be afraid to be alone with him?"

"No." Actually, I sincerely loved the idea of being alone with him.

"Good. Now raise your glass."

I raised it, then he clinked his glass to mine.

"Cheers to my sister dating a hot, virile werewolf. May the fates send one my way soon."

I laughed. "You'd date a werewolf?"

"Why wouldn't I?"

"They seem kind of, I don't know, wild for your taste."

"Oh, sweet sister of mine, you don't know my taste."

"That could be true. Apparently, I didn't even know my own until very recently."

He chuckled. "Wait till Samara hears about this."

My cousin Samara was my best friend. Smiling, I said, "Yes, I think she'll enjoy this bit of news. But don't tell Dad or Diego. I'm not ready for all of that nonsense yet."

"Your secret is safe with me." He stood and walked to the counter. "Now how about some of my shrimp and sausage pasta? I think it will go better with the wine than chips and salsa."

Finally relaxed, we settled in to eat, while I tried to figure out a way to meet up with Ronan Reed again.

CHAPTER 4

~RONAN~

"It's not street fighting. You can use more than your fists."
I stepped up and took Zack's place to face Bowie, while they
both watched. "Don't forget to use your legs."

I demonstrated a sweep, taking Bowie to the ground quickly,
then put a knee to his chest and raised my fist, all in about
three seconds.

"Daaaamn," drawled Zack on a laugh.

Bowie's eyes glinted bright green, his wolf surfacing. I was
used to seeing that in the ring. I stood and held out a hand to
help him up. He took it.

I was grateful both Zack and Bowie had agreed to join my
team, but neither had formal fighting experience. Bar fights on
occasion, yes, but not cage fighting, which was a much more
complex animal.

"Why don't we just shift and then really take care of business?" Bowie combed a hand over his close-cropped dark hair.

He was built with more muscle, which made him tougher but slower.

I'd wondered about his unusual name. He said his Creole grandmother, who mostly spoke French, used to call him her little "beau," meaning *handsome man*. He started calling himself bo-ey which eventually became what everyone called him. His real name was Marcelle.

"If someone shifted, then it would turn to murder," I explained simply. "Werewolf form is forbidden. You can use claws if you want, but that's it. If you shift, you automatically lose the match and the fight is over."

"Has anyone ever shifted in the ring with you?" asked Zack, leaning back against the old, gutted mustang, which had apparently been forgotten here behind the painting shed.

Zack was built leaner than his best friend Bowie. He kept his light brown hair a little long and shaggy. He always seemed to be smiling, but the kind of smile that looked like he was up to something, even when he wasn't.

"Yeah." I grinned. "I'm pretty good at pissing off my opponent." Bowie chuckled. "I bet."

"This one guy, he was from New York. Was considered the best of the best. My opposing team in Austin brought him in to take me down."

Zack and Bowie both grinned, then Zack said, "But he didn't."

"No way, man. This guy thought he was king of the mountain. He was about as big as one, though. Built like you, Bowie. But he was arrogant. I danced around him in the ring, getting a jab or a kick in, then circling." I laughed. "He was big but slow, so I started mocking him for it. Trash-talking. Saying how I thought New Yorkers were quick when he was slow as fuck. Shit like that."

Zack and Bowie laughed.

"It didn't take long before that fucker was sprouting hair and shifting into his fifteen-foot-tall monster."

"Damn." Zack shoved Bowie. "He does sound like you."

"What happened?" asked Bowie, seeming concerned. "How'd they keep him from killing you when he shifted?"

"There are handlers at every bout who carry tranquilizers that would knock down a rhino."

"They tranquilized him?" Zack's expressive eyes widened in surprise.

"Oh yeah. And everyone knows the rules. You fully shift, you'll get darted. And that shit will knock you down fast and hard. You won't wake up for a day or two and will have the nastiest fucking headache. At least, that's what they tell me."

"So you've never shifted in the ring?" Bowie asked.

"Nah." I shook my head, my gut tightening. "I never needed to. I can beat anybody." It wasn't bragging. It was true. "And I'm going to teach you two to do the same."

Bowie stood, ready to go again. "Well, let's get to it."

I spent the next two hours showing them different maneuvers, different combinations—kick and dodge, then punch as their opponent turns, double-punch, then sweep with the leg to get them on their back, corralling them to the cage so they could pin them and punch. We were all sweating by mid-morning.

"That's enough for today," I told them, panting as I picked up one of the bottles of Liquid I.V. I'd made this morning and chugged it.

I picked up the other two on the Mustang's hood and tossed them to the guys. We drank in silence for a minute, catching our breath.

It was Sunday so the shop was closed to customers, but that didn't mean there wasn't work to do. I'd told Zack and Bowie to come in early so I could show them some moves and see if they were really interested in wolf cage fighting. After Ty had introduced us yesterday, I'd talked their ears off about the underground cage fighting in Austin, and they were hooked.

While it was illegal in Texas, it wasn't here in Louisiana. They had their own league by region. This one called NOWFC—New Orleans Wolf Fighting Championship. That meant I could make a legit career out of it here without worrying about the local Enforcer shutting us down. I should've moved here with Uncle Shane a long time ago.

I was still waiting to hear back from this guy named Baron I found on Instagram. There were dozens of pics of him and his team—the Iron Claws, stupid-ass name—at actual fights, some in a gym sparring, and several of them holding up a championship belt that had a giant golden buckle with a wolf head howling at the center of a New Orleans skyline.

This guy Baron was at the center of almost every pic so I was sure he led the champion team here. He'd know where to register my team and when the next fight would be. The NOWFC website was temporarily down.

Until I heard from him, there was plenty to do. Train these two, find at least one more teammate, and find more time with that insanely beautiful witch, Celine. God. *Damn.* I needed to stop daydreaming about her and make my next move. I just still wasn't sure how aggressive I should be. She seemed so gentle and soft, and my instincts to grab and claim weren't the ones I should be listening to. Even as I thought about it, a deep, low growl rumbled in my belly.

What the fuck was that about? I hadn't heard my wolf—not fucking once—since my mother died.

"What's got your wolf all riled?" asked Zack, wiping his sweaty brow with his arm.

I chuckled, realizing they didn't know how strange that truly was. My wolf had been nonexistent my entire fucking life. And now, he wakes up after he takes notice of an awfully alluring witch.

"I was thinking about this girl I met the other day."

"Yeah?" asked Bowie, smiling for the first time. "Where'd you meet her? You haven't been here long."

"In the garage."

"No fucking way. That's just my luck," complained Zack. "Some hot chick brings a bike in the day I'm off."

"Nah. She wasn't a customer," I explained, drinking the last of my Liquid I.V.

They both froze and stared, then Bowie asked, "Who was this girl exactly?"

"Her name is Celine Cruz."

There was a second's pause, then Zack and Bowie broke out into hysterical laughter, Zack doubling over and coughing out his water. I think he hurt himself laughing so hard.

"What the fuck?" I asked. "What's so funny?"

"Dude," Zack finally said between laughter, "don't tell me you think you have a chance with Celine *Cruz*."

"If you prefer your balls attached to your body," added Bowie, grinning like a fiend, "I'd highly recommend you forget about her."

Forget about her? He was out of his fucking mind. I hadn't stopped thinking about her since we met.

"Yeah, yeah. Ty already warned me. Protective dad and shit."

"And brothers and uncles," said Bowie.

"And every wolf who works in this shop." Zack shook his head. "I get it. She's crazy hot, but no girl is worth all that trouble."

My entire body locked up like it did right before a fight, my wolf rumbling a warning. Just Zack's mention of calling her hot had set him off. It was a strange new sensation to feel my wolf's presence.

"Whoa, whoa." Zack held up his hands, grinning. "I see how it is. Just be careful, man. Seriously."

Bowie shook his head. "You just might be the bravest mother-fucker I've ever met if you face that firing squad."

"Ronan!" Uncle Shane stood in the open back door of the paint garage, looking surly as always. He waved me over.

"Let us know if you hear from that guy about registering our team," said Zack as I was walking away.

"Sure thing."

Uncle Shane turned and walked off before I reached him so, of course, I followed. He kept going through the main garage until he was in his office. Then he closed the door behind me. The office contained a small computer desk and a table where he sat with clients to go over designs and price quotes.

He sat at the head of the table and clasped his hands—not a good sign—so I took a seat next to him. I had no idea what this was about unless. Maybe Celine? If he was going to give me another warning speech like all the others, I would get up and walk out of here.

But the fiddling of his thumbs as he scowled at the table told me it was something else. He was anxious and nervous, not angry.

Finally, he cleared his throat and said, "So Sarah told me you still haven't ever shifted." He paused. "Since your mom."

Of course Aunt Sarah would tell him. "No. Never have."

"I think it's time we do something about that."

I almost laughed. "Like what? He's never come back. Not since Mom died." Which was a lie, because he apparently raised his head and sniffed the air the second I locked eyes on Celine Cruz.

"I want you to see someone." He leveled me with his scary uncle stare, the one that meant he was being serious.

"Are you saying you want me to see a shrink?"

"Hear me out." He raised a palm like I was about to bolt. I was. "She's a supernatural therapist, a witch, but she has medical degrees to back it up."

"I can't fucking believe this. And you think this shrink can make my wolf finally come out after being invisible my entire life?"

"I think you need to talk to someone about what happened with your mom," he said gently.

"I know it wasn't my fault," I snapped, even as regret and shame still lingered deep where I'd buried it. "I don't need a fucking therapist to hold my hand and tell me that shit."

He didn't respond to my anger with more aggression, which was what I expected. Rather, he appeared calmer and spoke even more gently, like I was an angry animal about to go rabid.

"Son, just do this for me. See her three times, and if you don't think it's worth it or helping, then I won't say another word about it. I swear."

I held his gaze, clamping my jaw shut, trying not to lose my shit over the fact my uncle thought I needed a therapist. Like I was mentally or emotionally damaged or something.

"You know, me fighting has nothing to do with all that," I told him. "I'm just really fucking good in the cage. And I enjoy being the best at something." At fighting.

He dipped his chin. "I get that." Then he slid a cream-colored business card toward me across the table. "I've got an appointment set for tomorrow morning."

My gaze dropped to my hands in my lap, realizing they were clenched into fists. I should've expected something like this. My uncle Shane was a fixer. Every visit to Aunt Sarah's for the holidays, he'd pull me aside and give me the man-to-man chat about responsibility and growing up and anything else he thought I needed to be doing better.

"What if I say no?"

His brow rose. I waited for him to tell me to find another place to live, but instead he said, "That's your choice. If you refuse, I'll cancel the appointment. But I want you to go." He paused. "I want you to try."

I remained still, stewing in my anger and frustration. It's not like I didn't want my wolf to come out. I realized a long time ago that I was a freak of nature. Of my supernatural nature. I was strong and fast but not nearly as much as if my wolf would wake the fuck up and come back into my life. For real. Not just to fucking growl at a pretty girl he seemed to like.

"You know, I understand what it feels like to be a little out of control," he started.

This was new. "What do you mean?"

"I didn't always have my shit together."

I huffed a laugh. "Since when?"

"Do you know how I got here to New Orleans?"

I shrugged. I was a baby when he left Texas. Mom always said Uncle Shane found his true home in NOLA.

"I came here to kidnap a woman," he said so matter-of-factly I thought I'd imagined it.

"Come again?"

His mouth ticked up on one side. "It's true. I was so fucking angry, full of rage. An old friend of mine who'd left Austin for New Orleans had met this woman, this witch, who could inject spells into the ink of tattoos. The kind that could help supernaturals connect with their magic."

I nodded. "I've heard of that."

"Yeah. Her name is Violet Cruz. She taught other witches how to do it. She's pretty famous for it."

"Violet *Cruz*?" I clarified, my brain fixated on her last name.

"She's a good friend of mine now too. Her husband, Nico, was the old friend I mentioned. They live here."

"Are they related to Celine Cruz?" It couldn't be a coincidence.

"You met Celine?" He frowned.

"Mm-hmm." I waited for another lecture, but it didn't come.

"Violet and Nico are Celine's aunt and uncle. Anyway, I'd been so angry because witches never gave us the time of day."

"Many still don't," I interjected.

"Old prejudices take a long time to die, son. But the Savoie family—that's Violet's maiden name—they've done a lot to turn that around. Anyway, I made a stupid move and kidnapped Violet, thinking that was the only way. So many of us in the Blood Moon Pack wanted more control over our wolves, so we wouldn't be prone to uncontrollable violence."

It was so interesting to hear him say this because I'd never been prone to it. Since my wolf had remained dormant and silent, I always had complete control over my emotions. It was the perfect ally in the ring since I was mostly fighting hotheaded werewolves. I'd gotten a reputation for being ice-cold in a fight. No one could ever provoke me into anger. And they hated it because that's where wolves made mistakes. And I always beat them when they did.

"Let me guess," I said, "it was a mistake."

He chuckled, wiping a hand down his close-cropped beard, darker brown than his blond hair that was the same shade as mine. "I learned real quick not to mess with a wolf's mate."

"Damn." I couldn't help but outright laugh. "I bet he wanted to kill you."

"He almost did. But Violet took care of herself just fine. Her telekinetic powers could smash a bus into a building like swatting a fly."

He laughed again, most likely at my surprised expression.

"Anyway, I'm just saying, I had a lot of anger built up inside me, and I let it take control. I made some stupid mistakes because of it."

The thing was, I wasn't full of anger. But I did hold a well of remorse and shame close to my heart.

He tapped the table with his index finger next to the business card still sitting on it in front of me. "Go see her. Eight a.m."

I didn't say I would or wouldn't as he stood and walked over, opening the office door.

The radio in the garage was playing "Fear of the Water" by SYML. A tool clanged against something metal. Uncle Shane stopped and turned before he walked through.

"And Ronan?"

I tore my gaze away from the card, wondering if I should go. "Hmm?"

"Texas *was* your home. This is your home now." He offered a small smile. "And I'm glad you're here."

Then he closed the door behind him, and I just stared at it. A little dumbfounded. Uncle Shane wasn't the sentimental type. Neither was I.

I swallowed hard, the emotion sticking in my throat. I'd moved in with my grandfather when my mom died, and I had driven him crazy, so Aunt Sarah had taken me in. She was kind and patient and she'd tolerated me for as long as she could. But I never felt like I belonged. For the first time since I was twelve, I thought maybe I finally found the place where I did.

My gaze lowered to the card still staring up at me, waiting to be picked up off the fucking table. I heaved a sigh and stood, taking the card and tucking it into my back pocket before I left.

CHAPTER 5

~RONAN~

THE PSYCHOLOGIST'S OFFICE WAS ON THE BOTTOM FLOOR OF A TWO-story building on Camp Street in the Lower Garden District. I hadn't visited this neighborhood in New Orleans yet, but it had a cool vibe. It reminded me of some of the areas in Austin where coffee shops, cool restaurants, and dog walkers dominated the scene.

I thought I had the wrong place when I walked through the wrought iron gate and up the few steps to an ornate glass front door. It looked more like a residence than an office building, but the metal plate next to the door inside the foyer on the left read *Dr. Ashlyn Theriot,* along with a string of letters behind her name.

When I opened the door, it was to find a comfortable waiting area with soft music playing and one of those diffusers spraying a scenty oil.

A young, smartly dressed man at the desk stood and smiled. "Good morning. You must be Mr. Reed."

"I am."

"We received your intake form online."

I hadn't filled out an intake form, so Uncle Shane must've done it for me. No telling what he wrote on that. Probably something like *troubled adolescent, a year in juvenile detention, multiple arrests, a regular all-around pain in the ass to his family.*

"You can come on in," the receptionist said politely.

I realized I was still standing in the doorway that led to the foyer, holding the doorknob like I might bolt. I was thinking about it.

"Dr. Theriot will be right out. You can have a seat."

But before I could do that, a middle-aged woman in pants and a blouse, her brown hair straight down to her shoulders, walked in from another door.

"Mr. Reed," she greeted me warmly, extending her hand. "Thank you for coming."

I took her hand and shook it, recognizing a familiar tingle of magic seeping into my body, calming my nerves. Though the last Aura witch I'd shaken hands with had had a completely different effect on me, I certainly recognized the similar signature of magic.

"You're an Aura," I said abruptly.

She smiled wider. "I am." She let go of my hand. "I hope you don't mind. It's instinctual for me to make newcomers feel comfortable."

She gestured to her open palm, knowing I'd sensed her using her witchy magic.

"It's fine."

"Good. Right this way, please." She led me into her office, which was similarly decorated as the reception area in cool blues, a comforting aesthetic.

She gestured for me to take a seat on her plush green love seat, and she sat in a velvet-covered club chair opposite me.

"Not what I was expecting," I told her.

"What were you expecting?" she asked easily. "A stiff, vinyl sofa where you'd have to recline while I picked your brain?"

Chuckling, I admitted, "Something like that."

"We try to make our clients feel as comfortable as possible while we're picking their brains."

She was teasing me. Another attempt to set me at ease.

"I didn't want to come here," I admitted abruptly.

Her smile smoothed into a calm expression. "Your uncle told me that you probably wouldn't want to. What made you decide to come?"

"I feel like I owe it to my uncle." I sat deeper into the sofa.

"But you don't owe it to yourself?"

She was good. I clasped my fingers loosely in my lap. "No offense. But I don't think there is anything you can do for me."

"Maybe there isn't," she said easily. "But maybe there is. We won't know until we talk it through."

I stared and waited for her to get started. When she realized I had no rebuttal because, fuck it all, she was right, she crossed her legs, leaving her hands in her lap, and said, "Why don't we start with an easy topic for most werewolves?"

"Shoot."

"What is it that makes you angry? Something that would normally awaken a wolf."

Smiling, I said, "Nothing. I don't get angry."

She blinked several times. "You don't get angry?"

"Never have. I'm not that kind of wolf."

"I see. What about other strong emotions? Fear or excitement?"

"Nope."

"You don't feel fear? Of any kind? Ever?"

I thought back, trying to remember a time I was afraid since the accident. "There was this one time I was babysitting one of my aunt Sarah's sons. He fell off the slide in the backyard."

"What did you do?"

"I picked him up and checked for injuries. He was fine."

"How did you feel?"

"What do you mean?"

"In that exact moment, did you feel that rush of panic, that sense of magic coursing through you."

It was known that werewolves shifted once a month at the full moon to let the wolf loose. But they shifted sometimes in reaction to danger or fear, emotions that would call him to defend.

"I was scared for him for a second," I said. "A momentary lapse in my own judgment in letting him try it on his own. He was still too young."

"Your wolf didn't rise to the surface? Sometimes, the wolf will come out to protect his loved ones."

I simply shook my head.

"And what about moments of extreme joy or excitement? You must have those emotions."

"Oh yeah. When I win a fight. All the time."

"No sense of your magic then?"

I huffed a laugh. "I always find it interesting when people refer to a werewolf's magic. You do know it's a curse, right?"

She gave me a small smile. "If you're asking if I know the history of how werewolves came into existence? Yes, I do. During the Spanish Inquisition, a powerful witch named Griselda hexed her captor and torturer, the Spanish officer Ortega, to be forever cursed by becoming the beast, the monster, she believed he was. And so it has been passed down that every male descended from that officer through the centuries has been forced to transform into a beast once a month to purge the monstrous instincts inside him."

"Exactly. So I'm not even quite sure why it matters if I connect with my wolf or not. If he awakens or not. I'm kind of a lucky one, aren't I? I escaped the curse."

"So you're saying you've never heard or felt your wolf? You've never transformed at all? Your uncle gave me little prior knowledge, wanting to respect your privacy. I know only the basics of your personal history."

My gut tightened. "Yes, I've shifted a few times, but it stopped."

"When was that?"

"When I was twelve."

"Do you know why your wolf may have retreated?"

I stared at her, all calm and collected, asking me about my most heinous nightmare. I answered coolly, "I don't want to talk about that."

She held my stare, then finally nodded. "Being a werewolf isn't all a curse, though, is it? The Goddess, or the Creator, whoever you believe in beyond our earthly realm, saw to it that wolves inherited not only the beast but also the gift of creativity. Every wolf I've ever known has had some kind of creative gift."

"You've met a lot of werewolves, have you?" I raised a brow, curious and dubious at the same time.

"I have," she said easily again. "And not just in my office," she added quickly. "I happen to be married to one."

"No shit?" I winced. "Sorry about the language."

She laughed. "I'm not offended. And yes, no shit."

I couldn't help but smile. She was pretty cool, this shrink.

"So I do know a little about wolves."

"I guess you do."

"What about lust?" she asked quickly. "Has that ever stirred your wolf?"

I flinched again. She had no issues getting personal fast. I opened my mouth to say no, because truly, my wolf had never reared its head ever for a woman. Except very recently.

"Yes and no," I finally answered, frowning.

"Why do you say yes?"

"Because a few days ago a woman's presence made my wolf growl."

For the first time, Dr. Theriot's expression was something other than calm and cool. She was surprised. "Really? What happened?"

"It wasn't lust, though. Well, not entirely. There was something about her that made him stand up and pay attention."

"I see." She stared intently but didn't add anything.

"What does it mean?" I asked.

"It could mean many things or one very simple thing."

I grunted in annoyance. "That's typical psychobabble—no offense. Can you tell me what you mean in plain English?"

Without missing a beat, she said, "It could mean that your change of scenery, this move to a new place that's unfamiliar and strange with people you don't know, has jolted your wolf into a defensive state. And he's decided you need him. Or it could mean you've simply reached an age where your past trauma isn't as sharp and your wolf finally feels safe to come out, though I don't believe that's the case. Or it could mean you've met your mate and your wolf noticed her first." She paused. "Right away, actually, I'd imagine."

The ensuing silence was almost suffocating. Blood rushed feverishly through my body, and my chest heaved with labored breaths.

"That can't be true," I said dumbly.

"Why not?" she asked in that annoyingly calm voice.

"I just met her last week."

She smiled. "That doesn't matter. You know that."

"I do know that, but fuck, I shouldn't be told by my damn shrink that I met my mate last week."

"I said it was a possibility. And I much prefer therapist or counselor, please."

"Right. Sorry."

I stood and paced to the window, propping my hands on my hips. A red cardinal hopped from one branch to another on a crape myrtle tree in the front yard. It twitched its head back and forth, seeming to look at me for a split second before it hopped onto another branch.

"No," I said with conviction. "It's her. You're right. She's my mate."

"How can you be so sure?"

I grinned, remembering how many people had warned me off Celine since I'd shown even a tiny bit of interest in her.

"Because fate likes to fuck with me like that."

"I don't understand."

I turned, walked back to the sofa, and took my seat, but leaning forward, elbows on my knees, hands clasped. "How do you know I've had a past trauma?" I asked her. "Did my uncle tell you?"

"No. Your aura." She gestured with a finger, pointing around the perimeter of my body. "There's a layer of a darker thread among the brighter colors. That tends to mean a lingering trauma." Then she added with a smile, "Your aura is quite bright, though."

"I was told that recently."

"Really? By whom?"

"By my mate."

She smiled, then added, "She's an Aura witch? How interesting."

I shook my head. "When a shrink—I mean therapist—says 'how interesting,' that can never be good."

She laughed. "Or it could mean something very good."

"What do *you* think it means?" I turned the tables because I was genuinely interested.

"Aura witches are naturally and magically empathic. A partner like that would suit a wilder wolf who has a past trauma perfectly."

I sat back and considered what she was saying. I never needed anyone to calm me down as I rarely let anything offset my cool demeanor. But I was a bit wild, I'd admit. Aura witches used their innate magic to charm others with spells of happiness or serenity and such. That's why they made perfect therapists.

"But I don't need anyone to calm me down," I stated honestly. "I'm fine."

"So to be absolutely clear, you're *never* emotionally out of control?"

A flash of memory hit me hard—*a snarl, a squeal of tires, my mother screaming.*

"Ronan?" A soft touch to the top of my hand made me flinch. "Are you okay?"

I inhaled a deep breath and blew it back out. "Fine."

She studied me a few seconds, then nodded. "We'll talk more about this next week." She glanced at the clock on the wall. "Our time is up."

"Damn, that went by fast."

She stood and extended her hand for me to shake. "It usually does."

I shook her hand. "Thank you, Dr. Theriot."

"Will I actually see you next week? Or is this a waste of your time?"

I assured her, "I'll see you next week."

She walked me to the lobby where her assistant, Michael as he introduced himself, told me my appointment had been prepaid and my appointment was set for next week at the same time.

I couldn't believe it, but I was actually smiling as I walked out into the foyer of the building. Then I instantly froze at the sound of her voice.

"You did a wonderful job, Elijah. I'll see you next week."

There she was, Celine Cruz, ushering a kid and his mother out of the main doorway onto the outside steps. When she turned, her expression must've mirrored mine—round-eyed shock. But there was actually a touch of fear in her eyes that instantly called up my protective instincts. Until I realized it was because of me. "What are you doing here?" she asked, glancing around as if looking for an escape. My heart sickened.

She wore a pale green sundress with a tan cardigan, her wavy copper hair held back in one of those big clips. There was a loose lock hanging down one cheek, and I wanted to walk over and tuck it behind her ear and pull her close, then bury my nose against her skin.

Holy fuck, she truly was my mate. And she was currently a little afraid of me.

I didn't want to admit why I was actually there. The thought she might think me weak made me want to spill my breakfast on the polished oak floor. But I couldn't lie. Not to her.

"I, uh, had an appointment." I gestured to the door behind me.

"With Dr. Theriot?" Her auburn brows rose, softening her sweet face.

"Yeah." My voice was husky, my throat suddenly dry.

My gaze fell to the opposite doorway, the one behind her that was slightly ajar. The nameplate beside the door read *Celine Cruz, MS, LPC.*

"She's a fantastic counselor," she said quietly, which only made me more uncomfortable.

"So you're a therapist?" I gestured to the door leading to her office, wanting to change the subject but also wanting to know more about her.

"I am." She finally smiled, and I remembered how to breathe again.

"But for little kids?"

"Yes. I actually use art therapy with children who have anxiety."

I glanced through the open door and saw a table with paints and teacups set on them. I couldn't help but walk closer, drawn to her, lured in by everything about her.

"Will you show me?"

She gulped hard, much more nervous than the first time we met. "Of course."

She guided me into her office, which was set up differently than Dr. Theriot's space. There was no reception desk, just the open room with several separate spaces. A sitting area with three comfy chairs in a circle, another area with stuffed animals and toys, another with an easel and a white dry-erase board. Currently, there was a childlike picture of a butterfly and a flower and someone's rudimentary handwriting with *I love you, Miss Celine* on the whiteboard.

My entire chest caved in at the sweet beauty of this room and the love it evoked. With the woman at its center, how could fate possibly have assigned her to be my mate? I wasn't good enough to wash her pretty feet.

"Your patients don't call you Dr. Cruz?"

"I'm not a doctor. I'm a licensed counselor."

"But you teach art therapy?"

"I double-majored in art and science as an undergrad."

"I barely graduated high school." Somehow, that was easy to tell her. Perhaps because I knew there were other ways than formal education to learn life lessons. Or that I innately knew she wouldn't judge me for it.

"Not everyone needs a college degree to do well in life." And there she went proving me right.

I chuckled, turning to face her. She looked more like the brazen angel in the garage now, her cloak of confidence hanging back around her shoulders where it should be.

"That's what I always believed too."

That air of knowing lingered between us, twining and weaving. We seemed to get one another even though we came from very different backgrounds and walks of life.

"What if your patient isn't an artist?" I asked.

"You don't have to be an artist to enjoy painting or drawing or weaving."

She gestured to a table in the corner where a square loom sat with an unfinished tapestry on it. The kid who weaved it had missed a loop or two and had pulled the thread too tight on one side where it was bunching up.

"And how does the art help them exactly?"

"It's soothing to the brain and relaxes emotions. It's a calming activity that helps them open up and allows me to help them work through their anxieties, to develop coping skills when they're out in the world."

I let that soak in a minute. "Can I try?"

"Painting teacups?" Her brows shot up.

I nodded.

"Of course." She didn't mock me or seem shocked that a big oaf like me wanted to paint. Again, I was surprised and not surprised by her.

She gestured for me to sit, so I did, while she opened a cabinet along the wall where I could see a line of plain white teacups. She brought one over and set it in front of me, then took her seat next to me where she'd been painting her own with the little boy, Elijah.

"So what am I supposed to paint exactly? Like leaves or something."

"Whatever you want. Abstract designs, leaves, flowers, kittens."

"Flowers and kittens, huh?"

She smirked.

I picked up the paintbrush. "I'll probably fuck this up."

"It doesn't matter. We all make mistakes. The important thing is to keep going. To keep moving forward."

Damn, she was amazing.

I dipped my brush in the sky-blue and started to paint. She did the same. I noticed her design was feminine and precise, a chain of green leaves connected by a delicately looped vine.

We painted in silence for a while, only the sound of her soft classical music on low volume and of an occasional passing car disturbing our quiet. It was remarkably soothing. So much so that I fell into an easy rhythm, finding the design that made sense. While we both focused on our work, I couldn't help but want to confide something.

"I do draw, you know."

"Do you?" she asked casually as she dipped the tip of her paintbrush into the forest-green paint. "That doesn't surprise me, though."

"Why's that?"

"All werewolves have a creative talent."

"You know a lot about werewolves?"

She stopped painting, her hand frozen in the air as she looked up at me. "You didn't do much homework about me, did you?" When I didn't know what to say to that, she went back to painting and said, "My father is a werewolf. My two brothers, Diego and Joaquin, are too. We're triplets. Well, Joaquin is actually both a werewolf and a warlock. Not many of them according to history. Oh, and my uncle."

I did know that her uncle Nico was a werewolf, but I hadn't asked enough questions about the rest of her family. I'm sure I stared like an idiot. "No, I guess I didn't do my homework. I had no idea."

I'd just assumed her witch mom had married a warlock. No one had mentioned her dad was a fucking werewolf. No wonder he was overprotective. Most wolves were of the women in their lives. This new knowledge didn't deter me at all. Rather, it was encouraging.

I settled back to painting, finding my rhythm in the design quickly. "So you're not opposed to dating werewolves then."

She kept painting, a pretty blush pinking her cheeks. "No. I'm not opposed to dating anyone who is a good person."

Interesting and acceptable answer. "I'm a good person."

She laughed as she dipped her brush again, the sound spreading warmth through my chest.

"Okay, Mr. Good Person. What is it you needed a fresh start from?"

While continuing to paint, I said, "I'm a wolf cage fighter, and that's illegal back in Texas. I might've worn out my welcome on the supernatural scene by being in a few bar fights in Austin, but let me explain." I dipped my brush in the purple paint. "I never started the fights in the bars. I only finished them. I just made a lot of enemies in the underground ring."

"I've never even heard of wolf cage fighting before. What is it exactly?"

"Similar to UFC fighting, but a bit more . . . brutal."

She set her teacup and brush down. "So you moved here to find a new career?"

"Oh, no." I finished the last flourish of the artwork on my teacup and set the brush down, wanting to look her in the eyes. "I'm a fighter. That's what I was meant to do. In Louisiana, it's legal. I want to organize my own team. Wolf cage fighting always happens in circuits with a team. I want to climb to the top, become the champion in the United States. Then maybe even go to the international circuit."

She stared at me with a mixture of wonder and a touch of fear yet again. I hated seeing that look in her eyes.

"You're afraid." I could hear her speeding pulse. "But there's no need. It's just a sport like any other."

"It's not like any other. Your goal isn't to get a ball in the end zone. It's to beat your opponent into submission."

"True. But every man who fights understands that. It isn't as if we are stepping into the ring ignorant of the pain."

"What about the danger? The danger of severe injury or death."

"No one dies in the ring."

"But they could."

"I won't."

"Why not?"

"Because I'm the best. I never lose."

"There's a first time for everything."

Holding back the sigh of frustration I wanted to let out, I asked, "So you won't date me because I'm a fighter?"

"I never said I'd date you at all, even before I learned your profession."

I stood from the table. "But you will, Celine."

She stood, too, lifting the teacup, and turned as if to put it on the back shelf to dry.

"Celine," I said softly, touching her forearm.

She gasped and dropped the teacup, which shattered into several pieces.

"Shit, I'm sorry." I bent with her to pick up the shards.

"It's okay. I'm a little jumpy."

"Because of me?" I asked, both of us crouched and facing each other.

She held my gaze. "Yes."

"I don't want to make you nervous." A small pang pinched me on the inside.

But then she smiled. "I can't help it." Her gaze swept over my face with obvious admiration. "You're . . . you."

Now my heart was racing. The thought that these feelings were mutual and charging forward with dramatic speed was both euphoric and terrifying.

I took the broken pieces from her hands and dropped them in the trash can next to the table, then I returned to her side. I took her hand slowly in mine and lifted it to press a light kiss to the inside of her wrist where her pulse beat wildly.

"I'm sorry about the teacup." I reached down and lifted my teacup carefully off the table and handed it to her.

"You don't have to give it to me."

"I want you to have it."

Her mouth slightly ajar, she slowly took the cup, careful not to touch the wet paint. The design had come to me quickly. They were a series of interconnected and overlapping feathers. I'd used two shades of blue, the darker for the detailing, creating a trail of wispy feathers all the way around the rim. On one side, I'd painted a line drawing of a female angel with a golden halo, the only color other than the blues.

"It's how I see you," I admitted boldly.

She remained frozen, those heartfelt green eyes on me.

"Elegant and beautiful." Tucking my hands in my jeans pockets, I backed toward the door. "I'll see you soon, Celine." Then I turned and forced myself to walk away, cherishing that small smile that tilted her pretty mouth when she gazed down at the fragile teacup in her hands that I'd painted for her.

CHAPTER 6

~CELINE~

I STOOD AT THE BAR OF JOAQUIN'S CAFE, WATCHING MY COUSIN SAMARA make a cup of tea for a customer. For the thousandth time, I thought about the teacup Ronan had painted that I'd set on my office desk and stared at endlessly between clients.

I also berated myself yet again for not getting his phone number. I'd fully intended to the next time I saw him, but I was so floored by the frankness of our conversation, by my overwhelming attraction to him, and by the beauty of the teacup he handed to me with the words, *"It's how I see you,"* that getting his number completely slipped my mind.

"So just go to the body shop and get it," said Samara while she blended foam or milk or whatever it was she was doing.

"Samara. Like I can just stroll casually into the body shop, lean over whatever vehicle he's working on, and ask for his phone number."

She grinned over her shoulder and waggled her eyebrows. "Why not? I bet he'd enjoy seeing you bent over his vehicle."

"Shut up. You look so like your dad when you make that face."

"Which one is that?" She dusted cinnamon onto the foam-topped tea.

"The cat-got-the-cream look."

Setting the tea on a saucer, she turned and paused on the other side of the counter in front of me. "I've never seen you gush and grin over a guy like this. Not ever. So I say, let the cat get the cream. Now, I need to get this to the professor before he starts glaring at me. Oops. Too late."

I watched her meander in between the tables to the back wall of booths where a dark-haired, pale-faced man was frowning in her direction. Samara set the tea in front of him, her long hair in a thick plait falling in front of her shoulder, then she stepped back, asking something, gesturing to the laptop and books strewn on his table.

His gaze softened only slightly as he responded in a deep, clipped voice, though I couldn't hear what they were saying. I did notice, however, that when Samara turned and walked back to the counter, his gaze lingered on her a touch longer than proper before he returned to his laptop and books.

I couldn't blame him. My cousin was gorgeous. She had the warm brown skin of her father, Uncle Devraj. Her eyes were green like her mother's, my aunt Isadora. The same shade as mine and my mother's too. She was curvier than Aunt Isadora, though, built more like our aunt Livvy.

Glancing beyond her to the professor, I noted his aura glowed with the magic of a supernatural, though I wasn't quite sure what he was.

"Is he a vampire?" I asked as she wound back behind the counter and wiped it down with a cloth.

"The professor?" She smiled and shook her head. "Warlock, though he does have the look of a vampire, doesn't he?"

Now she was the one doing the staring.

"Samara, is there something going on between you two?"

Her dark brows shot up. "Goddess no." She started drying the line of coffee mugs in the dishwasher tray and put them away in a neat stack. "He's just a regular. He likes my chai. Gets it every Saturday."

"Every Saturday? Seems like he might want more than your chai."

She laughed. "I doubt it. I've tried flirting with him. He never takes the bait. He's all about his studies and books. He teaches at Loyola and works on his weekly lectures here every weekend."

I observed the professor, his serious expression intent on his laptop as he typed away. He was extremely good looking but also sort of intimidating. "Isn't he a bit old for you anyway?"

"Meh. He's in his eighties. For a warlock, that just means he's good and experienced." She winked at me.

Seeing as supernaturals lived much longer than humans, a warlock in his eighties was still in his prime. In human standards, he looked more like late thirties or early forties, having that confident, distinguished air.

Two new customers, young women, stepped up to the counter so I moved out of the way. It was mid-afternoon, between lunch and dinner, the slow part of the day. The Silver Moon Café was solely a breakfast/lunch place. Joaquin closed at seven, giving customers time to stop by for one more caffeine fix and perhaps a pastry before the end of the day.

Once Samara had served their foamy lattes, she turned back to me. "So when are you going to tell your parents about this new guy?"

"Never."

Joaquin stepped through the swinging door, untying the apron he wore when he cooked. "Tell Mom and Dad what?" he asked me.

"About Ronan," I admitted, taking a seat at the side bar while Samara greeted another new customer. "The new guy I told you about."

He raised a superior brow, dark auburn like his wavy hair. "Celine, you should just get it over with."

"Bringing a guy home to meet Mom and especially Dad is a big deal, and you know it. It's not like I see you bringing any men home to meet the parents."

He leaned on the counter across from me. "That's because there are none to bring home. I've given up on dating."

"What a cynic. Giving up before you're even thirty?"

"It's too disrupting," he admitted honestly.

I couldn't even laugh, because I knew it pained him to have his life in any sort of disarray. My brother hated anything messy or disorderly. He was what my mom always called an *old soul*. I just called him an old man. If anyone needed someone messy and disorderly in his life, it was my serious, stoic brother Joaquin.

It didn't help that he was both a werewolf and a warlock with the powerful Enforcer designation. One day, he would inherit my aunt Jules's place as ruler of New Orleans, one more thing to take super seriously. Like he needed it. Sometimes, I wished a man would come along, knock him off his perfect pedestal, and rock his world.

"What's been bothering you?" he asked quietly.

"Are you psychic too?"

"I can just sense it. Tell me."

He was right. Something had been nagging at me since I saw Ronan at the office. I hadn't told Samara or anyone, because I liked to believe I was completely past all that.

"I saw Ronan at my office this week, right outside my door."

Joaquin frowned, leaning closer. "He followed you to work?"

"No. He actually was seeing Dr. Theriot."

He waited and listened carefully and didn't ask why Ronan was seeing a therapist. But that was his way. He only poked into someone's personal life if he thought it was necessary.

"It was a coincidence. Or fate. Whatever you want to believe. But for a few seconds, when I saw him there, I was afraid."

He reached a hand across the counter and tugged on my fingers, giving them a squeeze. "Bit of a flashback?" he asked gently.

I nodded. "Only for a few seconds. Then I realized Ronan was nothing like *him*. Actually, I believe it was my magic telling me so. The fear vanished pretty quickly. But, for a moment, it was there."

"That's perfectly normal. If it was able to overtake you then there would be more to discuss or worry about. But your instincts are clearer now. What's good and right is guiding you." He squeezed my fingers between his. "Don't you think?"

He raised his brows, willing me to admit that I was still okay now, that I was in control and could trust myself and my magic.

I inhaled a deep breath, then blew it out and sat up straighter. "Yes. You're absolutely right."

He smiled wide. My brothers both had the best smiles, but Joaquin rarely gave his away. "That's what I like to hear."

He walked through the barista prep area and the opening of the counter to where I stood from my stool and pulled me into a hug. His casual hugs were my favorite, and he knew it.

"This is good, sis. You're doing fine."

He smelled like spices and lemon from the kitchen. It was a comforting smell.

"Thank you." I hugged him back.

"That's what I'm here for." Then he let me go and turned to Samara who was handing over another foam-topped latte. "Can you lock up? I've got to run by the bank and do some errands. Devon and Miranda are closing up the kitchen."

"Sure thing."

He untied his white apron and hung it on a hook beside the kitchen entrance before leaving through the café door out onto Magazine Street.

"So when are you going to see him again?" asked Samara.

I thought about the teacup. And then about the fact that Ronan was seeing Dr. Theriot. She treated people with anxiety, depression, and past trauma. I wondered what category Ronan fit into.

Of course, I would never ask her. Doctor/patient confidentiality was a tenet I held very dear myself. And Dr. Theriot would never tell me if I asked. She was my mentor and my friend, but that didn't mean she'd betray a patient to appease my curiosity.

"I don't know," I finally answered.

"Do you *want* to see him again?"

"Oh yeah." I smiled. "Most definitely."

"So just make that happen."

Easier said than done. Samara was far more extroverted than me. She had her father's charming and charismatic personality. I was quite the opposite. As much as I'd like to take her advice and show up at the garage unannounced and boldly get his phone number, that wasn't going to happen.

But there was something that resonated with my Aura magic when I was near him, a rightness I felt trembling through my flesh to my bones. Aunt Clara, who was an Aura witch like me, always told me to listen to my magic. Our magic knew better than our human instincts.

If she was right, then the Goddess would throw us together again. If that happened, then I wouldn't waste the opportunity, no matter that he was the exact opposite kind of man my family, in particular my father, would want for me. My magic knew best, and she was beaming a spotlight on this particular rough-around-the-edges werewolf.

CHAPTER 7

~RONAN~

ZACK AND BOWIE WALKED SLIGHTLY AHEAD OF ME AS WE STROLLED through the parking lot to this place called Howler's. There was a live band playing tonight. The marquee above the door read *Tonight—Silver Bane.*

"You'll love this band," Zack was saying as we paid the cover fee at the door. "The singer and the drummer are werewolves. The bass guitarist is a vampire."

I nodded, paying the cover and following them inside. Howler's was on the Westbank where a lot of werewolves lived. That was because there were actually some woodlands close to the area and wolves, even in between their full-moon shifts, often liked to run in wolf form.

The place was already pretty packed, though the band didn't start for another half hour. The crowd ranged from twenties to forties. I sensed a lot of wolves in the crowd, but other supernatural signatures as well. Some humans thrown in the mix too.

"Come on," Zack called back to me, grinning, "I'll introduce you to the band."

He zigzagged through the crowd toward the stage where the guitarist stood, plucking at some strings, checking the sound as he adjusted them. There were two guys sitting on the edge of the stage, one had drumsticks in his hands and was twirling them and mock-playing a set in his head while the other guy was laughing with a couple of girls.

"Hey, Diego," said Zack as he maneuvered up into their small circle, the girls stepping back to make room for us. "I'd like you to meet a new friend of ours. This is Ronan Reed." Zack gestured toward the one I knew was the singer, but then my gut tightened when Zack said, "This is Diego Cruz."

Ignoring the devilish grins Zack and Bowie shared at my expense, knowing full fucking well this surprise introduction might throw me off, I reached out a hand to shake Diego's, calm as ever.

"Hey, man. Welcome." His tone was cool and casual, but I noticed the way his eyes flashed gold when his hand met mine.

This wasn't uncommon when two werewolves met for the first time, especially two dominant ones. The interesting thing was that my wolf never showed himself, and yet, this had happened to me more times than I could count when I met other alphas. They saw me initially as a threat. And in the ring, they learned that I was one.

"Nice to meet you," I said, withdrawing my hand and sizing up Celine's brother.

He was sitting, but I could tell he was as tall as me, maybe taller. His longish hair that fell almost to his shoulders softened his hard edges. He was packed with muscle, and the wolf I detected laying beneath his skin was a fierce animal.

"He's Shane Reed's nephew. Just moved here from Austin."

"No shit," said Diego, still observing me keenly. "My uncle Nico lived in Austin for a while."

I nodded, having nothing to add to that. Quite frankly, I was reeling slightly from meeting some of her family so abruptly. I was going to kick Zack's ass when we left this place because I was sure it was his idea.

"This is Boomer," Diego introduced the drummer who'd been mock-drumming a set the whole time, barely noticing us.

He gave me a head nod, and that was his greeting, I supposed.

"Don't mind him." Diego grinned. "He's in the zone right now." Then he called back to the guitarist, "Hey, Morgan! Come meet Shane's nephew."

The vampire stopped what he was doing and walked to the edge of the stage, but he didn't sit.

"This is my cousin, Morgan." Diego gestured over his shoulder.

"Your cousin?" I asked, wanting clarification because he was definitely a fucking vampire, not a werewolf.

"His mom is my aunt Jules. She's the Enforcer in New Orleans if you hadn't heard." Diego watched me for any reaction, but I wasn't going to give him any.

"Cool," was all I said.

Again, I was taken aback. Ty had mentioned that Celine had grims and vampires as uncles as well as werewolves, but I suppose it hadn't really sunk in. They were truly a melting pot of supernaturals in this family. That wasn't all that common. At least, not where I was from. But it also was highly encouraging for my chances with Celine.

As if I'd conjured her, I smelled her on the air. I had to bite back the instinctual growl at the jolt of sensation when she waltzed right in front of the other girls still standing near Diego and gave him a hug.

"Hey, sis," he said, giving her a one-armed embrace. "Glad you made it. Hey, Lauren."

He smiled at the pretty brunette who trailed behind Celine. "Hey, hot stuff."

They started chatting, but I couldn't focus on anything, my entire being wholeheartedly fixated on the red-haired witch standing only feet away.

I did not acknowledge Zack off to the side, shaking his head at me, giving me all the *no* signals he could manage. That was when I realized I hadn't stifled my wolf as well as I'd thought. There was a steady low rumble vibrating in my chest.

When Diego heard it and turned in my direction, so did Celine. I coughed quickly to try to cover it up.

"You okay, man?" Zack patted me hard on the back.

"All good." The rumbling warning of my wolf had stopped. Apparently, he didn't like her among all these other wolves.

The vampire Morgan was plucking at some strings, but his silvery gaze was on me. Fucking vampires. They noticed everything.

"Hi, Ronan," said Celine casually, though I noticed her suck in a deep breath. Her friend grinned like a fiend next to her, which told me she'd been telling her buddy about me. I liked that.

"Hey, Celine." That sounded good, casual, not obsessive or aggressive at all. By some miracle.

Still, Diego frowned, sitting up a little straighter. "How do you two know each other?"

"The body shop," I said quickly.

"Yeah. I dropped some designs to Rhett," she chimed in quickly.

Then it was awkward and quiet except for the bar music playing "I Like the Way You Kiss Me" overhead. And then I was irrationally drawn to Celine's mouth.

Diego's frown deepened, but then some guy, who must've been a bar manager, came up between us. "Five minutes. Let's go."

Diego and Boomer hopped up onto the stage to get ready to start. Zack and Bowie cackled to themselves like schoolgirls while I stepped closer to Celine and her friend.

"Buy you ladies a drink?"

Celine glanced at her friend, then turned back to me. "Sure."

I couldn't help but gently guide her in front of me, my hand at the small of her back. She was wearing jeans and a dark green top that was silky to the touch. I bet her skin was softer.

As we made our way to the bar, most of the crowd was pushing forward toward the stage. I turned to look at her, really drink her in. She and her friend took seats on stools at the bar. I leaned in close to her ear.

"Fucking hell, you're beautiful," I murmured low.

Her mouth dropped open partly, her gaze wide and jewel-green. After a few seconds of the two of us being lost in each other, she leaned back slightly on her stool. "This is my friend Lauren."

"Hi, Lauren." I shook her hand. "What would you two like to drink?"

"Lemon drop martini," said Lauren, twisting backward on her stool and facing the stage as Diego stepped up to the mic and welcomed everyone out tonight.

A chorus of cheers erupted as Morgan twanged his guitar.

"And you?" I turned to Celine, stretching my forearm along the bar behind her since she'd twisted to face the stage too.

She placed her phone in her lap. "Double old-fashioned."

My brows shot up.

She laughed. "Does that surprise you?"

"Yeah. I kind of thought you'd be a lemon drop martini kind of girl too."

"Nope. I'm a whiskey girl. Bourbon, preferably."

"You've got surprises." Leaning closer, I said, "I like that."

She simply smiled, then I hailed the bartender and ordered our drinks. The band lit into the first one, which instantly caught my attention. It was a song by one of my favorite bands, Bad Omens. Diego sang "Just Pretend" with raspy emotion. I liked the band's vibe.

Once we had our drinks, her friend sipped hers and then hopped off her stool. "Thank you, Tex. I think I'll give you two some privacy." Then she winked at Celine and maneuvered through the crowd to talk to someone she apparently knew.

Leaning close to Celine, my arm now draped along the bar behind her, I said, "Alone at last."

She laughed. "Hardly alone." Then we were both caught again, staring inappropriately too long. I simply didn't care who noticed. I was well and truly hooked.

In an attempt to act normal, I sipped my beer and turned to face the stage with her. We watched them play. Well, she watched them play, but my attention was riveted to the sweet-smelling witch next to me.

With her head focused straight ahead, she said, "You're staring."

"I am," I admitted. "Can't help it."

"Well, you need to stop."

"Why's that?"

"My brother might actually notice."

"Nah. He seems pretty cool."

"That's because he doesn't know your intentions." She was smiling now.

"And what are my intentions?"

She turned her head, our faces intimately close as she answered, "Me."

"Well, you've got that right, angel. My intentions are you."

She held her phone in her lap with one hand, and I glanced down obviously at it, faking concern. "Damn, did you drop your phone in the parking lot? It's cracked."

"Shit." She instantly examined her phone. "Where?"

I took it from her hands and quickly input my digits, then sent the call to my phone, which vibrated in my pocket.

"Ronan," she said in an almost scornful tone, like she was trying to mean it, "that was pushy."

"A wolf's gotta do what a wolf's gotta do."

"Just like an alpha." She paused, then added, "I would've given it to you."

That surprised me. "You didn't the last time I asked."

She shrugged. "I changed my mind since then."

"Why's that?"

"Because you painted me a teacup," she said, biting her lower lip to keep from smiling too wide.

"If that's all it took to get your number, I would've painted a dozen teacups. See what that might get me."

She arched a reddish brow at me. "And what are you expecting?"

"Not expecting. But hoping."

She pressed her lips together, trying to suppress her smile. "What are you *hoping* for then?"

"A date."

The song ended and everyone erupted into applause. Celine turned to clap and ignored my request.

"Okay, fine." I exhaled a sigh. "I'll paint you the perfect porcelain teacup with pink flowers all over it. I owe you one anyway."

She burst out laughing, but the roar of cheers drowned her out as they started playing the next song.

"Pink flowers?" She shook her head in mock surprise. "That's awfully tempting."

"And butterflies," I promised. "That's my final offer."

She stared at me, smiling that scintillating smile that made my heart pound wildly and my knees go weak. The hold this woman had on me was ridiculous.

"What if I'm more of a dragon kind of girl?"

"Are you?" I loved the way she surprised me.

"Yeah. But I like pink flowers too," she teased.

"What about wolves? Do you like them?"

A blush spread into her cheeks. Rather than answer, she asked, "Are you leaving town this weekend with your uncle?"

"Why would I?"

"It's the full moon," she explained on a little laugh. "My dad and brothers usually leave town together. They have a cabin in north Louisiana. My mom goes, too, since she likes to go with Dad."

Of course. I didn't watch the calendar like my fellow wolf family and friends. There was no need.

"I won't be leaving town," I told her honestly.

Her expression shifted to concern. "Isn't that sort of dangerous? Uncle Shane lives close to residential areas, even though there are some woods around his place."

"Yeah, that's true. But I won't need to leave town."

"Why not?"

"Go on a date with me, and I'll tell you."

She held my gaze, that tightening in my chest increasing tenfold while I waited for her answer. Then the softest "okay" left her lips, and I suddenly felt like I could conquer the world.

"This Saturday?"

She nodded, then sipped her drink. I'd left my beer on the counter the whole time, but I took a moment and downed half of it in a few gulps.

While we faced the stage, watching the throng of fans sing along and cheer the band on, she said, "It might be a good idea to circulate the bar and not keep so close to me."

"Because of your brother?" I asked.

"Mm-hmm."

"Celine, it is very hard for me to walk away from you."

She exhaled a breath. "The things you say." Then she took a deeper gulp of her drink.

Zack and Bowie made their way through the crowd toward me. I'd expected them to be gloating over the fact that they'd blindsided me with an introduction to Celine's brother, but they weren't smiling at all. Bowie actually had that scowl he often wore when he was annoyed.

"What's up?" I asked Zack as they drew close.

"Remember that guy Baron you were trying to contact? The head of the Iron Claws team?"

"Yeah."

"He's here."

I'd shown Zack and Bowie the Instagram of the team I wanted to compete against, the champion team we'd have to beat.

"Where at?" I asked, standing straight and peering around the room.

"Right over there." Bowie gestured to the far left of the room where there were some booths and a couple of pool tables set away from the stage area.

Sure enough, that was definitely him, laughing with another teammate as he set up a shot at the pool table.

Turning to Celine, who now wore a puzzled expression, I told her, "I'll be back in a few minutes."

When I stepped in their direction, Bowie grabbed my shoulder and leaned in. "Be careful. I've had words with that big fucker before."

I paused to find who he gestured to. It wasn't Baron. "The one leaning against the wall with his arms crossed?" The same guy who was now glaring at us from across the room.

"Yeah. We've almost come to blows before. He tries to start fights all the fucking time with me."

"Y'all have some history?"

Bowie scoffed. "Not really. They're not from the Westbank. They just like to hang over here. It was over some girl he was manhandling in another bar once. He's a big, dumb fucker."

Shit, I hadn't planned on there being built-in animosity with the team I intended to climb over to the top.

"Just let me do the talking," I told him and Zack, who was on my other side.

Then I made my way behind the roaring crowd to the pool tables. Baron noticed me first since I approached him directly. His brows pinched when I finally came to a stop. His whole team of four was here. I recognized the guy Nate sitting in a booth with a girl on his lap as the one who used his claws most often in his past fights. I'd done my due diligence on what kind of fighters they were.

Baron gave me an arrogant look. "Can I help you?"

He wasn't quite as tall as me, but he was well-muscled. We'd be a good match.

"Yeah, I was hoping you could," I said coolly but as friendly as I could fake. "My name is Ronan Reed. I recently reached out to you about the NOWFC."

Baron stared another few seconds before he smiled, but it wasn't a nice one. "Yeah, that's right. I got your message. But you said you don't even have a team."

The big one on the wall shoved off and stepped closer, obviously shooting a death glare at Bowie.

"I'm getting one together." I nodded to Bowie and Zack.

"Three isn't enough," he said, that cocky grin still spread wide. "You need four minimum on a team."

"We'll fight you out back right now, three on three," added the big one.

Bowie was right. He was a dumb fucker. But I suppose my still-healing bruises targeted me as the kind who'd fight in a back alley. Of course, I had done that in Austin, but most of the time it was because we had to fight an underground ring. And people liked to mess with me outside of it.

"I've got nothing against you, man," I told the idiot, then turned my attention back to Baron. "I want to compete legitimately. Who's on the circuit against your team next?"

Baron smiled, his dark eyes glittering. It didn't go unnoticed that every stitch of his clothes was high-end, including the Nike Jordans he was wearing that I knew cost in the two-grand range.

"No one at the moment. We've beat every regional team. Unless another one steps forward, it'll be us going to the state tournament in the fall."

I nodded. "Give me a month, and I'll have my team ready."

I heard Zack make a disgruntled sound beside me, but I didn't look at him to acknowledge it. Baron and the rest of his team on the Iron Claws snickered.

"Let's do it, Baron," said Nate, glaring at us from his seat in the booth.

Fucking hell, these wolves were filled with some nasty, pent-up aggression.

"Okay then. What was your name again?" asked Baron, reaching one hand out to shake mine.

"Ronan Reed," I repeated, knowing full fucking well he'd heard my name the first time.

We shook hands, and I definitely felt like we were having a pissing contest over strongest handshake before we both let go.

"When can you bring in your full team to register? Everyone has to sign for themselves. Death waivers and all."

"You're in charge of registry?" I would've assumed it would be someone unaffiliated with a team.

"My father's company sponsors the events."

"And owns the stadium ring," added Zack with a bit of snark.

Baron's smile slipped, but he didn't admit there might be some favoritism toward his own team winning since Daddy owned and ran the events.

"How about Monday?" I suggested, trying to defuse the tension. I knew who I was going to convince to be my fourth team member.

"Monday's no good," he said.

"Why not? Your father's office isn't open on business days?"

Okay, that might've been a bit out of line, but this douchebag was rubbing me wrong.

He scoffed. "The full moon is Saturday." He might as well have added "you fucking idiot" at the end of that sentence with the amount of disdain he injected. "Nobody will be in my father's office until at least Tuesday."

"Yeah, right." I nodded, wanting to kick myself for forgetting. "Next Wednesday then."

"I'll message you the address." He turned his back on me as if I were a nobody and bent to take his shot. "You can go now."

Any other night and any other place, I would've pounded this fucker's face into the pool table. I didn't get in bar fights near as often as my uncle Shane thought, but yeah, I had been in a few.

Strangely, it was never because someone had pissed me off. It was always simply because someone I'd beaten in the underground ring in Texas had sought me out to prove he could beat me. And I always obliged to prove that they couldn't. But this asshole. The burning sensation that crawled up my chest stirred me to anger. My gaze drifted back to the bar where Celine was watching us. Perhaps that was why this guy had gotten to me. She was close by, near these lesser wolves. I didn't like them. They smelled wrong. And they were near her. For the second time in a week, my wolf made himself known.

A deep, feral growl rumbled up my throat. It wasn't made by me, but definitely by my wolf.

Baron took his shot with a crack of the ball, then swung around to face me, puffing himself up as he held his pool stick.

"You wanna fucking go right now, Reed?"

I clenched my fists, while Bowie stepped forward and planted a palm to my chest and eased me back.

"No, we're not going to fight here," said Bowie calmly.

But I wasn't moving. The very idea that these assholes were in any vicinity near Celine had dug a feral claw into my gut and was ripping upward, climbing through my body like the growl that wouldn't stop growing louder.

I hadn't realized it, but the band had stopped for a break. That was the only reason Diego Cruz was suddenly shoving me and Baron apart. His eyes were bright, wolf-gold, and his voice was dangerous and low.

"No fucking fighting in Howler's," he warned. Then he said to Zack, "Get your friend the fuck out of here now."

"No one needs to hold my hand," I said, taking a step back.

Without another word, I turned and stormed through the crowd, not looking over at Celine once as I exited the bar, Bowie and Zack right behind me.

"What a goddamn idiot," I muttered.

"Yeah, he totally is," agreed Zack.

"Not Baron," I said, spinning around to stare at the door I'd just exited. "Me. I let that asshole bait me. And now Celine's brother thinks I'm an asshole."

Zack heaved a sigh. "If it makes you feel any better, you didn't have much of a chance with Celine regardless."

"So you said."

I knew I had an uphill climb with her, but my first, or rather second, impression with her obviously alpha brother was that I was a shit-stirring bar fighter. And I wasn't.

"Goddamn it." I turned to head to the curb, pulling up the Uber app. "Y'all can go back in. I'll Uber home."

"Hell no." Bowie grabbed me by the shoulder and turned me toward his SUV. "Ain't no damn way we're going back in there. Those guys are itching for a fight."

We piled into Bowie's SUV. I took the back seat.

"Well, we're going to give him a fucking fight, I can tell you that," I swore.

"But we need a fourth team member. And apparently by Wednesday since that's when you said we'd register the team."

"I'm going to convince Ty to do it," I told them.

"Ty at the shop? You think he'd do it?"

"He'd be a good match for that Nate asshole. He's fast."

"He fights?"

"Taekwondo actually. And Krav Maga. I kind of secretly interrogated him while we were working on that Camaro last week."

Zack laughed. "Does he know you've been interviewing him for the position on his team? He may not want to do cage fighting. Not as sophisticated as his style of fighting."

"We'll see. But I have a good feeling. I looked him up on some of the video posted from his competitions. He's pretty fierce. Very competitive."

"That would be fucking awesome," said Bowie. "We'd have a solid team."

I leaned back and wondered how a night that had started so great had ended so horribly. Pulling out my phone, I quickly shot off a text to Celine, apologizing that I had to leave suddenly.

A minute later, the dots popped up, then a text from her.

Celine: Who were those guys? Are you okay?

My heart beat faster knowing that she was worried about me.

Me: I'll explain on Saturday. On our date. If you still want to go.

Celine: Of course I still want to go. Text me the details, and I'll give you my address.

Me: I'll text you tomorrow.

I paused a minute, then added:

Me: It was such a good surprise seeing you tonight.

That was an understatement. Sitting next to her at the bar, drowning in her intoxicating scent, and listening to her laugh, her voice, was the happiest I'd felt in ages. But if I told her all that, she'd think I was crazy.

A few dots popped up, then a text.

Celine: For me too. Talk to you tomorrow. :)

CHAPTER 8

~CELINE~

I sat on the bench in our courtyard, petting Petunia. She was the sweetest tabby cat ever. My mom said their own Zombie Cat, who'd died when I was around five, had been the best cat in the world. I barely remembered the all-black cat who seemed so old and fragile when he died, but I do remember my mom being very sad.

Petunia was currently curled in my lap while I went through some work emails, all from Michael, who took care of my appointments as well as Dr. Theriot's. I had a few patients who needed to move appointments and one new patient.

While I was replying to Michael, a text notification popped up. Ronan.

My heart flip-flopped in my chest at seeing the notification.

Ronan: I'll pick you up Saturday night at 6:00.
Is that good for you?

Me: Perfect. What do I wear?

Ronan: Anything you want. Or nothing at all.
That would be fine by me too.

I laughed, disturbing Petunia, who hopped off my lap since I was paying too much attention to my phone and not her. I quickly sent him my address.

Ronan: Yes, I know where you live. That
reminds me, go check your front porch.

How did he get my address? The old fear sparked for a split second before I pushed it away. His uncle could've easily given him the address. Or anybody else in the body shop. Almost all of the Blood Moon Pack had been here for one reason or another over the years—parties, Christmas gatherings, Guys Game Night. Just because he found it didn't mean he was stalking me.

Quickly, I hustled toward the kitchen door, texting him that I was heading to check my porch now. I rounded the kitchen into the living room, texting and walking.

"Stop right there!"

I jumped, froze, and looked up to see Joaquin and Mom sitting on the couch with to-go coffees from Silver Moon Café. He came over once a week, bringing coffee and pastries, to chat with our parents. But it was Diego sitting in the wingback close to the fireplace with a half-eaten pecan cookie bar in one hand who'd shouted at me when I entered.

"Who are you texting?" he asked with a scowl before he devoured the other half of his pecan bar in one bite.

"None of your business."

"It's a guy, I know it," he said around a mouthful.

"How do you know?"

He huffed. "Because I know what a girl's face looks like when she's thinking about or texting a guy she's into."

"Leave her alone," said Joaquin, sipping his coffee. "Give her some privacy."

Diego snorted indignantly. "You know who it is, don't you?"

"It was Lauren," I said.

"Liar," snapped Diego. "I may not be a psychic, but I know what I know."

"Stop harassing your sister." Mom set her coffee mug shaped like the Death Star on the coffee table. She then unclipped her dark auburn hair and retwisted it tighter in the clip on top of her head as she walked toward me.

"Would you like to stay and have coffee with us?"

This was Mom's way of gently suggesting I stay and chat so she could prod information from me. Normally, I'd be fine with that, but I was still super protective over this very new, fledgling of a relationship I had with Ronan. Besides, she still worried about me when it came to dating.

Diego picked up another pastry—something chocolatey, so it was probably made by Samara. "It's not that werewolf I saw you talking to at Howler's, was it?"

"Werewolf?" My mom's eyes lit up excitedly.

"Will you butt out, Diego?" I shouted past her. "Mom, I'm going to take a hard pass on coffee. Sorry."

I gave her shoulder a squeeze. If I happened to send her a calming spell when I touched her, well, that was pretty normal for me. I didn't want her to worry about me. And this time, there truly wasn't a need to.

"It's that Ronan guy, isn't it?" asked Diego.

Then I heard Dad open the back kitchen door. He'd been out back working in his art studio. I hurried over to Diego and twist-pinched his arm.

"Ow!" He jumped back. "Fuck, sis."

"Don't you say another damn word," I hissed in whisper.

"About what?" He stuffed his mouth with the chocolate truffle or whatever it was, grinning like the devil while he chewed.

"Don't." I pointed a finger as Dad rounded the corner and stopped right next to Diego, a puzzled expression on his face.

He propped his hands on his hips. "Do you smell another wolf?"

My dad, Mateo Cruz, was the gentlest, most affectionate, and loving father a girl could want. But his wolf, known as Alpha, lived simultaneously in his head. And he was the exact opposite.

Unlike most werewolves, whose wolves were silent except that one time of the month, my father lived with Alpha's intrusive thoughts fairly regularly. And Alpha was . . . well, he was *insanely* dominant, protective, and possessive when it came to family. Especially when it came to me, the baby girl. Though I wasn't a baby anymore.

Diego swallowed his mouthful of chocolate and inhaled a deep breath, now mirroring Dad's position with his hands low on his hips, looking like a younger carbon copy of him. "Yeah. I do."

"Where is that coming from?" asked Dad.

"Could be the mailman," Diego replied, taking a big whiff.

"The mailman is a warlock," said Dad.

Then he sniffed the air again, and I realized with shocking horror that Ronan must've delivered a package to my front door himself, not knowing that my father had the best sense of smell of any werewolf in the damn city.

I was already hurrying through the living room when Diego called roughly, "Celine, I still want to talk to you." At least he didn't mention Ronan's name in front of Dad. Small mercy.

"Later, Diego! I've got some patient work to tend to," I lied, fleeing the room like my ass was on fire.

Hurrying, I grabbed my purse and keys on the side table and raced to the front door to find a small brown box on the mat with only my name scrawled across the top. I picked it up and rushed to my car before my family could hassle me any more, and especially before my father could locate the scent of the strange werewolf who'd been on our premises.

Without thinking, I drove to Samara's studio apartment a few miles away. Thankfully, her car was parked on the street outside the building, which was really an older house that had been reno-vated and divided into four nice apartments. Taking the box with me, I walked up and knocked on her downstairs door.

Samara opened it, wearing a T-shirt and yoga pants. "Hey." She stepped aside, puzzled. "What's up?"

"I had to get out of the house fast."

"Why's that?"

After she closed the door behind me, I sat on the sofa with the little box in my lap. It was taped shut with packaging tape.

"This. Ronan left me some kind of a gift, and my dad and Diego started sniffing around, *literally*, wondering who the strange werewolf smell belonged to."

Samara leaned forward and took a whiff. As a vampire, her sense of smell was nearly as good as a werewolf's. Except my dad's. She grinned and waggled her brow. "He smells delicious."

"Stop, Samara." Still, I shivered. The thought of his scent surrounding me made my pulse race. For once, I wished I was a damn werewolf or vampire with those heightened senses. "Do you have a knife to get this open?"

"Of course."

She popped into her kitchen and returned, slitting it along the top seam and the sides for me.

I opened the lid to find some packaging paper wrapped around a small item, carefully cocooned in wrapping paper.

"What did he send you?" Samara sat next to me, peering into the box I'd set on her coffee table.

I lifted the object out of the packing. "I don't know." When I unwrapped it and realized what it was, I started laughing while holding it in my hands.

"A teacup?" Samara seemed bewildered. "That's an odd gift."

He'd painted it with these beautiful pink flowers all around the rim. There was actually a pot of pink flowers painted on the front with the tiniest purple dragon sitting on a leaf, his wings open. "I can't believe he did this."

"What?"

"It's a personal joke he was teasing me about. He accidentally broke one of my teacups, and he promised to replace it." Then it hit me as I swept a finger over the tiny dragon with a mischievous look in his blue eyes. "He had to go out pretty early to find the supplies and make this, let it dry, then wrap it and deliver it to my doorstep."

"Damn, you've already got private jokes with each other. I thought you'd only met twice."

"Three times actually. He was at Howler's last night."

"Dammit. I knew I should've gone."

"You said you had an important paper to work on."

She gestured toward her desktop in the corner of the living room where the screen showed she was working on something in Microsoft Word.

"Still am."

Samara was working on her master's degree. And though she was excellent in school, she still wasn't quite sure what she wanted to do in a career.

"Tough paper?"

"Forget about that." She took a seat on the sofa, facing me, her legs crossed underneath her. "So tell me what happened at Howler's."

My mind went instantly to the end of the night when Ronan left the bar in a hurry after nearly getting in a fight with some guys by the pool table.

"Well, that's not a happy face. What happened?" asked Samara.

"Actually, it was a great night. Being with him is like . . ." I shook my head, trying to find the words. "I don't know how to describe it. Just standing next to him and talking, I felt like I was right where I was supposed to be, like I was always supposed to be within Ronan's orbit."

"Whoa. That's kinda deep. You are an Aura, though."

Like that alone explained my romanticizing what it's like to be with him. Still, I was being honest. I couldn't understand it myself. Only that I felt more alive, more alert, even happier when he was near me. I just felt . . . more.

"So what's wrong?" she asked. "Why the long face?"

"Toward the end of the night, he went with two of the guys he works with at the body shop—good guys, Bowie and Zack. They all went to talk to some others I didn't know in the bar, and it was obvious Ronan nearly got into a fight with one of them."

"No shit?"

"The worst part was that the band were taking a break, and Diego rushed over, had a few words with Ronan, who then left with Bowie and Zack in a hurry. Thankfully, Diego and the band started back up not long after, and I left early."

"Did Diego tell you what the altercation was about?"

"The first I saw him since last night was just a little while ago when he and my dad were trying to figure out where the werewolf scent was coming from." I pointed to the box.

"Ahhh. I see."

"Diego did yell at me as I was leaving that he wanted to talk to me about Ronan. But I don't want to hear his overprotective bullshit."

"You're going to hear it anyway."

"Regardless," I said, heaving a happy sigh, "I'm going on a date with Ronan tomorrow night."

"Really?" Samara gave me that wicked smile. "Where are you going?"

"No idea. He's picking me up at six."

"At your house!"

"Calm down." I grinned. "My parents and Diego will all be gone. It's the full moon Saturday."

Samara frowned, and she didn't have to ask because I knew what she was thinking.

"Ronan told me he doesn't shift on the full moon."

"Like ever? What's wrong?"

Also concerned about the same thing but knowing it was too personal to ask yet, I told her, "I don't know. But I'm pretty sure that's why he's going to a supernatural psychologist."

We both grew quiet a minute, knowing there must be something deep going on with him for his wolf not to shift. I wasn't sure if this was a recent issue or if it had been going on for a while. He'd promised to tell me on our date.

"Well, then." Samara patted me playfully on the knee. "The more important question is, what are you going to wear?"

"I have no idea," I admitted.

"Something sexy, girl. Don't hold back. You want to see his jaw drop to the floor when he picks you up."

I laughed. I usually kept to my comfortable, more modest, attire on dates. But for Ronan, I truly did want to wow him. "I think you're right," I admitted.

"I'm always right. Come on." She hopped up and walked toward her bedroom, the only room off the large open living space and kitchen. "There's a great boutique store down the street that will have just the thing."

"But what about your paper?"

"I was looking for a reason to procrastinate," she called from the next room.

A minute later, she returned with shoes on, then we set off to buy me something spectacular for my date with Ronan.

CHAPTER 9

~CELINE~

T HE KNOCK AT THE DOOR SOUNDED AT EXACTLY SIX O'CLOCK. I'D BEEN sitting in the living room, anxiously waiting for him. And now it was officially real. I was going on a date with a werewolf. And hiding it from my family.

A twinge of guilt twisted in my chest, but I pushed it away as I walked through the foyer to the front door.

My nerves were a wreck until I opened the door and saw him standing there. If his jaw dropped like Samara said it would, I didn't notice because I was stunned still myself, drinking him all in.

He wore black slacks and a navy-blue button-down, rolled up at the sleeves. His usually mussed blond hair was styled more neatly, revealing the sharp, lovely features of his face clearly. His ocean-blue eyes shone darker as he devoured me from head to high-heeled feet.

At that boutique shop Samara had taken me to, I'd tried on at least ten dresses before finally finding this one. I never wore red, always thinking it clashed with the copper color of my hair, but this shade was deeper and a touch toward orange in a way that complimented my freckly, fair skin and made my eyes appear even greener.

With the way Ronan stared, sending a shiver of goose bumps along my arms, I knew I'd picked the right dress.

"Hi," I finally managed to say. "You look very nice." Quite the understatement.

He shook his head and stepped right up to me, taking my hand in his as he leaned down and brushed a light kiss on my cheek. My heart catapulted faster.

"You look stunning," he said in a low, sultry voice, his face close to mine.

"Thank you," I murmured, breathless.

It was a little brazen to kiss me on the cheek at the opening of a first date, but I didn't mind one single bit. I stood there, staring, just as he was. We both seemed a little shaken, my stomach flip-flopping at his close proximity and the way he was still gently holding my hand, rubbing his thumb over my knuckles.

"Did you like my gift?" he finally asked.

"Yes. I didn't expect you to replace the broken one. You didn't have to do that."

"Did it make you smile?"

There was a beat of silence while we stood there staring, locked in place. "Yes," I finally answered. "It did."

"Then you're wrong," he said gently. "I did have to do it."

There was something about Ronan that was wildly unpredictable. Both in words and actions. Perhaps that's why my pulse was pounding so hard. There was also something deeply genuine about him. Other guys always tried to impress me in some way, but Ronan wasn't trying to impress. He was simply being himself—highly impressive.

"I know my old Bronco isn't exactly fancy"—he held on to my hand as he finally took a step backward and tugged me toward the walkway and the curb where his Bronco was parked—"but she's tough and reliable."

"Like her owner?" I teased as we passed through the wrought iron gate.

He stopped and opened the passenger door for me, his voice deep near my ear as I passed him. "You can count on it."

I settled in the seat and put on my seatbelt, taking the ten seconds it took him to round the car to the driver's seat to catch my breath. It definitely wasn't enough time because then he was right there, filling the small space with his masculine presence and delicious scent—clean and sharp. Perfect for him.

"Where are we going?" I asked, noting the nervous edge in my voice and hoping he didn't.

"You'll see," he assured me, reaching across the console and taking my hand in his, threading our fingers together like it was the most natural thing in the world. And it felt like it.

I looked over at him, surprised. He gave me a soft smile. "Is this okay?" he asked, giving my hand a squeeze.

"Mm-hmm," was all I managed to say.

The radio played a croony Lana Del Rey song, and I relaxed into the seat and into the company of Ronan Reed. It was so natural, while at the same time my skin pebbled with goose bumps and my body felt warm and soft. Something about being next to him in the quiet of his car and the radio playing a smooth and lovely melody, my hand held firmly but gently in his, had my soul at ease.

He drove down Magazine Street, heading toward the French Quarter. I surely hoped we weren't going to be navigating the uneven streets of the Quarter. It would be precarious for me in these heels. But thankfully, he turned left on Julia Street in the warehouse district before we ever reached the touristy part of the city.

I couldn't help but look over at him while he concentrated on taking the next turn down a narrower street and marvel at the fact that he had no idea what a revelation this was. With Ronan—a large, strong, alpha male—I felt *safe*, not afraid of his dominance or strength over me. And that alone was something worth smiling about.

The only men I'd dated after high school and that nightmare of a warlock had been soft-spoken, passive, and one-hundred-percent beta guys. I loved beta guys—sweet, kind, and non-threatening in any way. But they also weren't my type. Therein lay the problem.

But here I was on a date with a definitively dominant male, feeling like I was in heaven.

Ronan parked along the side street. "We're here." Then he hopped out.

I looked around and saw nothing but the back entrances to a hotel and a dumpster. As I went to open the door, Ronan was already there and swinging it open.

"I've got it."

I smiled to myself at his overly gentlemanly manners. Southern born and bred, I suppose.

"Thank you." I smoothed my dress. "I guess your mama taught you right."

His gaze met mine, a fleeting frown pinching his brow before he smoothed it away. "She did." He closed the door and took my hand, guiding me back toward Julia Street.

"So where are we going?" I asked for the second time.

"Right there." He pointed to a sign hanging above a nondescript door that read *Jolie.* "Have you ever been here before?"

"No."

He opened the door, plunging us into a dimly lit interior and a narrow hallway that led up a small ramp into the restaurant and to the hostess station. I gasped.

Ronan spoke to the hostess while I marveled at the interior. "Reservations for two under Reed."

"Yes, sir," said the hostess in a sleek sheath dress. "Your table is right this way."

To our right, there was a private area for large parties curtained off by dark velvet drapes. The chairs at the center of the restaurant were all plush club chairs covered in rich textiles. The unique chandeliers and wood beams together with the decor gave it a bohemian, art deco vibe.

"Here you are, Mr. Reed." The hostess smiled at us both as I sat and scooted around the circular green velvet booth to the back. "Your server, Valerie, will be right with you."

She set drink and dinner menus on the table as Ronan sat next to me, his left knee bumping my right.

"Sorry," he murmured.

"It's okay."

I almost told him he could leave it right there. He could scoot even closer and let his thigh rest right up against mine if he liked. Hell, I wouldn't have minded climbing into his lap, but I figured that might be a tad forward and inappropriate. What could I say? Ronan Reed had me thinking vastly inappropriate things.

Goodness, what was wrong with me?

"What do you think?" he asked.

"This is one of the coolest places I've ever been to. I can't believe it's just a few miles from where I live, and I've never heard of it."

"Yeah, I thought you'd like it."

"Why did you think that?"

He gestured to the surroundings. "It's pretty artsy, don't you think?"

"Very. Didn't you just move here? How'd you find it? Zack or Bowie?"

He laughed, the deep, rich sound matching our intimate and lovely surroundings. "I'm sure those two have never been here. No, I asked a work buddy named Ty, who's a little older, knows the NOLA scene better."

"Oh, yeah, I know Ty. He's a great guy. He and my uncle Nico go way back, apparently, just like with your uncle Shane."

"He's helped me settle in at the body shop a lot."

Our server stepped up, and we ordered some of their specialty cocktails. I opted for the citrusy vodka drink called Glitter, and Ronan ordered a smoky bourbon drink.

"This is actually more of a cocktail lounge," he said as the waitress went to the bar to get our drinks, "but Ty said the food is excellent."

He tapped his fingers on the table, scoping out the place. Of course, my gaze was now riveted to those hands, just like when he'd painted the teacup.

It should be illegal for a man to have hands as sexy as Ronan's. The way the veins rose over the back, his long fingers—not too thick, not too thin—tapping lightly on the table. There was a definite callus on the edge of one thumb, and all I wanted was to feel it scrape across my skin as he ran his palm up my thigh.

"Are you okay?" he asked, jolting my attention back to him and away from his sinfully provocative hands.

He frowned with concern. He *should be* concerned. My dirty mind had gone from hand-holding to thigh-holding in a matter of seconds.

"Yes, fine. I'm fine."

The server set the drinks down and offered to give us a few minutes since neither of us had even looked at the menu. I distracted myself by sipping the glittery cocktail.

"How is it?" he asked.

"It's as delicious as it is pretty."

He froze with his drink halfway to his mouth, his blue gaze dark and intense. "I'll bet it is," he said, then licked his lips before he took a swallow.

A flush of heat swept up my neck and cheeks so I took another sip to try to cool my thoughts.

He cleared his throat. "So how did you get into art therapy? Did you always want to counsel kids?"

"I've always loved kids. I used to love babysitting Aunt Clara's brood or Aunt Violet's twin girls when they were little. I thought I might go into teaching, but I changed my mind after high school."

"What changed your mind?"

His voice was low and steady, his gaze fixed and attentive. Rather than make me nervous, I found it intoxicating. And while I wanted to get to know him and for him to get to know me, I wasn't quite ready to spook him with the big, scary skeleton in my closet. But I also wanted to be honest, so I told him enough.

"I used to suffer from anxiety as a teenager. It got to the point that my parents sent me to a therapist. Anyway, I found the experience so helpful that I knew I wanted to help others in that way."

He smiled. "I like that."

My stomach flip-flopped at the small compliment. "How so?"

"That you discovered your career path in that way. Someone helped you so it inspired you to help others."

I lowered my gaze and opened the menu finally. He did the same.

"And what about you?" I asked while skimming the entreés. "Did you always want to do auto bodywork?"

He laughed again, once more causing swirls of excitement to spin in my belly.

"Why are you laughing?" I asked, unable to keep from smiling with him.

"I, in no way, want a career in the body shop."

"Oh. I just figured you'd come to work for your uncle because that's what you're interested in."

"Not at all. For me, it's just a job, a way to keep my uncle happy while I pursue my real goal."

"And what's that?"

"To be the champion of the New Orleans Wolf Fighting Championship. Then to go on and win at state, and then hopefully move on to the national ring. Maybe go international."

He'd already told me he was into fighting, but I hadn't realized he was pursuing it as his career. Before I could respond, he went on excitedly.

"What's so fascinating is that the WFC is illegal in many states. Texas is one of them." He huffed out a laugh. "I can't believe I didn't leave Texas sooner. But I was doing well in the underground ring. Rose to the top quickly. Then some of the guys started bringing the fights outside the ring. That caused me some trouble."

I nodded. "Is that why your face was bruised last week?"

"Yeah. But I'm done with barroom brawls and underground cage fighting. I want to be a legit champion."

The excitement was clear on his face, and I couldn't help but smile with him, even if I didn't understand the lure of fighting or violence.

"It takes a lot of training and skill to be good in the ring. Even more to be the best," he said, seeming to want to convince me of something.

"Oh, I'm sure you're right. I've just never known someone who fought for a living."

"It bothers you?" His gaze was softer now, more vulnerable.

"I suppose I just don't quite understand it." I offered a sincere smile. "But I'm eager to learn more about it."

I was being honest. If this was something he was passionate about, then I definitely wanted to learn more. "So how does it work? When is your first fight?"

"Actually, the other night at Howler's, you remember those guys I went to talk to?"

"Yes."

"One of the guys on their team is the current champion, Baron Hammond. I'd been trying to reach him on social media, but the guys recognized him at the bar. So I went over to talk about registering. The website for the local chapter is down right now."

"Your chat didn't seem to go well from where I was sitting."

"Yeah. They were being assholes. Got under my skin a little." He frowned deeper. "Which doesn't usually happen to me."

"No?"

His smile returned, and my body instantly relaxed. "I'm known for being cool under pressure. I was just a little off the other night." He took another gulp of his drink right as the server returned.

We both ordered the steak with herb compound butter and Parmesan fries. When the server asked how I wanted it cooked, I answered, "Medium rare, but closer to rare, please. I like it a bit bloody."

Ronan grinned as she walked away, pressing his palm to his chest. "A woman after my own heart."

I laughed. "Of course you'd be impressed by a girl who eats her steak bloody."

"Can't help it. The wolf likes a carnivorous lady."

He kept grinning while my cheeks grew hotter.

"You promised me something at Howler's," I said, trying to calm my heart rate and stop blushing.

"Did I?"

"You said you'd tell me why you wouldn't be leaving town on the full moon."

"You're a smart woman, Celine. I'm sure you've figured it out."

I blinked, wondering if I'd hurt his feelings, but he didn't seem put off by the conversation at all. In fact, he was smiling contentedly as he waited for me to answer.

"I can only guess that's because you won't be shifting."

"Correct."

"And do you . . . ever shift?"

"I did. A few times actually," he answered casually. "But I stopped shifting when I was twelve."

"Do you know why?"

"Yes, definitely," he said, still with that casual tone. "My mother died, and my wolf simply"—he flitted his fingers in the air—"disappeared."

I stared for a moment, mouth hanging agape at his casual confession that his mother had died and his wolf had abandoned him. I'd heard about the time my own father couldn't shift. It was actually how my parents met, when a hex was put on him and he could no longer change once a month, so his wolf had pushed into his psyche. My father basically now had two personalities living inside his head at all times.

What I do know about that time was that not shifting was like torture for him. I'd never known another wolf who couldn't shift. It was a release that every werewolf needed to do in order to remain sane, basically.

But here was Ronan. Perfectly well and seemingly content.

"Is that why you're seeing Dr. Theriot?"

He brushed the condensation on his glass with his index finger, drawing me back to his perfect hands for a moment.

"I'm seeing Dr. Theriot to make my uncle happy. He's worried that I haven't shifted since Mom died."

"And you're not worried?"

"No." He smiled, staring intently again. "I'm perfectly fine just the way I am."

"Does your wolf speak to you?"

His dark brows shot up. "Does he *speak* to me?" He chuckled. "No. He's just gone. Or . . . he was anyway."

"What do you mean?"

"I heard my wolf growl recently." He leaned back against the velvet bench and draped an arm along the back behind my shoulders. "Haven't even sensed him in about fifteen years."

My pulse quickened. "I was pretty sure that was your wolf growling at me the day we met in the garage."

His eyes were more midnight than blue in the darkened lounge, their keen watchfulness studying my every move.

"You're right, Celine." He leaned closer, a lock of blond hair falling partly across one eye. "That was him."

He was confessing quite easily that he hadn't heard his wolf in fifteen years, yet he had the second we met. I could hardly keep my breath under control as he leaned close, surrounding me with his sultry scent and his dominating presence and his easy confession that it was *me* who had awakened the wolf who'd been hiding deep inside him.

I wasn't brave enough to address that for the moment. I switched to something deeply personal, but something I wanted to know. "How did your mother die? If you don't mind me asking?"

With the hand draped at my back, he swept my hair over one shoulder. "She died in a car accident."

The collar of my dress was a wide oval, revealing much of my bare shoulder. He played with a lock of my wavy hair, then let his knuckles softly caress the bare skin near my collarbone.

"Does this bother you?" he asked, eyes on my throat.

"Not at all." I swallowed hard, trying to focus. "I'm sorry about your mother, Ronan."

"You don't need to be. It was a tragedy, yes, and I still miss her. She was a great mother." His mouth ticked up on one side, but his gaze was on my shoulder where he gently swept the backs of his knuckles. "I loved her dearly, but I've accepted her loss."

"And the loss of your wolf too?"

He raised his gaze to mine. "I don't need him," he said with confidence, not defiance. "I've been doing just fine without him for a long time."

"But you're still going to see Dr. Theriot."

"To appease my uncle, yes." Then his smile turned wicked. "And maybe to pop in and see a certain pretty therapist across the hall when I leave."

I couldn't help but return his smile. Then his smile faded, as did mine, our gazes locked. We stared for an unnaturally long time, both of us seemingly content in this silent, intimate connection.

"Here we are." Our server Valerie finally broke the intensity of the moment as she delivered our meals. "Can I get you anything else?"

"Just some water, please," I said, placing my napkin in my lap.

"Same for me," said Ronan.

We ate quietly for a few moments. Valerie came and went with our waters.

"Is it rare enough?" he teased lightly, checking out my steak.

"Yes. It's delicious." Before he could tease me again about how I liked my meat—and all the insinuations that can go with that—I asked, "So tell me about how the training is going with Zack and Bowie."

He launched into a rather detailed explanation of their sparring sessions and how quickly the guys were learning and improving. There was pride shining in his expression as he talked about it. And while I wasn't crazy about fighting, it was pleasant listening to his voice, his Texan drawl luring me in.

Having finished his steak, he leaned back and watched me, his mouth tugging up into a semi-smile.

"What?" I asked.

"I want to ask you something, but I don't want to offend you."

"Well, now you have to ask me." I set my silverware down and dabbed my mouth with the napkin, giving me his full attention.

"What's it like having a witch for a mom and a werewolf as a father?"

"Why would that be offensive?" I laughed.

"It's strange is all. Where I come from, witches don't mingle with wolves. They sure as hell don't marry them."

Proud of the fact that my parents—and my entire family really—were open-minded, I said, "To answer your question, it's awesome. I don't find it strange at all. My parents are perfect for each other. The fact that my dad is a werewolf is normal to me, not odd."

"I like that," he admitted, that tantalizing smile and those hypnotic eyes sending a shiver over my skin.

"Why?" I asked breathlessly.

"That you see your parents, a wolf and a witch, as the perfect match."

I knew he was thinking about us now, and I couldn't do anything but stare dumbly. He broke the tense silence first.

"So when do I meet your family?"

"Not yet," I snapped quickly. I wasn't quite ready to face the firing squad.

Ronan's expression blanked, then he nodded and waved at our server and asked for the bill. I couldn't help but note that his aura had dimmed to a deep, dark purple. It wasn't anger or anxiety I was sensing. More like frustration.

After Ronan paid the bill, he politely escorted me to the car, taking my hand and walking closest to the street.

Again, there was silence on the short drive back to my house and up the walkway to the porch where he gently pulled me to a stop.

"I hope you had a good time tonight." His expression was austere and serious, no hint of the playful smile he so often wore. "Because I certainly did."

"Yes, thank you. I had a wonderful time." How could he doubt it?

"Does it bother you that your family will find out you're dating me?" he asked with directness.

"Yes," I answered honestly. But then the sudden hurt look on his face made me jump forward and grab his upper arms. "But not because I'm dating *you*, specifically. It's just a hassle." Especially when my father found out.

His brow pinched into a frown. "I don't understand why your family is so insanely protective of your dating life. You're a grown, intelligent woman. You seem quite capable of making your own decisions."

"Yes, you're right." I bit my bottom lip, still not wanting to admit my past that had turned our whole family upside down so long ago and had made them overly cautious whenever I brought a new guy home.

I realized I was still clutching his upper biceps while he had his hands in his pants pockets, as if he was trying to distance us. I didn't want him to pull away.

"All I need to know," he said, licking his lips, "is if you like me. That's all that matters to me. I don't give a shit what your family or friends or anyone else thinks. Just you."

Squeezing his arms, I stepped closer, now well within his personal space. "I like you, Ronan," I admitted softly. "Very, very, very much." My gaze dropped to his mouth, then back to his hauntingly beautiful eyes. "Do you like me?" I teased with a small smile, though my voice shook a little.

He dropped his forehead and pressed it to mine, his hands still stuffed in his pockets as he heaved a weighted sigh. "Celine, Celine," he repeated in a low whisper, "I can't tell you what I feel for you. Not just yet."

"No?" I slid my hands up his strong shoulders. "Then why don't you show me?"

On a deep rumble, he finally raised his hands and cupped my face, tipping my chin higher. He swept the pad of his thumb across my mouth once, twice, then on the third pass I opened my lips wider and touched my tongue to his thumb.

A purring growl vibrated in his chest as he angled his head and brushed his mouth softly and slowly against my lips. My entire body lit up like a raging bonfire. I whimpered as he nipped and coaxed and teased my mouth wider, finally licking inside with his hot tongue and melding his mouth to mine.

The sweep of gooseflesh over my skin and the shiver down my spine made my knees go weak. His kiss was like the first time I'd felt magic, a heady sensation full of promise.

One of his hands slid to my nape and the other around my waist, holding me still as he pulled my entire body to his. I moaned into his mouth, completely obliterated by the arousing sensation of his kiss. It was maddening and delicious, and I never wanted it to stop.

Fisting his hair in my fingers, I rubbed against him, certainly noting his large erection against my belly, while I kissed him back with all the passion I felt for him.

Did I like him? *Goddess above.* I was completely, insanely obsessed and besotted.

His tongue in my mouth, his hands on my nape and my waist, had me wanting to climb him like a tree. Or better yet, take him inside.

He nipped my bottom lip with his teeth, then sucked on it, and I felt the tug pool heat between my legs.

"Ronan," I murmured, leaning forward to kiss him again.

He softened it this time, easing his hand to cup my jaw as he swept his lips lightly up that line to my ear. "Can you feel how much I like you?"

I laughed heartily. "Yes." Then I pulled back and traced my finger over his mouth. "Can you feel how much I like you?"

"Let's just say I'm a lot happier than when we left Jolie."

We were silent for a moment as I let his hurt sink into me. My magic recognized it quickly, wanting to soothe and take it away, but I knew he had every right to be hurt. I wasn't going to charm him with magic to forget that I was the one in the wrong, who'd made him feel unwanted in any way. It was my place to make it right, but not with magic.

"I'm sorry, Ronan. I didn't mean to make you think that I was ashamed of you. I'm not. Not at all."

He nodded, both of his hands on my waist now where he gave me a squeeze and eased me away from him. "I get it. Your family is a handful."

I heaved a sigh. "You have no idea."

"I'll find out at some point, right?"

"Yes, of course. Let's just hold off that hurricane as long as we can."

"Whatever you want." He leaned his head down and pressed a soft, sweet kiss to my lips. "So when do I get a second date?"

"When do you want one?"

"Tomorrow."

I laughed. *How about tonight* almost escaped my mouth, and I wondered what had gotten into me. I was the ever-cautious, good girl Celine Cruz. But when it came to Ronan, I didn't want to be cautious or to be good. I didn't want slow and steady. And it wasn't simply lust that had my entire soul lit on fire. Still, I tried to maintain some self-control and thought about what I had on my plate tomorrow.

"Damn, I can't tomorrow. I have a new client to meet."

"On a Sunday?"

Shrugging, I added, "I don't have any free spots right now, and the mother was referred by a family friend."

"I have to catch up at the garage anyway. I've been falling behind and pulling Zack and Bowie off their jobs. Uncle Shane won't like it if we don't have that Camaro ready this week."

"Why don't you text me, and we can set a date?"

"That's a good plan." He leaned down for another kiss, taking his time with a soft, lingering goodbye. "I'll text you later." He grinned before he backed away.

My heart sped at the promise of more later. I was completely gone for this guy. He stopped halfway down the walkway and frowned at the house.

"You're here alone?"

"Don't worry. My aunt and uncle live next door."

"Is that the werewolf uncle or one of the vampire or grim reaper uncles?"

He *had* been looking into me, but it didn't bother me at all. "My three-hundred-year-old vampire uncle. He'd be in the house in two seconds if I called."

"What if you can't reach your phone?"

"No, I mean, if I called aloud. As in screamed for help. He's got really good hearing." I peeked to the right, seeing the kitchen light on at Aunt Isadora's. "Actually, he likely just noticed us making out on the porch." One more who might report me to the rest of the family.

Ronan kept his serious face on. "All right, then. Get inside and lock the doors."

"Yes, sir."

His only response was that deep rumbling growl I recognized as his wolf.

Smiling, I turned back to the door, fumbled with my keys, unlocked the door, then shut and bolted it. When I peeked through the side window, Ronan nodded and finally turned to leave.

Leaning back against the door, I grinned to myself and surveyed my emotions. No fear, no hesitation, nothing at all hindering me from wanting to launch myself headfirst into this relationship. And that's exactly what I planned to do.

CHAPTER 10

~RONAN~

IT WAS SUNDAY, AND CELINE WAS BUSY TODAY. THE HOUSE WAS QUIET since my uncle was still gone. So I was busying myself in my room, sketching Celine's portrait while listening to Hozier on my phone.

I realized how pathetic this might seem—listening to sappy music while pining in my bedroom and sketching pictures of her—but I simply didn't give a good goddamn. And if I happened to be replaying in my mind our first kiss on her doorstep, it couldn't be helped. The devil take me, but I couldn't stop obsessing over the sweet taste of her, the scent of her, the softness of her skin. I was truly, deeply undone.

My door popped open, and I jumped, shocked to see my uncle Shane standing there in cargo shorts and a T-shirt.

"What the hell?" I tapped my music off. "I thought you were gone for the full moon."

He shrugged, like that was enough of an answer. "What are you doing?"

I closed my sketchbook. "Nothing."

"Good. Get your ass outside. It's a beautiful fucking day and I'm grilling."

Then he turned and walked off, leaving the door open.

Okay, that was weird. Werewolves usually stayed in the woods and shifted for several days around the full moon, needing time to let the wolf roam. But Uncle Shane had only been gone since yesterday morning.

Shoving off the bed, I padded barefoot in my jeans and T-shirt through the house to the back door leading to the small deck. When I passed through the kitchen, I noticed several plastic bags of groceries on the dining table. The scent of burning charcoal wafted from the back as I stepped out onto the deck.

Uncle Shane was lighting the pit, a bottle of Abita in one hand. "Grab a beer."

He gestured to the outdoor table where he'd left a six-pack. I took one and twisted it open. Some country music was playing on his portable speaker, his phone sitting on a station next to it. The music reminded me of Texas. Even in the city of Austin, you'd hear country music playing in plenty of bars more often than not.

"Your wolf doesn't need more than a day?" I asked, curious.

That hadn't been my experience with other friends back in Texas. They typically left for at least three or four days around the full moon.

"Ah. One day was enough." The pit lit, he settled into one of the chairs with a sigh and swallowed a few gulps of his beer.

There were dark circles under his eyes and he hadn't shaved. "You look a little tired," I mentioned as I took the other chair at the table.

He shrugged. "Didn't like the idea of you back here on your own."

I chuckled. "Doesn't bother me." I spent most of my time back in Texas alone too.

"It bothers me," he stated emphatically, holding my gaze.

His eyes were somewhere between the wolf and the man. He should've stayed gone another day and let his wolf do what he needed to do.

"Look, you don't have to worry about me. I'm fine."

He made no comment, turning to look out at the woods that extended behind his property. The pit began to smoke more as the coals burned.

"How is it going with the doctor?"

"My therapist?" I clarified with a smile.

He nodded.

"Good, actually. I should thank you for that."

"No need."

We settled into a bit of silence, drinking our beers, listening to the music. Uncle Shane drummed a finger on the side of his beer. He was anxious about something.

"Better get the meat on that pit." Then he headed back into the house.

This was odd. Uncle Shane and I didn't spend quality time together, but he'd called me out here. And obviously for some specific reason. Rather than worry about it, because he'd get it off his chest sooner or later, I relaxed and let the noonday sun warm me on the deck and enjoyed my cold beer.

Uncle Shane took his time piling what smelled to be spicy sausage, pork steaks, and burgers on the grill.

"Are we expecting company?" I asked.

"Nah." He laughed, closing the pit and setting his tongs on the side. "Figured I could get some cooking done for the week."

"Good plan." I reached over and opened two more beers, seeing as he had finished his first as well. I handed it to him as he took his seat again with a sigh.

Though he seemed pensive about something, we sat in companionable silence for a bit. From here, I could see the back of the paint barn and the smaller shed for storage. Beneath the overhang of the storage shed was the Harley I'd seen Rhett drive into work the other day rather than his regular truck.

"What's the story with that bike over by storage? Is that Rhett's?"

Uncle Shane followed my gaze. "No, that's actually all of ours."

"How's that?"

"Last year, we had this corporate guy drop off that Harley Frontier. He wanted some custom work done. But before we'd even gotten to work, he said he'd changed his mind. Went out and bought a Roadmaster instead. Said he wanted something better to tour across the US." He shook his head on a snort.

"That one wasn't good enough, huh?" I asked sarcastically. The Frontier was a seriously nice bike.

He chuckled. "Apparently not. He was in a hurry. He said I could have it for a quarter of its value."

"Damn. Why'd he let it go for so little?"

He shrugged. "Rich people. Guess he didn't want the hassle."

"That was lucky."

"Yeah. So we keep it here and any of the guys can use it when they want." He sipped his beer. "You know how to ride?"

"Yeah. I've never sat my ass on a bike that nice, though."

Smiling, he said, "Well, you're welcome to use it whenever you like."

"Thanks."

Another country song came on that I recognized right away, "Keep The Wolves Away." I couldn't help but laugh.

"What's funny?" he asked.

"That song. My friend Malcolm and some other guys"—ones I used to fight with in the underground ring—"we would sing this one at the end of the night at our favorite bar. It was owned by a werewolf like Howler's is, and he found it funny to play it at closing time."

Uncle Shane nodded and smiled. We sat quietly a minute, sipping beer and listening to the song about trying to survive, finding a better life, and keeping the wolves of the world away.

"You know, growing up, we didn't have much," said Uncle Shane. "My mom was sick for a long time and died when I was in my teens."

I'd never met my grandmother. Mom used to say how loving and sweet she was. Cancer took her before I was born. She was human and didn't have the genes to fight diseases like super-naturals did.

"Our dad worked hard, but it wasn't enough," he continued. "I went to work right out of high school to help keep things afloat. Stacy was still in elementary school, and Ella, your mom . . ."

He paused and observed me carefully. I knew he was seeing my mother's features in my face. I favored her a lot.

He cleared his throat. "Your mom never went to college like she'd planned. We needed her at home, especially Stacy, and she knew it." He took a sip of his beer. "She'd wanted to be a teacher. Did she tell you that?"

"Yeah." My voice was rusty.

Mom used to teach me at home when I was little. She'd gotten pregnant with me not long after her sister Stacy had gone off to junior college. So yet again, life threw more adversity in her way. But she never let me feel like a burden. She always made sure I knew that I was the most important thing in her life. I never doubted it.

"She was a fantastic cook," he said. "She made the best damn chicken enchiladas I ever had."

I chuckled, my throat a little thick. "Those were my favorite. She made them for me all the time."

"Lucky son of a bitch," he teased.

We both laughed, but it turned somber quickly.

"Every year on my birthday, she made me a homemade red velvet cake. My favorite. Even when I moved away from Amarillo, she'd package it carefully and ship to me every year wherever I was living. Can you believe that?"

I couldn't answer at first, too overwhelmed with these specific memories of her. I hadn't talked about her with anyone who knew her in years. My aunt Stacy never talked about her with me. It was too hard.

Clearing my throat, I said, "I can believe that. She always thought about everyone else."

"She did." He set his beer on the table. "I miss those cakes." He stood and walked over to the pit and turned the meat.

It was a clear day with wide blue skies above us. It wasn't nearly as hot as usual, a balmy breeze rustling the leaves in the trees behind the house. Mom loved that sound. I'd never gotten to reminisce with anyone who knew her before.

When he sat back down, I told him, "She used to say all she needed for the perfect day was a hammock and a breeze and a salty margarita."

Uncle Shane laughed. "She always enjoyed the simple things."

We both grew quiet again. My mom was an amazing, wonderful woman. I'd dealt with her loss, but it always hurt when I thought about her in this way—all the moments we'd had and all the ones we never would.

"I should've been there." My uncle's voice had gone deep and serious.

"When?" I asked, unsure what he was talking about.

He held my gaze, his expression tense with emotion. "After she died. I should've been there for you."

Never in my life had I expected this. I didn't know what to say.

"Your mom was the most selfless person I've ever known. And when her son needed someone, I wasn't there. I've been so absorbed in my own life. I have no excuse." He heaved a sigh and combed a hand through his hair. "Anyway, I'm sorry, Ronan. I should've come around a lot sooner to help out."

"It's okay. I'm fine."

"I suppose you are. Hell, I can't blame you for all your cop troubles, because I was the same way when I was your age."

I shrugged. "I've done all right on my own."

"Yeah. But you don't have to be on your own anymore. That's all I'm saying."

He suddenly seemed a little uncomfortable. That was a lot of emotion for my rather gruff uncle Shane.

He clapped his hands together and stood. "How about we eat?" he suggested abruptly.

"Sounds good to me. I'm starving."

"Grab us some plates, would you?"

"Are there any vegetables or just meat?"

"Just meat and beer."

I chuckled. "I'm good with that."

After I fetched the plates and we settled outside with piles of pork steak and sausage, we ate in silence. Neither of us felt the need to talk anymore. Nothing but the sound of the wind in the trees to keep us company. It was a beautiful day.

CHAPTER 11

~RONAN~

Bowie, Zack, Ty, and I walked toward the warehouse office building at the port. This was the physical address of the NOWFC according to the website. It was also one of the many port offices for Baron's father's company, Hammond Industries.

I'd expected at least something that appeared to be unaffiliated with Baron and his championship team, the Iron Claws, but apparently not.

It had been far easier to convince Ty to do this than I'd thought. On Monday, I'd pulled him aside and explained what I was doing. When I mentioned the NOWFC, he said he already knew about it. I started to explain that he was an ideal candidate because he was already trained in multiple martial arts.

"So that's why you've been interrogating me on my extra-curricular activities," he'd said. After an in-depth discussion where he asked quite a few questions, he finally agreed to be on the team.

"This is pretty sketchy," said Ty as we approached the building. The sound of boats on the Mississippi River and men working the port and large machinery echoed around us.

"Just a bit," I agreed. "But his daddy can't help him win fights, so it doesn't matter."

I opened the door, and we entered. The office was one room with about five desks and computers squeezed inside. There was a middle-aged woman—a witch of some kind—at the first desk, typing away. She wore glasses and looked a bit like a no-nonsense librarian.

She stopped when we entered. "May I help you?"

"Yeah. We're actually here to register for the NOWFC. This was the address I was given."

Baron had finally answered my DM on Instagram and sent me the address yesterday.

She briefly eyed the guys behind me. "Is your entire team present? You can only register with everyone to sign their own waivers."

"Yes. This is the whole team."

She spun on her wheeled chair and opened the second drawer of a filing cabinet. After rummaging a minute, she finally pulled out a file and spun back to her desk while taking out a sheet of paper. The logo for the NOWFC, the wolf's head with the skyline of NOLA behind it, was at the top of the sheet.

"You'll need to fill out everyone's names and contact information. And I need to copy your driver's licenses."

The four of us pulled out our licenses while I took the waiver form and stepped over to a table with a couple of chairs against the wall. Ty sat next to me, Zack on the other while Bowie remained standing.

"In case of injury or death in the ring, I will not hold NOWFC responsible or file civil suit against NOWFC," Ty read. "They're not playing around."

"Have you ever seen this before?" Zack asked me.

"I've never signed a contract because I've only fought in illegal rings." I turned to the woman copying our licenses on a printer. "How many fighters have died in the NOWFC?"

"None," she replied dryly. "Severe injuries, though. A few broken arms. One was in the hospital for a week. But we provide top-rate healing witches following the fights for anyone who needs it."

"Is this waiver normal?" I asked.

She turned with the licenses and walked over to set them on the table. "Same waiver they all use in Louisiana. You're not from here?"

"Texas."

She chuckled. "Yeah, the cowboys over there need to make it legal." She leaned over and pointed down at a line below the contact information. "You probably didn't see this part, did you? This form guarantees your payment of winnings to be deposited to your bank within seven days of a winning fight."

I read that part carefully, smiling at the percentages of the house earned by each champion of the night.

"All fighters get paid, though. The losers just get paid a much smaller percentage of the house."

"Well, hell," said Zack, "hurry up so I can sign."

We chuckled as I filled out my contact information, my emergency contact information—Uncle Shane—then finally signed the waiver below and slid it to Zack. After we'd all done our part, I stood and handed the form over to the woman at the desk.

"So what happens now?"

"I'll input your information into the NOWFC database, and once I get the approval from the central office in Baton Rouge, which usually takes one business day, you'll be registered as official fighters in the WFC of Louisiana."

Zack made a *woot* sound and clapped.

"I think that means we'd better start training harder," added Ty.

"Definitely," I agreed, then asked the gatekeeper of this organization, "When will the first fight be scheduled?"

"That will be decided by the board of the NOWFC. Since the current champions have fought and beaten all of the other competitors this year, you'll be fighting them. The Iron Claws. Oh!" She frowned, looking at the form. "You didn't put a name for your team."

I glanced at the guys, one by one. "What do y'all think?"

Bowie shrugged. "The Blood Moon."

"Yeah," added Zack. "The Blood Moon Crew."

"That'll work," agreed Ty.

She wrote that down, then looked up at me. "Are you the leader of the team?"

"Yeah."

"They'll be contacting you with the fight schedule. All right, boys." She reached out and shook my hand, then the others. "Welcome aboard. And good luck."

We left, walking through the lot toward Bowie's SUV in silence. While I was filled with hope and excitement, for I was finally on a legitimate WFC team, I wondered what the guys were feeling. I wished I had Celine's Aura ability so I didn't have to ask.

We piled into the SUV, me and Ty in the back seat.

"So what are y'all thinking?" I asked as Bowie turned out of the port gate.

"I think we could make a lot of money," said Zack with a smile.

"We need to get training harder," added Ty.

"Agreed. I was hoping you could teach them more on the kickboxing end, Ty." I tapped open my phone and sent the screenshot I had to all three of them. "I actually pulled the shop schedule and worked out a training schedule for us on our days and afternoons off."

Ty read the schedule. "That'll work for me."

"I know this will take up a lot of your free time, but we need to train hard from here on out."

"I've got nothing better to do," added Bowie.

Zack chuckled. "Me neither."

I sat back and sighed, looking out the window as we headed into the Lower Garden District toward Ty's house to drop him off. Celine now weighed heavily on my mind.

Since our date Saturday night, we'd texted daily, both of us unable to meet up for that second date yet. She'd been immersed in work, and I'd been either in the shop or out behind it with these guys.

So strange that my dream was finally taking shape. This was the first step, but it was still a move forward and upward. And yet, all I could do was think about how much less time I'd have to be with Celine.

"Damn." Ty looked over at me. "Now that's a heavy sigh."

"Wouldn't have to do with a certain redheaded witch, would it?" chuckled Zack from the front seat.

"No way." Ty shook his head. "You're really trying to date Celine?"

"Not trying." I smirked. "We went on our first date Saturday night."

"And she's giving you a second date?" asked Bowie.

I smiled, not about to give these nosy asshats any details. "Yeah. She is."

"Interesting," said Ty.

"Why do you say it like that?" I asked, annoyed.

"She's just very particular."

"Never gave me the time of day," said Zack.

"Like that's a shocker," added Bowie.

"And quite frankly," said Ty, ignoring them, "few guys want to deal with her father and brothers."

"And uncles and aunts and cousins," added Zack.

"They don't intimidate me." I made that clear.

Ty gave me a look of respect along with a somewhat mischievous smile. "Good for you, Ronan." He glanced out the window, then tapped on Bowie's shoulder in front of him. "Hey, why don't we grab a bite right here. That café's got the best brisket sandwiches in town."

I checked my watch. "Yeah, let's get some food. But we'll have to make it quick. I've gotta finish that paint job on the Camaro."

Bowie pulled over to the curb and parked. It didn't escape my attention that he flashed a grin at Ty as he got out on the driver's side.

"You two got a private joke you want to let me in on?" I asked as we walked into the Silver Moon Café.

They just laughed as we made our way into the café, which also seemed to be a coffee shop. There were several loners set up with laptops and coffee at booths and tables.

A pretty woman with black hair, brown skin, and green eyes greeted us, breaking out into a big smile. I read the vampire designation buzzing off her, but also a little something more. Strange.

"Hey, Ty! It's been a while since you've been in here."

"Hi, Samara. Yeah, we were on this side of town, thought we'd get some of Joaquin's famous brisket sandwiches."

"Great. So is that four of the special?"

Ty turned to us, and we nodded.

"What can I get y'all to drink?" she asked.

Zack and Bowie ordered. I got a bottled water, needing to hydrate after my early run this morning.

"Oh, Samara," said Ty suspiciously, "you haven't met Shane's nephew, have you? This is Ronan Reed, new to town."

Her green eyes widened, as did her grin. "*You're* Ronan Reed?"

Frowning, I nodded. People knowing my name before I knew them hadn't always been a good thing for me. It usually led to a bar fight. But this was a pretty witch, and she didn't seem pissed off on hearing my name. Quite the opposite.

I shuffled uncomfortably. "Have we met?" I asked to be polite, knowing we hadn't.

"No," she said on a laugh. "But you've met my cousin, Celine Cruz."

Zack and Bowie chuckled. I rolled my eyes at them.

"Yeah. I know Celine," I told her.

"Oh, I *know* you know her." Then she completely checked me out from head to toe. "Celine told me."

At that moment, the kitchen door swung open, and a tall, supernatural man wearing an apron walked straight toward us. He had dark red hair and familiar looking green eyes that flicked to Ty first before swiveling to me with a scowl.

"You're Ronan?" He propped his hands on his hips.

I definitely read a werewolf signature pumping off him with some aggression, but like the woman beside him, he also seemed to have some witch in him.

"As I just confirmed, yes, I am," I answered firmly. I'd already figured out who he was. "You're Celine's brother, aren't you?" The other triplet.

He continued to examine me, as if he could determine whether I was a good guy or a piece of shit by staring me down. Hell, maybe he could. This family seemed to have a mixture of magic I hadn't ever seen before.

"I am," he answered gruffly.

I wanted to punch Ty in the face for blindsiding me and kick Zack and Bowie in the balls for snickering off on the side like children. But I needed all three of them in good health to fight on my team.

My team. A sense of pride swept through me. Then I stepped forward and stretched out my hand. "Ronan Reed. It's a pleasure to meet you."

His intense gaze flicked to my hand. I waited, wondering if he was actually going to leave me hanging. But he didn't. He shook my hand. "Joaquin Cruz."

I knew that, but I said, "Nice to meet you" anyway.

He looked at Ty. "Did you know he's chasing my sister?"

"I'm not chasing her," I said emphatically. "We're dating."

That green-eyed gaze came back to me, and he crossed his arms. "Is that so?" But rather than seem angry, he actually seemed pleased.

"Yep," said Samara. "That is so much so."

We all turned our attention to her.

"It's true," she added. "They're going on a second date soon. Isn't that right?"

I hid my smile because, apparently, Celine told her cousin quite a lot about us, and we hadn't even met. Also, she was defending me. I liked this cousin a lot.

"We sure are," I confirmed.

Joaquin looked at me again, pensive and grave. "You don't look like her usual type."

"Thank the Goddess," muttered Samara.

My body locked up at the mention of other men. I mean, obviously a woman as beautiful as Celine had dated lots of men, but I didn't like thinking about it. Not one bit.

I shrugged. "I'm dating her all the same." And unable to stop myself, I added, "I ain't going anywhere either."

"Good," Joaquin said rather emphatically, which surprised me, then he huffed a small laugh. "You're going to need balls that big to date my sister."

"That's what I understand," I answered, shooting Ty a death glare. "Some warning might've been nice."

Ty smiled. "More fun this way." Then he looked at Joaquin. "Good to see you again."

"Yeah, you too." Then he turned back to me. "Good luck."
He turned abruptly for the kitchen. "I'll get those orders," he
called back.

"You're not going to spit in mine, are you?" I yelled after him.

He stopped with the door open and looked back. Then he
laughed a real laugh. "Nah, man. But I'll do worse than that if
you hurt my sister."

"It'll never happen," I swore, feeling the truth of it down
to my bones.

"Then we're good, Reed." He nodded and left, letting the
door swing behind him.

Zack, obviously put out, stepped forward. "What in the hell
was *that*? That's it? That's all? Joaquin's just going to let him
date her?"

Samara scoffed. "Celine is a grown-ass woman. She can date
whoever the hell she wants."

Zack laughed. "But come on, no punches thrown? No death
threats?"

"There was a bit of a threat there," interjected Bowie. "And
Ronan hasn't met Mateo yet. Or his wolf."

Samara set our drinks on the counter for us to take. When I
took my bottle of water, she leaned forward and whispered con-
spiratorially, "Hang in there, Ronan. Celine needs a man like
you in her life."

"I was being truthful to her brother. I'm not going anywhere."

She stared for a second, then dipped her chin. "You're exactly
what she needs." She winked, then turned to take the next order
as a couple had come in behind us.

"I hate you," I said as I sat down next to Ty.

"No, you don't." He nudged my elbow. "You need some allies. I knew Samara would be on your side. And I had a feeling about Joaquin. Celine is closer to him than Diego when it comes to personal matters. He understands her more."

There seemed to be something else he wasn't saying. "Understands what more?"

I also wondered about what Samara said, that I was the kind of man she needed. It made me think there was more to that statement too. Some secret behind it.

"Nothing." He shook his head.

But it wasn't nothing. I was quickly realizing that Celine's family wasn't blindly overprotective. There was a catalyst for this type of overbearing behavior. Whatever it was, it wasn't going to stop me. That was something the whole damn family needed to realize right quick.

Celine was mine. Or she was going to be. And no one was going to keep me from getting my girl.

CHAPTER 12

~CELINE~

An entire flock of butterflies exploded in my belly as I walked up to the body shop. The radio was playing some Billie Eilish song when I entered the garage, looking for a particular werewolf.

Ty stepped from underneath a hood and wiped his hands on a rag. "Hey, Celine. You looking for Rhett?"

Clearing my throat, I shook my head. "No. I was looking for Ronan. If he's not too busy."

Ty's mouth ticked up on one side. "He's not too busy for you."

The afternoon sun was dipping behind the trees, but it was still hot. Hopefully, he thought my flushed cheeks was from the heat.

"Can you tell me where he is?" I saw Bowie working underneath another hood. He gave me a nod and went back to work.

"He's out back at the paint barn with Zack. You can walk right on through that back door."

I hurried around the cars, thankful Rhett was in the office. I didn't see Ronan's uncle Shane either, so all my prayers to avoid the awkwardness of dropping by for no other reason than to see the man I was completely infatuated with were answered.

Once through the back door, there was a well-tread path in the grass leading to the paint barn. I could hear Zack rambling about something as I stepped closer. He seemed to be recounting some sci-fi show I'd seen on Netflix, but he stopped talking before I reached the barn. The sound of the paint machine stopped too. Of course, they were werewolves and must've sensed me.

As I walked in, Ronan was removing a mask to protect his mouth from the fumes, but I froze at the sight of the rest of him. He was wearing one of those onesie coveralls, but he had his unzipped to the waist, the arms of the onesie tied at his hips. Underneath, he'd been wearing a threadbare white T-shirt that was soaked through with sweat, adhering to his muscular chest like a second skin.

When I finally caught his gaze, it was obvious he recognized the desire in my eyes. He tossed the painting tool aside that looked like some sort of gun with a wide nozzle at the end. Then he removed the glove he'd been holding it with and let it drop to the barn floor.

"Zack, why don't you take a break," he suggested, though it sounded more like a command.

His voice fell to that deep register, sending a spray of goose bumps up my bare arms. Then he stalked toward me, his hair a mess, his body dirty and drenched in sweat, spots of red paint on his arms and covering one of his hands.

"Yeah, good idea. I'll take a break," said Zack, though neither of us even looked at him as he left through the open double doors of the barn on the far end.

"Why didn't you wear gloves on both hands?" I asked dumbly as he drew closer, those piercing eyes tracing down my body.

He shrugged. "What did I do so right to get this surprise visit?"

"We haven't gotten our second date, and I . . ."

He was almost to me.

"I missed you," I admitted freely.

I was rewarded with a wide grin. "Celine." He heaved out a sigh along with my name, shaking his head as he stopped right in front of me. "You can't say things like that when I'm already so weak for you." He lowered his head and brushed his lips over mine, pressing forward, only touching me with his mouth.

I threaded my fingers into his messy hair, fisted my hands, and pulled him forward as I stepped back. He followed with a groan, kissing me until my back hit the barn wall.

He broke the kiss and planted one hand above my head, his eyes dark and intense. "I missed you too."

"Show me," I teased, thinking of our first date.

"I don't want to get you all sweaty."

"Maybe I *want* you to get me all sweaty."

And that was all it took. He opened his mouth on my neck on a moan as I curled a hand in the side of his shirt and pulled his body against me.

I whimpered as he nipped and licked his way down my throat. "Ronan."

"You smell so good," he murmured into my skin, surrounding me with his heat and his musky masculine scent. "Taste so good."

"Yes." I curled my fist tighter in his hair as he skated his mouth down the vee of my dress.

He'd been avoiding putting his hands on me, but he finally gave in, reaching around and cupping my ass. He grazed his mouth over my breast. I'd worn a thin bralette under my summer dress, which meant I could feel the heat of his mouth on my nipple.

When he grazed his teeth over the peak, I urged, "Yes, more."

I'd been pressing and pulling him, simply needing so much I didn't know what to do. But then he fell to his knees, nudging his nose and mouth against my mound before he peered up at me.

Heavens, the feral look in his darkened eyes made me shiver. As if of their own volition, my hands inched up the hem of my dress, slowly, boldly, until I held all of the material at my waist, giving him a good look at my white satin panties.

Holding my gaze, he eased forward and opened his mouth on my mound, tonguing me through the thin material.

"Oh God." I clutched his shoulder with my free hand as he sucked and groaned, his eyes having lost all of their blue.

"Open your thighs wider," he commanded.

I did, watching him slide my panties to the side with his long fingers. He sat back, biting his bottom lip as he glided the pads of two fingers along my slick slit and around my throbbing clitoris.

"So fucking pretty all over, Celine." He gripped my bare thigh with his paint-stained hand and continued working my clit with his other one.

When he leaned forward again and flicked his tongue around the tight bud, I made a sound I was a little embarrassed by, but I rocked my hips forward anyway, seeking more of his hot mouth.

Groaning, he lapped at me, then slid his two fingers inside me and pumped, the wet sound of my arousal on his fingers as he fucked me with them sending me closer and closer to climax.

"You're so fucking sweet," he whispered, his hot breath on my clit as he circled it with the tip of his tongue. "I wanna eat you and drink you all damn day."

I clenched his shoulder. "I'm going to come way before that."

He smiled against my pussy. "I want you to come in my mouth, baby. Need to taste more of you."

"That won't be a problem," I panted as he began thrusting his fingers faster.

Then he opened his mouth over my slit, flicking my clitoris with his tongue. I clutched a fistful of his hair and held his mouth to me.

Within a minute, I was crying out. "Yes! Ronan, I'm coming."

I spasmed and continued to rock against him as he groaned, that low wolflike purr vibrating from his chest as he licked me clean. When I was nothing but a panting mess, one hand still clutching my skirt at my waist, I finally let go of his hair, but he wasn't done.

He licked and kissed my swollen lips, now being careful to avoid my sensitive clit, then he righted my panties and planted a soft kiss to my mound before standing in front of me. Shamelessly, he thrust his fingers that had been inside me into his mouth and licked them clean, holding my gaze.

"Ronan," was all I could manage. A swirl of heat spun again just at the sight of him licking my taste off his fingers.

"When is our third date?" he asked, curling one arm around my waist, the other hand planted firmly on my ass where he gave me a squeeze.

"This was a date?" I asked, still breathing heavily.

"If I had my tongue in your pussy, then it was a date to me."

I laughed, a heated blush creeping up into my cheeks.

"Oh, she's shy now? After lifting her skirt and tempting me so wickedly."

I glanced away, embarrassed. "I couldn't help it."

"I'm so glad." He pressed his lips to mine, my scent mingling with his in an oddly pleasurable way. "I loved it."

I buried my face into the crook of his neck. He laughed and pulled me close, his hard cock pressing against my belly. I wanted to do something about that.

"Is there anywhere private we can go?" I reached down between us and slid my hand over his erection.

He hissed and gently gripped my wrist before pulling it away. "No way. The guys can listen to me getting you off, but no way we're giving them a full show."

"They can't see us! Can they?" I looked around, wondering if there were cameras out here or something.

"No." He chuckled. "They can't see us. But they're wolves. They can hear well enough, and you weren't exactly quiet."

"I can't believe I didn't think about that. I'm so embarrassed."

"Don't be." He eased back, gripping my waist, rubbing his thumbs at my hips. "I'm glad. Now they'll stop telling me I don't have a chance with Celine Cruz."

"They didn't say that, did they?" I scowled.

"*Everyone* has been saying that," he assured me, his playful smile wide and sweet.

"Well, they're wrong."

"I know." He squeezed my hips again, looking down and making a disgruntled sound before releasing me. "Fuck, sorry about your dress."

There was red paint on the waist on one side and a handprint of red fingers on my thigh, still visible when I smoothed the skirt down.

"It's okay." I smiled up at him. "It was worth it. I'll keep my stained dress in memory of our second date."

He laughed, the pleasant sound rolling through my chest and filling me with warmth and happiness. His aura was the brightest pink, and I couldn't help but smile. I was pretty sure I'd made him light up from within.

"So when do I get my third date?" he asked again.

"My brother's got a gig in Mid-City tomorrow night. I could meet you there."

I still hadn't told my parents about Ronan, and by some incredible miracle, none of my uncles or nosy brothers had mentioned him either. I suppose they all knew that I'd never forgive them if they ruined this thing I had going before it really got started.

Not that my dad would ruin it, but he might dampen the moment, this lovely beginning between Ronan and me. I was in this euphoric, joyful, exciting place. And though I'd experienced this sort of excitement at the beginning of other relationships, nothing and no one had compared to this. I wanted Ronan all to myself for a little longer before I had to deal with my parents. Well, mostly my dad. He always meant well, but I just didn't want to take the chance of anything spoiling this for me right now.

"Send me the address." He eased closer, pressing one last kiss to my mouth. "I'll see you there," he promised.

I nodded. "Walk me to my car?"

"Of course." He offered his arm along the grass trail to the garage. "I don't want to get you any dirtier with my hands."

"I really like the way you get me dirty with your hands." I nudged his arm with my shoulder. "And your mouth."

"Celine," he warned.

I laughed. "You're actually blushing," I accused.

"No way. I don't blush."

But he totally was, and I loved it.

He didn't take me back through the garage, thankfully. I didn't want any side-eyed looks or grins from the guys. When we got to my Honda, he opened the door for me, and I slid in.

"I met your brother Joaquin," he said abruptly.

"What? He didn't say anything to me. When was this?"

"Yesterday."

"How was he?" My stomach clenched, wondering what Joaquin said to him.

"Better than I expected actually." He chuckled, holding my door open. "I met your cousin Samara too. She was really cool."

"Yeah, she is."

For the first time, I thought maybe my family was going to behave completely normal about me dating a rather rough-around-the-edges werewolf.

"See you tomorrow night, babe," he said casually as he leaned down and pecked my lips before shutting the door.

A giddy excitement thrilled through me at his casual and perfectly natural use of the endearment *babe*. Like it belonged on his lips and only when he addressed me.

I watched in the rearview as he stood in the gravel drive, then finally turned and headed back to the garage.

"Can't wait," I said, smiling at his retreating reflection, "babe."

CHAPTER 13

~RONAN~

"So why fighting?" Dr. Theriot sat in her plush club chair across from me, cross-legged and attentive.

"Why not?" I shot back, more defensively than I intended.

"Most werewolves tend to lean into a creative field, being the gift that came with the curse of transformation of wolfkind."

"Fighting can be a creative art form," I explained gruffly. "It requires skill and finesse and sometimes creativity to beat an opponent."

She nodded in that sage way of hers, then kept pushing. "It's just that you could've gone onto a thousand different career paths. But you chose wolf cage fighting, which was illegal where you were born and lived the majority of your life."

"It's legal here."

"But it wasn't where you first chose it."

"Maybe I didn't choose it. Maybe it chose me."

She smiled that doctorly smile. "That's a thought. Let's follow it. Why would fighting choose you?"

I leaned back all the way, my fingers clasped loosely between my legs. "Maybe I had to fight."

"Why?" she asked gently.

I snorted and turned my head toward the window. No cardinals on the tree outside today. "Because nobody was going to fight for me."

"You said that your grandfather took you in after your mother died."

"He did. And when I was too much for him, he gave me to my aunt. And when I was too much for her, she kicked me out."

"But that was for more than a decade. And now you're living with your uncle."

I shrugged, not knowing where the hell she was going with this. "And?"

"Perhaps you're right," she added. That was a shocker. "Perhaps fighting chose you. Your feelings of abandonment needed an outlet."

"I never said I felt abandoned," I argued gruffly.

She paused but didn't comment on that. "Your wolf went silent as an adolescent, but that doesn't mean he hasn't been there for you all along. He's a fighter, that's certain, so he's been fighting for you, *with* you, all this time."

I stared at her, unable to say a word, my knee jumping as I tapped my heel nervously on her soft carpet, my throat feeling thick as I swallowed.

"When was your first fight?" she asked. "Not in the ring. I mean, after your mother died."

My leg still jumping, I slid my palms to my knees and squeezed, willing myself to calm down. "About a month after I went back to school."

"What happened?" she asked gently.

I hadn't thought about that incident in a long time, so it was strange to recount, even when I could see it as clearly and feel the anger as if it had happened yesterday.

"This kid named Patrick in my seventh-grade class had never liked me. Maybe he somehow sensed the wolf in me and saw me as a threat. He was human, of course, and Mom had made sure that no one knew what I was. She'd wanted me to have a normal upbringing, she always said."

"Yes, you're different," my mother said as I was curled up on the floor in the kitchen, my head in her lap. She calmed me with soft words, combing her fingers through my hair as I battled the first signs of the wolf emerging, my fingernails curled into black claws.

"I'm a freak," I mumbled.

"No, Ronan. You're special. There's nothing wrong with being different. You're as fine a son I could've ever hoped for, and you'll be an even finer man. I love you no matter what."

Pressing a palm to my chest, I could feel my heart beating wildly at the sudden, jarring memory. It wasn't the one I was recounting, but it had popped into my head unbidden. My mother had even apologized to me for my father not being there. He'd left her shortly after I was born, saying he wasn't fit for family life. I'd never bothered or cared to find him. I was happy to have her last name and not his. I didn't want anything from him. Even so, she lamented I didn't have the proper influence I needed.

"We were actually planning to move from Amarillo to Austin."

"Why did you plan to move?"

Clearing my throat, I said, "Mom had wanted to be closer to family. And I wasn't adjusting to middle school very well." Because my wolf was finally coming out. "Her father, brother, and sister lived in Austin. She thought they could help me adjust to this new transition in my life."

Dr. Theriot nodded but said nothing.

"So this kid Patrick had been bullying me."

"Why do you think that is?"

"I was a loner. I didn't fit in, and it got worse when I went to middle school. Anyway, the day after we buried my mom, he and his friends were standing behind me at my locker. Patrick was running his mouth as always. It never bothered me before. But that day he said, 'Your mom is probably happy to finally be rid of you.'" I scoffed. "I fucking snapped. I turned on him and beat him bloody. It took three teachers to get me off him."

She stared a moment before saying, "It was a reasonable reaction. Anyone talking about your mother would've set you off so soon after her death."

It was my turn to go silent.

"And the wolf didn't emerge then?"

I shook my head. Not since the day my mother died.

"Did you believe him?" she asked.

"Believe what?"

"That your mother was finally happy to be rid of you?"

My gut clenched and my stomach flipped at her question. It was ridiculous, and yet, it poked at me and made me feel raw, like a tender bruise not yet healed.

"Of course not," I answered softly.

She raised her brows. "You said you had to fight for yourself because no one was there to fight for you. Not your grandfather or sister or uncle. Or your mother."

Or the piece of shit who'd been my father.

"My mother didn't abandon me." My voice was rough as I choked out the words.

"No, Ronan." She reached across the space between us and placed her palm over my hand, her empathic magic softening my hard edges and the beginnings of despair that had begun to spiral through me. "Your mother did not abandon you. And she never would have. She was taken from this world too soon. It was a tragic accident. That is all."

Closing my eyes, I let her words and her Aura magic sink in, forbidding myself to think about the accident, to wonder if maybe she was wrong. I let my feelings of powerlessness and that sharp emotion that liked to haunt me—abandonment—wash and roll away. When I'd calmed down enough, I opened my eyes.

Dr. Theriot leaned back, offering me that kind, soothing smile. "Also remember that your uncle is here for you now. He cares so much that he's sending you to a phenomenal therapist."

A bark of laughter escaped me, breaking the bubble of tension. "Yes. He certainly is."

"There's nothing wrong with fighting as a career. I only meant for you to look at the reasons you've chosen this path."

"You may be right about why I chose this career. But I don't fight now because I feel I have to. I fight because I'm good. Because it makes me feel good to compete and win at the highest level."

"And those are very healthy reasons," she reassured me. "But look at the greater picture too. Every step we take in this life, every choice we make is guided by an intrinsic motivation. Sometimes they are positive, healthy instincts. Sometimes they are not."

"You think when I first started fighting, it was a bad instinct?"

"Not at all. I think you were surviving, you and your wolf. Somewhere along the line, it became not about surviving but about winning, about thriving."

I nodded, because that's exactly how I felt about it now.

"Did you have to leave Austin and come here? Were there no other options?"

I thought about it for a second. "I'd been living in my aunt's extra bedroom, and she made it clear I couldn't stay there anymore."

"But you had no friends at all you could've moved in with?"

"I had plenty of friends. A couple of teammates." I chuckled, remembering how pissed Malcolm was with me for moving.

"So you could've stayed there, but you came here instead."

"Uncle Shane called me up, offered me his extra bedroom on the condition I work in his garage to earn my rent."

"You've always been close to your uncle?"

"Not especially. I was when I was younger, but as I grew up, he was a bit of a hard-ass with me."

"And you took the offer anyway, even though you knew it might be difficult living with him. Why?"

"I don't know. I just wanted to start over, get out of Austin. Something told me this was the right move."

"And perhaps a chance to rekindle a relationship with some-one who you knew deep down did care about you."

I pondered that a moment. "Maybe."

Because the minute I landed in Louisiana on his front porch, the sun setting nicely behind the trees that surrounded his house, I felt like I'd found my way. It had felt right.

She checked her watch. "Our time is up, Ronan." We both stood. "But I want you to think about that a little between now and our next session."

"Will do, Doc."

"I'll see you next week?"

"Yeah. See you next week."

She walked me out into the lobby, and I waved to Michael at the reception desk. Once in the foyer of the building, I could hear the muffled voices on the other side of Celine's office door. I couldn't help it. Even though I didn't shift into my wolf once a month, my senses were heightened just like any other werewolf. The scent of her lured me closer, and I nearly whimpered at the sweetness of it.

But then I paused, pressing a palm to my stomach. The session with Dr. Theriot today had left me feeling raw and vulnerable. I'd never been good at hiding my emotions, and I wasn't quite ready to dump all my baggage at Celine's feet. I wanted to tell her about my mother, but not yet.

Knowing I'd see her tonight was the only way I was able to force my feet to turn and walk the other way. As I made my way to my Bronco, Dr. Theriot's observation came back to me.

Yes, I'd come here for the fresh start and perhaps to bond with a male who was my blood and who did, in fact, care about me. But perhaps my wolf led me here for other reasons too. Or for one very specific reason.

When I'd stood on my uncle's porch for the first time, I'd taken everything in, inhaling deep, filling my chest with the sounds and scents of the summer in the Deep South. A golden sunset, the buzzing of cicadas, the call of a crow in the pine trees along the back of the house.

Something resonated with me, a rightness I couldn't exactly put my finger on, but one that I felt down to my bones. It was like Uncle Shane had told me. I was home.

And a few days later, I was working in the garage, scenting her on the wind, seeing her standing there in a halo of sunlight. Like the universe had literally dragged me here for that moment, to see her, to know, to recognize who she was to me the second I laid eyes on her. My beautiful, radiant mate.

The only problem was, she didn't know. And I wasn't sure how a woman, even a witch raised around wolves, would feel about that.

I suppose there was only one way to find out.

CHAPTER 14

~CELINE~

THE PLACE WAS PACKED, BUT MOST OF THE CROWD HAD PUSHED toward the stage. I'd never been here, some bar where a lot of the college students hung out. It was dark, but the stage spotlighted where Diego was singing his heart out, his eyes closed, strumming the guitar.

My cousin Morgan plucked at the bass, his head down and focused as always while girls drooled and stared and sang the song with them. Apparently, they had groupies now. Go figure.

Skirting along the back of the club where it was less crowded, I peered over the throng, trying to find Ronan. I'd texted him I was running a few minutes late. He'd texted back he was already here, but I couldn't find him, and he was pretty recognizable. A tall, sexy-as-sin blond usually stood out in the crowd.

I decided maybe I would need to push my way to the bar on the far side when an arm wrapped around me and pulled me back into the shadows. I yelped, then instantly laughed, knowing the scent and the feel of the man's arms around me.

He buried his nose into my hair, nuzzling it aside to get to my ear. "Got you."

"Yeah, Ronan." I turned my head to look up at him over my shoulder since he had my back glued to his chest. "You really do."

Smiling, he dipped his head at an angle and kissed me sweetly, a swift, brief sweep of lips. He still held me tight like he'd captured his prey and he wasn't letting go. I didn't want him to let go. Not ever.

The song ended in a wild crescendo, then a slower melody began.

"You look beautiful in this dress."

I'd found this dress online and instantly bought it, thinking of Ronan. It wasn't my usual type. It was a black shift dress with angel-wing sleeves and a loose hem that hung elegantly against my frame. The scoop neck reminded me of our first date and the way he liked access to my neck, and I liked giving him access to my skin.

"I wore it for you."

He dipped his mouth close to my ear. "What color are the pretty panties you wore for me?"

I smiled. "I didn't wear any at all. For you."

The gruff sound he made in his throat sent a tingling shiver across my skin. "The things you say."

Then Diego said, "Here's one for those falling hard. It's called 'I Wanna Be Yours.'"

Then he began to croon softly, while Ronan dragged me backward, deeper into the shadows until we were tucked into an alcove, and I was standing between his spread legs. He reached up and turned off the sconce lamp above his head so that we were steeped in shadow.

"Do you know this song?" he whispered close to my ear.

"No."

"Listen closely."

He began to sing the lyrics in my ear, his hold on me softening as he spread a palm across my ribs, my heart melting when I realized the song was all about the desperate need to fall in love, to be someone's everything.

I leaned my head back until it hit his chest, watching the band and the mass of the crowd sway in the dim light near the stage, seeming entirely separate from us in our private corner.

Ronan continued singing softly in my ear, sliding his one hand down to the hem of my skirt. He glided his fingers back and forth over my skin along the loose hem of my silky dress. I reached back and down, grabbing the sides of his jean-clad thighs, needing something to hold on to.

Then he slid his hand under my skirt and between my legs, finding me bare. He groaned but then kept singing, no one paying any mind to the couple in the dark in the back corner, as he slid one finger through my wetness, then slowly circled my clit.

I'd never done anything in public before. I'd never kissed a boy or made out or had sex anywhere but in private. Of course, the guys I'd dated since high school would never dare to do more than hold my hand in public.

But this was Ronan. And here I was, pressed against him, his hand up my skirt, stroking my arousal to the point where I was already breathing heavy, and I didn't care if the whole place caught on fire. I wasn't moving, and I sure as hell wasn't stopping him.

Closing my eyes, I leaned more heavily into his arms, arching my spine so that my backside rubbed against his hard dick. His hand at my ribs slid farther around my belly, holding me tight. I clawed my nails into his jeans, soaking in the sensation of his hands on me, his hard body at my back, his mouth at my ear, singing about need and want and obsession.

When I opened my legs wider, he took the hint, sliding one finger to my entrance where he pumped slowly inside. At this point, I was writhing, desperate to orgasm.

"Are you close, baby?" he whispered in my ear, thrusting slowly, then sliding out to press and circle my clit.

"Yes." I turned my head to look up at him, his eyes glittering in the dark. "I need you to go faster."

He dropped his head until our mouths brushed while he slid a second finger inside me. "No, you don't. Nice and slow."

"Ronan," I whispered against his mouth as he continued to torture me with slow slides and easy strokes.

All the while, the band played loud and the crowd never noticed, entirely focused on the stage. It was daring and exhilarating, and I couldn't believe I was doing it.

"You're so pretty when you come, Celine." He kissed me, sliding his fingers deeper and rubbing my clit in that agonizing slow movement, but pressing a little harder. "You're driving me crazy."

I reached up and gripped the hair at his nape and held him so I could kiss him hard. I wasn't going to be able to orgasm like this. Then he stroked his tongue deep and suddenly, I was coming, moaning into his mouth as it ripped through me.

The song was ending and the crowd screamed and cheered, but I was in another world, engulfed by sensation and heady emotion, coming on Ronan's fingers in the dark.

He stroked his tongue gently against mine, tasting me thoroughly as I continued to come, his fingers working me, my sex pulsing.

I pulled away sharply, gasping for breath. He pressed his forehead to mine as he slid his fingers from inside me, cupped my mound, and gave it a light squeeze before removing his hand from beneath my skirt.

Laughing, I whispered, "What was that last squeeze for at the end?"

He wore that sinful grin that made me feel warm and melty. "I'm going to miss her. Had to give her a little hug."

I laughed, turning to fully face him, reaching up to wrap my arms around his neck. "I'm sure you'll see her again soon."

"Is that a promise?" His hands were light and soothing at my waist, one palm rubbing up and down my spine.

I nodded. "You need to go wash your hand."

"No way." He shook his head and leaned down to whisper in my ear as the band started up the next song, something harder. "I wanna smell you when I go to bed. When I fuck my fist, I'm gonna inhale deep and think of you when I come."

I dropped my head forward, pressing my forehead to his chest. "The things you say."

He chuckled since we'd both been throwing that phrase back and forth a few times.

"Come on." He took my hand and guided me along the back wall to a narrow staircase, then led me upstairs.

"Where does this go?"

"It's a little quieter where we can talk," he called back, finally pulling me to an outdoor space on the second floor.

There was a small bar with a single bartender and a few others laughing around the tall tables scattered across the rooftop.

"Over here," he said, guiding me to a small booth in the corner.

I slid in, and he slid in on the same side. From here, we had a view of St. Charles Street and the traffic zipping past.

"Oh, you want something to drink?" He started to move back out of the booth.

"No," I said. "I just want you."

He stopped and held still. He wrapped both of his hands around one of mine, his gaze dark and serious. "This is pretty intense, Celine."

"Mm-hmm," I agreed, unable to say more.

"Has this ever happened to you before?"

"What, exactly? Do you mean have I ever been so into a guy that I can't stop thinking about him every waking minute of the day?" For some reason, I had zero reservations about laying my feelings on the table. Perhaps that was because I knew he felt the same. Then he proved me right.

He stared with obvious admiration for a few seconds before he said, "Yeah. That's what I mean."

"No." I smiled. "Never."

"Me neither."

We sat in silence another minute. He held my hand on his lap, rubbing his thumb over my knuckles. "So when do I meet this scary dad of yours?"

I laughed. "Not yet."

He frowned. "What's wrong? You don't think he'll like me?"

"It's not that. It's that I'm afraid he won't even give you a chance."

"Your dad is that much of a dick?"

"No. He's just . . ." I shrugged a shoulder, staring down at our hands. "He's overprotective."

Another beat of silence. "What made him that way?"

"What do you mean? He's a werewolf," I explained, as if that was obvious. But I knew what he was really asking, my pulse speeding faster.

He leaned back against the booth and raised a hand, brushing my throat with his finger. "Your heart rate is racing, Celine." He held my gaze, somber and patient. "What is it you aren't telling me?"

For a moment, all I could do was stare back. He remained quiet, waiting. I'd never told any guy I dated about my high school catastrophe. And while I was embarrassed, still struggling to get over my naivete, I wanted him to understand.

"When I was a sophomore in high school, I dated this guy. He was a warlock. An Influencer."

Ronan clamped his jaw, and I wondered if he already knew where this story was going with only a few words.

"He was really nice at first." I remembered how he was such a gentleman at the beginning, said and did all the right things. "He was a star basketball player on my high school's team. He was popular, and everyone loved him. It was easy to get swept away by his charm." Too easy.

Ronan had gone quieter and more still than I'd ever seen him. I couldn't look at him while I spilled the rest, so I kept my gaze on the traffic below.

"Anyway, things started to change slowly. If I had other plans when he had a game, he'd sort of guilt me into going. I started skipping family things to support him, to be a good girlfriend."

I scoffed at my stupidity back then.

"Then after one game, I was waiting for him in the parking lot, talking to one of his teammates. We were laughing about something I can't even remember when my boyfriend came out of the gym and saw us. We weren't doing anything."

I swallowed hard, pushing myself to get it all out even while I sensed the old fear tapping at my veins, speeding the blood faster.

"He was really angry. As he was driving me home, he pulled to the side of the road and started yelling, accusing me of cheating on him and fucking his teammate. He called me a slut." I huffed a bitter laugh. "I was still a virgin. I hadn't even had sex with *him*." Licking my lips, I continued, "He punched the dash so hard it dented. When I fell apart, crying and swearing I hadn't cheated, begging him to stop, he—" I shook my head at the chilling memory. "He went so cold and calm it was terrifying. He told me to 'shut up and stop crying.' He said he just had to scare me to see if I was telling the truth."

A deep, dark rumble vibrated from Ronan. When I turned to finally look at him again, his blue eyes glowed so pale I knew I was looking at his wolf. I wondered if he had any idea how close his beast was to the surface.

"He didn't hurt me," I assured him. "He took me home, and I told my mom what happened."

"Did you tell your dad?" Ronan's voice was gruff.

"No. He'd have killed him. Literally."

"I wish you'd told your dad."

I smiled, but Ronan didn't. "Anyway, that was definitely the final straw. He'd been pulling me away from my family and friends so slowly, I hadn't noticed until my mom pointed it out. She warned me that this show of violence was only a precursor of worse. Some men just had this sort of sickness with obsession and violence and control, and he'd never be a good partner."

"So you broke up with him."

"Yes. The very next day over the phone."

"How'd he take it?"

"Not well." I sighed. "He sent me texts, begging me to come back, apologizing and saying it would never happen again. He'd follow me around school, even when my brothers and cousins had warned him off. Diego even warned him enough to leave him with a black eye."

"Good," snapped Ronan.

"But the stalking had gotten even scarier than when I was with him. He'd show up at places when I was out with my friends shopping, just watching me. He'd leave flowers in my locker and in my car."

"So he was stalking you."

I nodded, my stomach turning with nausea.

"Then one night, I was doing a witch's round with my aunts. Do you know what that is?"

"Isn't that when witches commune with nature or something?"

Ronan didn't know a lot of witches, it seemed, so I didn't blame him for not knowing. "It's more about connecting with our magic and the Goddess of Nature. We recharge our magic in a witch's round, infusing energy with each other and nature. I'd been doing it all my life with my aunts."

"What happened?"

"Well, in a witch's round, the Goddess speaks to us, and our magic is often heightened or amplified by our connection to the other witches. And to my aunt Violet. She's a Seer."

"A psychic," he clarified.

"Yes. She's powerful. She can see the past and possible futures."

"What did she see?"

"My ex-boyfriend buying a lust potion from a witch who practiced dark magic."

His eyes flared brighter when he asked roughly, "What does the potion do?"

"They're illegal," I explained. "There are some potions, what some might call 'love' potions, that only enhance the mutual emotions of a couple who are into each other. They're legal because they don't alter someone's actual feelings. My aunt Clara even makes and sells them. But a lust potion made using dark magic is illegal. It's more than an aphrodisiac. It alters the one who drinks it, making them desire a particular person whose blood has been mixed into the potion. Even worse, the person who drinks a lust potion will act without their will. They'll know in their minds they don't want it, but they won't be able to help it."

Ronan's chest rose and fell faster. "Your aunt saw your ex buying this potion to be used on you."

I nodded. Ronan finally let go of my hand in his lap and combed both hands through his hair before wiping his hands down his face.

"But he never got to use it," I quickly told him. "As soon as Aunt Violet had the vision, she told all of us what she'd seen. My aunt Jules took it upon herself as Enforcer to not only find and arrest the witch who created it but also my ex-boyfriend for the buying and possession of an illegal potion with intent to harm. He stood trial in the supernatural court and was convicted, then sentenced to five years in prison on the West Coast. Before he was taken away, my father told him outside the courtroom that if he ever came within one thousand miles of me after his release, he'd kill him."

Ronan stared toward the street, his profile stark and hard, his aura now more red than pink. "I like your dad."

Smiling, I realized my dad would like him too. If he gave him a chance.

"Your ex would be out by now. What was his name again?"

"Oh no. I specifically left his name out. No need to worry about him. He lives somewhere in Southern California now."

"How do you know?"

"I have an uncle who makes supernatural tracking software. Apparently, he keeps tabs. I'm not worried anymore."

I truly wasn't. Fortunately, I didn't come to harm. My family had saved me in more ways than one. After my ex was sent away, they rallied behind me to make me feel safe and well. But it wasn't quite enough.

"Afterward"—I exhaled a deep breath—"I went to therapy for a while, just to get my mind straight again. That was the one good thing that came out of it. It gives me a new understanding for my clients now, having personal trauma experience and knowing how to cope with crippling anxiety."

Ronan tucked a lock of my hair behind my ear, his eyes having dimmed to a cool blue, the hue somewhere between wolf and man.

"You're amazing," he said in a low voice. "You took a nightmare of an experience and found the good in it. You found purpose in it. Only an incredible and strong person could've done that."

There was sadness in his voice and his gaze, and I wondered if he was thinking of his mother. But all I could say was "thank you."

Then he pulled me close. I instantly wrapped one arm around his waist, my other bent between us as I pressed my cheek to his upper chest. He rubbed a soothing hand up and down my back.

"I get it now. Why your dad is a little nuts about the guys you date."

"Yeah." I huffed out a small laugh.

"But I can take it, Celine. Whatever your dad dishes out, I can take it."

I hugged him tighter and smiled, knowing I'd finally found the one guy who truly could.

CHAPTER 15

~RONAN~

"Stop pacing," Ty commanded. "You're putting my wolf on edge."

I stopped and shifted from foot to foot, checking the tape wrapped around my fist for the twentieth time. Everything was just right, like it had always been before a fight.

I was excited to be competing in a legitimate fight for the first time. My boys looked good. All of us were in our dark red trunks, fists taped, and ready to go.

Bowie sat on the bench against the wall, his AirPods in, bobbing his head to his hype music. Zack was posting on social media.

"What's wrong with you?" asked Ty. "You're never nervous. If anyone should be, it should be me or those two."

"It's nothing."

"We're going to win," Ty added.

"I know we are."

We'd taught Zack and Bowie all that we knew, and they'd soaked it up like natural fighters. Even Bowie, with his larger physique, had perfected all of the swift take-down moves we'd taught him. It's like they were born for this. It was yet again another sign I was meant to be here.

We'd also studied videos of the Iron Claws on YouTube. We knew what moves they leaned into at the beginning of the fight, if they started offensively or defensively. We knew what defensive techniques they used when they got tired, and we'd practiced counteractive moves over and over again these past few weeks in preparation.

Between work and training, I'd only been able to sneak off to see Celine a few times for coffee and breakfast at her brother's on two mornings. She still hadn't introduced me to her parents—and I was pretending that didn't bother me—but she was also busy in her own right.

On one day, I'd taken a long lunch break, getting Ty to cover for me, to meet at a Mediterranean place called Misa's that had a romantic vibe, then we made out heavily in her car in City Park before we parted ways for work. We were like teenagers sneaking around. And while I cherished every minute with her, I wanted more.

"He's nervous because Celine isn't here yet," said Zack, finally setting his phone aside and leaning back against the wall, crossing his arms with his trademark grin, casual as fuck and not a bit worried about his first fight in the cage.

I didn't even argue. Not two seconds later, she peeked into the locker room. "Is everyone dressed?"

I jogged over and pulled her into my arms. She laughed and pecked a kiss on my lips.

"You made it." I beamed down at her, curling my fingers into the loops of her jeans.

"Of course I did. You thought I wouldn't?"

"Just didn't know if you could get away."

"I told my parents Samara wanted a girl's night."

Refusing to acknowledge the slight hurt that she still hadn't introduced me to her parents, I said truthfully, "I'm glad you're here."

"I wouldn't miss it."

"Did Samara come with you?"

"No. She's got finals for her summer class coming up. But Diego, Morgan, and Boomer came."

"Sweet," said Zack. "I thought they would."

"You told them about it?" I asked.

"Yeah. Why not?"

"No reason." Then I tugged Celine into the hallway. "So you told your brother about us?" My pulse had picked up speed.

"Actually, Joaquin did. And Diego isn't stupid. He pretty much figured out we've been seeing each other."

"And you're okay with that?"

"Why wouldn't I be?" Her brow pinched together. "I'm not ashamed of dating you, Ronan."

"How does Diego feel? Does he want to kick my ass or something?" Not that it mattered, but I needed to know what I'd be facing later.

"No. I told him I'd never forgive him if he started shit with you."

I slid my hands around her waist. "And that worked?"

"He's my triplet. He knew I meant it, and he hates it when I'm mad at him." She laced her fingers at the back of my neck. "Besides, Joaquin was on my side. He can't go against both of us. It's impossible."

"I knew I liked Joaquin." I lowered my mouth and brushed lightly, letting the taste of her sink in and give me strength.

I drew away from her when male voices echoed from down the hall. Behind me where the other locker room was, Baron and his teammates were walking this way. Immediately, my wolf growled, going on full alert. Interestingly, other than growl occasionally, I hadn't sensed the need to shift since he'd partly resurfaced.

I eased Celine out of my arms. "Go on back to your brother. I'll see you after."

"Okay. Good luck!" She pecked me quickly, then spun and hurried back down the corridor, her ponytail of copper waves swinging.

A whistle tightened my gut and pulled my attention to the assholes coming closer behind me.

"That's a pretty fine witch you've got, Ronan." Baron grinned. They were wearing matching blue trunks and short silver silk robes.

"Yeah," snorted Carter, the big oaf on their team. "How the hell'd you manage that?"

Ty, Zack, and Bowie pushed open the locker room door and joined me as the Iron Claws walked on past.

"I wonder if the carpet matches the drapes," said Adam, the one I was slotted to fight tonight.

My entire body was locked tight, including my jaw to keep from taking their bait.

"I'd love to find out," said Baron, winking at me over his shoulder, then they were heading through the swinging door, laughing, and out into the arena to the roar of applause. Music boomed at their entrance.

"Don't listen to them," said Ty. "They're just trying to get you angry. To get you off-balance."

"Yeah, I know." I fisted my hands, my knuckles cracking as I strode toward the door leading into the arena. "But I'm sure as fuck going to make Adam eat his goddamn words."

"They'll all be eating them," said Bowie, falling in line close behind me. "If they have any teeth left."

"That's what I'm fucking talking about." Zack laughed.

Post Malone's "Take What You Want" was blaring from the arena, the crowd screaming.

"Just focus on your training. Don't lose your cool," said Ty, now beside me. "And kick the fucking shit out of them."

Then we stepped through the double doors for our first fight.

CHAPTER 16

~CELINE~

I WAS LITERALLY SHAKING WITH NERVES. THEIR OPPOSING TEAM hadn't looked like much when I saw them playing pool at Howler's the other night, but dressed for the fight, you could see they were well-packed with muscle and ready to go. Not that Ronan and his guys weren't equally impressive, but the thought of Ronan getting hurt made me feel sick all over.

Of course, I'd never admit to him that I didn't care for fights or boxing on television whenever Diego and my dad watched them together. It just wasn't my thing. But now, knowing it was Ronan—gentle, charming, affectionate Ronan—down there about to be in the ring, I felt like my body was going to jump out of my skin. I was excited and terrified all at the same time.

The fighting ring itself, surrounded by fencing—an actual cage—looked so menacing. This arena was set in a giant warehouse near the port. Not exactly a fancy venue, but it was definitely making money. The stadium sat approximately five thousand people, and it was full. Concessions of beer and bar food were flowing.

"You okay?" Diego nudged my knee with his. "You look pretty pale."

"I'm just scared."

"Scared for your man?" he teased.

"Yes," I agreed.

Diego took a swig of his bottled beer. "Ty says he knows what he's doing."

"When did you talk to Ty?" I snapped.

"The day after I saw Ronan drooling all over you at Howler's."

"Why didn't you tell me?"

"And get my head bitten off like right now?" He faced forward, watching the ring as the referee was talking to both teams. "I didn't want to piss you off, but I had to check him out."

He avoided meeting my eyes so I wouldn't see the worry there, but I was an Aura so I could feel it anyway. Sighing, I linked my arm with his and gave him a sort of side hug.

"Thank you for looking out for me, but I know what I'm doing. And Ronan is a really good guy."

"Yeah. I know." He sipped his beer again. "I talked to Shane a bit too. He told me all about how he had a rough upbringing. No dad and that car accident they were in and his mom dying."

My entire body went cold. I didn't know he was in the accident that killed his mother.

"That'll fuck up anybody," Diego said, "but Shane says he's a good guy. He's just had a rough road."

I blinked back the tears pricking behind my eyes. "I wish you'd tell Dad that when I let him know we're dating."

"So you're dating? It's official? He's your *boyfriend?*" he teased. Ronan hadn't said so, but he didn't need to.

"Yes." Grinning, I turned back to face the cage as Ty stepped into it to fight one of the opposing team.

"Damn, sis. You've got it bad." He chuckled, but just then we were jostled as Joaquin shimmied down our row past Morgan on the end, then Boomer and Diego before he took the empty seat beside me.

"Since when do you like to watch fights?" I asked, openly shocked to see Joaquin here.

"I don't," he growled. "I'm just here for moral support for your new man."

Then the announcer was shouting into the mic. "Tonight, for our first bout, we have Ty Osborne of the Blood Moon Crew in red." An uproar of applause and cheers filled the enclosed arena. "And from our defending champion team, the Iron Claws, we have Carter Douglas." Even louder cheers erupted. Carter did a little grandstanding, waving to the crowd.

The referee said something quietly, and the two fighters went to opposite sides of the cage. The ref blew the whistle and the fight was on.

Ty bounced in place from side to side. Carter swaggered left a little, then swiftly attacked first, landing a hard punch to the jaw. Joaquin hissed in a breath next to me while I gasped.

Ty shook off the tough hit. I don't know what happened next, but Ty spun fast and popped up behind his opponent, locking him in a choke hold before he could even react.

The other guy, Carter, struggled and tried to kick back and twist away, but Ty was locked tight on him. When Carter's face began to turn red, I saw his claws come out. He scratched Ty's arm, then reached back for his neck.

The referee blew a sharp whistle and rushed forward. Ty released Carter, who spun and snarled, but his coach and another teammate hauled him back. The referee lifted Ty's arm. "The winner!"

We all screamed and cheered, but then I leaned toward Diego. "What happened? Why'd the referee stop the fight before he tapped out? I thought they could use claws."

I'd researched wolf cage fighting a little bit until it made me squeamish thinking about Ronan in a fight.

"They can, but they can't strike or even appear to strike their opponent on vital arteries. He was going for Ty's throat to make him let go. It's an automatic win."

The second fight was between Zack and Baron, the one Ronan had said was head of their team and the individual champion of the NOLA league.

Their fight went to the third round. Zack became trapped by Baron's wrestling moves against the side of the cage in every round before he finally managed to break free. Zack landed several kicks to his chest in the first two rounds. But in that third round, Zack swung a kick to his chest again, but Baron caught him by the calf and forced him to the ground on his stomach.

That was it. He had Zack's leg and arm pinned in such a way he couldn't get free. The referee whistled and declared Baron the winner, raising his arm for the crowd's applause.

"That's all right, Zack!" yelled Diego, clapping at my side.

My heart clenched at the dejected look on Zack's face as Ty and Bowie met him when he exited the cage. Ronan caught him, gripping him on both sides of the head. He told him something to which Zack nodded, then Ronan stepped around him and into the cage.

My entire being was fixed on him as Ronan walked to one side of the cage, turned, planted his feet apart, and held perfectly still with his arms at his sides. His opponent, who was announced as Adam Somebody, was grinning and pacing back and forth on the opposite side like a caged tiger.

While the referee made the prefight announcements that both teams had won one bout each, Adam walked back and forth, back and forth. Still, Ronan didn't move, his eyes glinting bright and silver as he watched his opponent.

"Daaamn," said Diego. "Ronan looks like he's going to kill that fucking dude."

It was true. There was something preternatural about Ronan's stance, like a tiger keeping still while the prey crept closer.

When the referee blew the whistle, I couldn't even breathe as Ronan launched himself at full speed across the cage. He spun and kicked Adam square in the face, knocking him on his back. Then Ronan was on him, straddling his chest and whaling on his face.

"Omigod!" I had my hands over my face, watching through my spread fingers.

The throng was on their feet, screaming and yelling for more.

I had to stand, too, to see over the people in front of us. Then the referee blew his whistle. Ronan shot to his feet, both arms over his head, his gaze sweeping the arena till he found me. That was when he finally smiled, and I could breathe again.

It was terrifying and incredible and my nerves were completely fried.

"Goddamn!" Diego yelled and high-fived Boomer and Morgan, then wrapped an arm around my waist and pulled me close. "Your man is legit, sis!"

I was sort of in shock because the crowd was still losing their minds. He had pummeled Adam into unconsciousness in less than ten seconds. The referee had blown the whistle the moment Adam became unresponsive and unable to defend himself because Ronan had completely annihilated him.

Joaquin clapped like a normal person and leaned toward me. "At least we know you're well protected around your new guy."

I laughed, because what else could I do? I'd just watched Ronan in action, and my new boyfriend was definitely an amazing badass.

ð❧

RONAN PICKED ME UP AND SWUNG ME AROUND IN THE MIDDLE OF Howler's where we met after the fight. I squealed and laughed at the vibrant, euphoric feeling radiating from him and into me.

Vaguely, I noted Diego and others congratulating Zack, Bowie, and Ty. When Ronan set me on my feet, he cupped my face and pressed a soft, chaste kiss to my lips.

"I missed you," he whispered.

"How? You just saw me before the fight."

"I always miss you when you aren't with me." His eyes sparkled a heavenly blue, his aura beaming a jubilant bright pink.

"You were absolutely incredible in the ring."

"Yeah," said Zack, butting in and handing us both a bottle of Abita. "That douchebag had it coming."

Ronan stiffened next to me. "Damn right, he did."

"Thanks, Zack," I said, "but I don't drink beer."

"Doesn't matter. You need something to toast with."

Zack pushed through the small crowd, all regulars of Howler's, hopped up on the bar, and pushed up to stand. "Hey, everybody! Let's all raise a glass to the Blood Moon Crew on our first win in the ring."

Everyone cheered and whooped. Ronan stood beside me, one arm around my waist.

Bowie had won the final round against the last opponent on the Iron Claws team, which meant it was three out of four, giving the overall win to Ronan's team. Apparently, in wolf cage fighting, the team of four fought and won according to how many total wins. And the individual fighter who won the most within the team was considered the overall champion. Currently, Baron was the champion of the New Orleans Wolf Fighting Championship.

"And also"—Zack lifted his bottle again and stared straight at Ronan, a purple bruise forming on his cheek—"to Ronan Reed, a really cool fighter and trainer. And a great friend."

More cheers went up. I tapped my bottle against his. "I'll toast to that."

He sobered at Zack's speech, his smile a little delayed before he raised his beer to his mouth.

"Hey, what is it?" I whispered.

"Nothing." He blew out a heavy breath. "That was just unexpected."

"What, your teammates never appreciated you back in Austin?"

He shrugged. "Maybe not like these guys." Then he stiffened, squeezing my waist where he still had one hand wrapped.

Diego was walking up to us, wearing his typical smirky smile. "Hey, Reed." He reached out a hand. "I'm not coming over to beat you up." He shook his head. "Not sure I could anyway the way you fight. I just want to congratulate you on the win."

Ronan let go of my waist to shake Diego's hand, still a little stiff and wary. "Thanks, Diego." He glanced at me cautiously.

"Yes, I know you're dating my sister," Diego added.

"And you're cool with that?" Ronan asked, as if he expected resistance.

"As long as she is, yeah, it's cool."

I laced my fingers with Ronan's hand. "Why, were you going to give me up if he wasn't?"

"Not a chance in hell," he told me honestly right in front of Diego. "I'm never giving you up, but I like to know who I have to fight beforehand."

"No problems here." Diego winked at me. "But now you've gotta tell Dad."

"I know," I admitted. "I plan to soon."

Ronan smiled, his body relaxing. I squeezed his hand reassuringly as Ty walked up.

"Great fight tonight, man." He clapped Ronan on the shoulder.

"You too. I knew you'd kill it in the ring."

"I've got some ideas to counteract some of Baron's holds."

"Cool. We can go over it tomorrow afternoon."

"See you at the shop." Then Ty headed toward the exit.

"Ronan!" Bowie called from the bar. "Come on, man. Celebration tequila shots."

"Hell, no. We've got to train tomorrow."

"Aww, man!" Zack whined. "One shot! I was the loser of the night. I need some consoling."

Ronan chuckled and tugged me by the hand toward them at the bar. "A consoling tequila shot?"

"Yeah, that's right." Zack grinned and handed me a shot and twist of lime.

"Celine can take mine if she wants. I'm driving her home soon."

"I'll take his shot," I told Zack. "Since you need consoling so badly."

"Sweet. I knew I liked you, Celine."

Then Zack handed the shots out to Bowie, Diego, and Boomer who'd been talking to some girl off to the side, one of their groupies. Morgan wasn't with them. He must've gone straight home from the fight.

"All right," said Zack, raising his shot. "To the Blood Moon Crew!"

"I'll drink to that." I smiled at Ronan, whose gaze on me was intense and heady.

I tilted back the shot and squeezed my eyes at the burn of liquor and tang of lime, not used to shots.

"Yeah, that's enough." Ronan set his shot glass on the bar. "No more shots," he commanded. "Training tomorrow."

Then he pulled me away from the crowd and toward the dance floor. There was no live music tonight, just one of their regular playlists I recognized. Currently, Katy Perry's "Dark Horse" pumped loud and strong, but Ronan pulled me into a slow dance.

He lifted my left hand in his right, placed his other hand on my hip, and hugged me close. Then he began moving and swaying, and I knew this man would be insanely good in bed. The way he held me firmly but gently, the way he led us in a slow dance that took hardly any motion at all, but somehow he commanded my body's attention.

I stared up at him, his hair still damp from the quick shower in the locker room, his sharp features stunning beneath the blue lights over the dance floor, his eyes magnetic as they held me captive. And, apparently, tequila made me brave.

"I'm falling for you, Ronan." I swallowed the lump forming in my throat. "Pretty hard and pretty fast."

He lifted the hand at my waist and cupped the side of my neck, brushing his thumb along my jaw.

"I fell for you the second I saw you, Celine."

"This feels kind of crazy, though, doesn't it?"

"No." He shook his head and lowered it till our lips were almost touching. "This is fate or heaven or whatever you want to call it, beautiful. You're my mate."

A shock rocked though me at the same time a tingling sensation buzzed through my blood like magic. It *was* magic. My mom had always told me that supernaturals, and even humans, had soul mates. But for a supernatural, especially a wolf, they knew instantly, long before their partner did.

"You're sure?" I asked, feeling dizzy, my knees wobbly.

He chuckled. "One thousand percent."

Then he brushed his mouth over mine, and I let him kiss me in front of whoever the hell happened to be looking. Even my brother. Because I wasn't going to hide my feelings from anyone.

"Yes," I whispered, nipping his bottom lip, making him groan and squeeze me closer. "You are my mate."

I laid my head on his shoulder, listening to Katy Perry sing about perfect storms and uncaged birds while magic sang through my blood, the euphoric sense of rightness buzzing through me like a drug. And I gloried in this sensation of falling in love with my soul mate, feeling utterly safe and perfectly content in his arms.

CHAPTER 17

~RONAN~

I WAS AGITATED AS I PARKED MY BRONCO AND HEADED INTO THE house. I'd dropped Celine off since she'd ridden with her brother to the fight, and he was staying out later with the guys. Besides, she'd wanted to get home before her parents, who were out for their date night.

The night had been perfect. The fight went better than I'd even expected. Zack's loss to Baron didn't even bother me because I knew Baron was their best fighter. The only one with advanced skills of the four of them.

Then seeing my girl afterward and holding her in my arms had been amazing. I'd even gotten the approval of her brother Diego.

On top of all that, Celine admitted she was falling for me. Tonight had been one of the best nights of my life.

So why was I so fucking annoyed as I made my way through the quiet house to my bedroom?

My blood was up as always after a fight. I was restless. I stripped down to my briefs, knowing good and well what this was. Sexual frustration.

But I didn't want just any girl or my hand again. I wanted Celine. Laying on my back, I draped an arm over my eyes and willed my body to calm down, trying to force myself to not think about how insanely beautiful she looked in those jeans and that red top tonight. She'd told me she was wearing my color, the team's color, and why that had gotten me so ridiculously turned on, I had no idea.

Maybe it was the fact that she was mine, but I didn't quite have her. She showed every sign of devotion, but she wasn't in my possession. And I wasn't in hers.

The strangest stirring had grown day after day since the second I met her, but now I knew what it was. My wolf was pacing inside me, waiting for me to claim her. But I wasn't an animal, even if one lived inside me. And Celine was . . . so fucking lovely it hurt. She needed patience and a gentle hand.

Suddenly, the back door opened and closed, the lilting sound of feminine laughter filling the house. Then the dark rumble of my uncle's voice.

I couldn't make out exactly what he said, but whatever it was only made his lady friend laugh. Then came the unmistakable sound of them kissing and clothes coming off.

His bedroom door shut. The only problem was that his bedroom was right next to mine. We shared a wall, and the walls of this house were pretty damn thin.

"Yes, right there," she told him.

My uncle's growl vibrated right though the wall, and then there was a high-pitched moan by the woman.

"You've got to be fucking kidding me," I mumbled to myself.

But it got worse. More moans and growling before a flopping sound as if they both hit the mattress. Next came the rhythmic thump of his headboard hitting my wall.

Thump, thump, thump was in perfect tempo with her loud, squealing cries, "Yes, yes, yes!"

No fucking way was I staying here for the full show. Hurriedly, I pulled on my jeans, T-shirt, and boots, then got the fuck out of there. I was in my Bronco, windows rolled down, and speeding off within two minutes.

I didn't know where I was going. I just drove. But it wasn't long before I realized my mind was on autopilot, going to the only place I wanted to be. Where *she* was.

The Lower Garden District still buzzed with activity. I passed her aunt's pub, the Cauldron, which seemed to still be pretty busy. It was right around the corner from Celine's house. I made the turn onto her street and passed by, noting that her parents and Diego weren't home yet. I parked a few houses away, then walked down the sidewalk past Celine's driveway and to the front of the house.

It took me no time at all to climb up the side trellis to the second-floor balcony of the bungalow-style home. I followed her honeyed scent directly to the second window on the right. I knew I'd find her quickly, but I didn't expect the window to be unlocked.

As soon as I raised the window, Celine popped up in bed. I couldn't help but grin as she threw off the covers and rushed to the window, where I was already stepping inside. It was one of those older homes with windows that went almost to the ceiling.

"You should keep this locked," I told her.

"What the hell are you doing?" she whispered, standing in front of me in a blue satin pajama shorts set.

I groaned at how pretty she was. "I couldn't help it."

"You're lucky my parents aren't home yet," she snapped back, her hair messy and beautiful.

I crowded her to her bed where she fell back onto the super-plush white comforter—so soft and girly—and then I crawled on top of her. "Yeah, I sure am lucky."

A tabby cat shot off the bed onto her desk near the door, which was ajar. The cat looked at me with narrow orange eyes and hissed.

"Uh-oh. Your cat doesn't like me."

"You disturbed her sleep. She always sleeps in my bed."

"Lucky cat."

Celine laughed. "Her name is Petunia."

I chuckled. It was so cute and girly. So Celine. "Come here, Petunia," I whispered gently. "Here kitty, kitty, kitty."

She hissed again and jumped down, then disappeared into the hallway. Celine stood, closed the door, and locked it. She turned to me with a sexy smile that had me hard as steel.

"Well," I lamented on a sigh, sprawled on my back, propped up on my elbows, "Petunia doesn't like me, but I know one pussy who does."

She smiled wider. "She sure does," she agreed easily.

"Come here."

JULIETTE CROSS

She crawled on top of me this time, her mouth meeting mine with desperate speed. When she ground down on top of me, I thought I saw stars, her heated arousal scenting the air. I kissed down her throat, sliding the thin strap of her pajama top down her arm. Grabbing her by the waist, I shifted her higher so I could lick and suck her perfect small breast, her nipple a tight bud.

She whimpered, pressing her breast closer so I could suck her good, grinding her pussy on top of the bulge in my jeans.

"Fuck, Celine. I need to taste you." I groaned at the same time. "Come sit on my face."

She pushed away and slid down my body on the bed until she was standing on the floor between my legs. When I sat up, my legs still hanging over, feet on the floor. I reached for her, but she batted my hands away.

"No way," she whispered, shaking her head. "It's my turn."

It took me only one second to understand what she meant before she knelt at my feet and starting working on unsnapping my jeans. I was too weak to protest. I hadn't planned this, not really. Maybe my wolf had been guiding me directly to her when I left my house. All I knew was that I needed to see her, be near her, kiss her, touch her.

I hadn't planned on fucking her for the first time in her parents' house, and that was still not on the agenda. But I sure as hell hadn't planned on her kneeling at my feet, pulling out my cock, and latching those perfect lips around the swollen head.

"Fuuuuuck," I moaned as she sucked the tip so perfectly. I reached down and cupped her jaw, sliding my fingers into her loose, wavy hair. "You're going to kill me with that mouth."

176

She let the head pop from her mouth and gripped my base tighter, pumping slowly. I hissed in a breath.

"That's not my intention," she whispered, her voice soft and raspy.

She tilted her head to the side, elongating her neck as she licked me from the base to the tip.

I was so fucking happy I was sitting, because that would've buckled my knees if I wasn't. Then she swallowed me deep, pumping her hand and mouth in the same rhythm.

"Baby, baby," I rasped, cupping the back of her head lightly, basking in this ecstasy.

I watched her work me, her little whimpers filling the quiet as she tried to take more. I didn't want to push. I could feel my climax coming already. There was something heady and hypnotic about her striving so hard to give me pleasure.

My past lovers were all takers. But not Celine. She was a giver. She'd already given me her gentle heart, her tender affection, her sweet admiration. Soon, she'd give me her body, and I wouldn't take it for granted. I'd give her everything right back. Hell, she already owned my soul.

I reached down and cupped her breast still exposed from when I'd lowered her strap.

"You're the most beautiful woman I've ever seen."

I mounded her breast, pinching the nipple lightly, which made her moan, her mouth vibrating around my cock. I fisted my other hand lightly in her hair.

"I want you always, Celine." My voice darkened, roughening with the wolf, though I hadn't expected him to make himself known right now. "Do you understand?"

She nodded, hollowing her cheeks before she let me slide from her mouth, still pumping me with her fist.

"You have me," she promised, and I knew it was true, the reality of my great fortune glittering in her jade-green eyes by the moonlight through the window. Then she deep-throated my cock, and I flinched.

"Goddamn, Celine. I'm going to come down your throat if you don't stop."

I gripped her shoulder to push her off, but she batted my arm away with her free hand, then dug her nails into my bare thigh. She stared up at me, sucking hard and fast. She wanted me to come down her throat. My sweet Celine was a sexy-as-fuck witch.

"Oh, fuck, baby."

I couldn't help but curl my fingers tighter into her hair, fisting the loose waves as my cock pulsed with release into her mouth and down her throat. She moaned and kept bobbing her head, sucking me all down.

"Yes, just like that. Can't wait to come inside you like this."

That seemed to make her moan louder, her own arousal heightened. The fact that she was turned on by getting me off twisted me up inside.

"Come here." I pulled out of her mouth, scooped her up beneath her arms, and twisted, tossing her onto the bed behind me.

She squealed. "Ronan!"

My jeans were still open and halfway off my ass as I readjusted my dick in my briefs. "Now it's *my* turn," I told her right as there was a slam of a door downstairs.

Celine jolted upright, her eyes wide as we listened.

"Could be Diego," I told her, sniffing to see if I could identify who'd come home.

But then there was a definite pounding of boots of someone coming up the stairs and drawing closer.

"Mateo!" called a woman's voice from downstairs. "What is it?"

"Holy shit!" Celine was off the bed and shoving me toward the window. "Get out, get out!"

"It's your dad?"

"Yes! Omigod! Get out, Ronan."

"I'm going to have to meet him sometime."

Her mouth dropped open in complete shock, then she hissed, "Are you *insane*? He'll kill you. Like literally, *kill* you." She was at the window, shoving it back up.

I half-heartedly pulled my jeans up my hips, ready to face this mean old bastard even though Celine was having a heart attack.

"Celine!" a deep-barreled man yelled, then pounded on the bedroom door. "Open this door right now!"

"Just a minute, Dad," she called, her eyes wide as she pulled and shoved me toward the open window.

"All right, all right." I laughed.

"I can hear that wolf in there, Celine! Open this *door*." The word *door* was drawn out into a guttural growl, and his next words were full of the wolf. **"I'll rip the pup limb from limb."**

"Is he shifting?" I asked, staring at the door as he pounded again, the door cracking beneath his fist.

"Alpha! Stop that right now," came the woman's voice, obviously Celine's mother now in the hallway with him.

"Please, please go. I don't want him to hurt you." Celine was near tears now, and I couldn't have that.

"Don't worry, baby." I straddled the windowsill and cupped her by the nape, then pulled her in for a swift kiss, my tongue teasing her lips before I let her go, all while that insane werewolf pounded on her bedroom door and her mother shouted at him. "I'll be just fine. I've got you to live for now," I teased.

Then the door splintered, and I slipped out onto the balcony, holding my jeans up as I leaped off the second floor to the grass. Zipping up and running at the same time, I heard the old man roaring from her window. Probably too fucking big to get through it without breaking that too.

"Stop, Dad!" Celine yelled.

"You shift back right now, Alpha," her mother's voice rang out, "or you'll be sorry."

I didn't bother to wait around to see what happened next. If that werewolf caught me with my pants half down and Celine's scent all over me, particularly below my waist, his fucking head might explode.

I raced back to my Bronco, hopped in, and drove away. I left my windows down, letting the balmy summer night whirl around me. I tilted my head back against the seat and laughed all the way home.

CHAPTER 18

~CELINE~

I sipped my coffee at the booth while Samara stared at me with sympathy.

"So how long did it take before he shifted back?" asked Samara.

"Oh, Mom was furious, so he shifted back pretty fast."

"And what did he say to you?"

"Mom didn't give him a chance to talk. She practically shoved him out of my bedroom and told me to get some sleep."

"Then you woke up and tore out of there first thing?"

"Yep." I sipped the coffee. "I texted Mom, though, and I could use some breakfast."

"What'll you have?"

I didn't need to look at the menu. I'd tried everything on it, and it all was good. But I wanted a little comfort food after last night's debacle.

"Give me the Cajun Eggs Benedict and don't tell Joaquin I'm here, please."

She snickered. "Coming right up."

Thankfully, the cafe was kicking, even at seven a.m. on a Saturday. My brother had made quite a reputation with the locals for having some of the best breakfast food and sandwiches in town.

I was enjoying my coffee when Diego entered the cafe, looked around, spotted me, grinned, and marched straight over.

"You're in trouuuuuble," he sang annoyingly as he slid into the booth across from me.

"What are you talking about?" I asked while my heart beat faster.

He snorted. "I could hear Mom and Dad arguing in the kitchen a little while ago."

"What were they saying?"

Yes, I was a grown-ass adult, but even adults were usually terrified of their parents when they upset them. It wasn't something you grew out of.

"Dad was pissed that you'd allowed some wolf in your bedroom, someone he didn't know. And Mom told him it wasn't his business. Then Dad said, 'It sure as hell is my business.'" Diego was pretty good at doing our dad's voice. "You were his daughter and that was his house, and you should know better to invite a stranger inside. Then Mom said you wouldn't invite a stranger. And Dad said, *'Then why the hell haven't I met him?'*"

"Hey, Diego," said Samara with an empty tray in hand, having dropped another table's plates at a booth. "You want breakfast?"

"Always. Give me two of the special on the board."

Diego had always eaten a mountain of food at every meal. Fortunately for him, he had an insane metabolism because he was lean and fit as always.

"A coffee and large milk like usual?" she asked, completely unshocked by the pile of food he'd ordered. She knew him too well.

"You got it." Then his gaze flitted across the room. "Samara, your professor is here."

She instantly turned her head to the door where that same hot warlock strode toward the booth he'd sat in last time, his austere gaze meeting hers for a brief second.

"He's not *my* professor," she said in a low voice.

"Sure." Diego chuckled. "Whatever you say."

She huffed and left, aiming straight for the professor, who was pulling his laptop from his leather bag.

"So when had you actually *planned* to tell Dad about Ronan?"

Of course, Diego knew the only person I was hiding him from was Dad, not Mom.

"Soon. I just hadn't planned on him finding out *that* way."

"Yep. You totally bungled that shit, sis."

"I know. You don't have to rub it in."

"Oh yes. I definitely do. This is classic. Little princess is in the hot seat for once and not me."

"Don't you have a guitar to strum or a girl to chase or something?"

Diego chuckled, not letting up. "Sneaking in bedrooms at night like teenagers."

"I never allowed someone to sneak into my bedroom as a teenager, Diego. That was all you."

"Oh yeah. I let lots of girls sneak in."

"Shut up. Gross."

He laughed as Samara delivered his coffee and a gallon-size glass of milk as well as my Cajun Eggs Benedict—a warm, crispy cheddar biscuit layered with andouille sausage cut lengthwise and topped with a perfectly poached egg and creamy, spicy hollandaise sauce.

"Yum. Let me have a bite." He reached for my plate.

I smacked his hand with the back of my fork. "You have, like, a whole pig about to be served up to you."

The special included a giant pork steak and sausage with two fried eggs, cheese grits, multigrain toast, and sliced avocado. I'd seen him eat the double-portion mound of food before.

"No worries." He glanced sideways, then picked up his coffee and milk. "Think I'll go hang at the coffee bar with Samara for a while."

"Why? What did—?" I stopped short when I saw my parents walking across the café to my booth. "Shit."

Diego laughed as he slid out of the booth, then pecked a kiss on Mom's cheek as he passed them. He was obviously irritatingly gleeful I was on the chopping block for once instead of him.

I clasped my hands in my lap and exhaled a deep breath as Mom and Dad sat in the booth where Diego had just vacated.

I expected Mom to start. She was always the mediator when Dad's wolf got out of hand. The interesting thing about this was that it usually involved Diego. Like the time he wrecked his brand-new Jeep they'd bought him or that time he and his wolf buddies decided to do some daredevil climbing on the Mississippi Bridge for fun and almost killed themselves.

My dad was typically calm and levelheaded, but when Alpha took the reins, he could be extremely intimidating.

Like last night. That was downright scary. By the time he busted through my door—literally—he was all twelve feet of snarling, angry wolf. I knew he'd never hurt me, but I was terrified he'd chase after Ronan and slice him to pieces.

Fortunately, he was happy enough that he was gone, and my mom practically ripped him a new asshole for going full wolf and breaking down my door like a maniac.

Right now, I was sitting across from my poised yet dour father. He laced his fingers on the table and spoke first. "I'm sorry about last night." He cleared his throat while my mother watched him expectantly. "I shouldn't have burst into your room like that, and I apologize for my . . . beastly behavior."

Mom nodded and then turned to me, all sympathy and concern. "Your father and I both want to respect your privacy. We know you're an adult now. The other night shouldn't have been handled the way it was, but neither of us knew you were seeing someone you might have over at the house."

I was grateful Mom didn't emphasize my *bedroom* in the house, but I could slowly feel a certain edge to this conversation that I didn't like.

"Because you hadn't introduced him," Dad began, "I did feel the need to ask around."

I crossed my arms. "And what did you find out?"

"Well, we know this guy Ronan is new in town. He's running from a checkered past with multiple arrests for assault and at least one drunk and disorderly back in Texas. I also know that he's a bit of a wanderer. Hasn't held down the same job for long. Was caught up in the illegal wolf cage fighting ring in Austin." He shook his head. "He doesn't have a great reputation."

"You don't know him," I snapped defensively.

"We don't," Mom agreed before adding, "but you've never been interested in a guy like him before, Celine."

"No," I scoffed. "I haven't. I've only dated very safe, extremely nice guys who I wasn't really attracted to."

They both frowned, then Mom asked, "So you're trying the exact opposite now? Are you testing yourself after what happened in high school? To see if maybe this is your type or something?"

"No." I forced my voice to remain even and calm while a hornet's nest of emotions swarmed in my belly. "I'm not testing myself. This isn't an act of rebellion. And I'm not trying a different kind of guy, the bad boy, on for size. It's none of those things. Ronan is a *good* man. He's a *good* wolf. And yes, he had a shitty upbringing. He had no father, and his mother was killed in a car accident when he was twelve. So he's probably not made a lot of good choices. But I care about him a lot. He's my . . ." I paused to lick my lips. "He's my boyfriend."

I didn't tell them he was my mate, the one marked by the Goddess as mine. Best not to overwhelm them too quickly. They both stared at me with mirroring concerned expressions.

Dad chimed in then. "We just want to be sure that you're making the right decisions, sweetheart. You say he's good, but we want to be sure he's good enough for you."

"I know what you're both thinking," I said softly. "I'm making some sort of self-destructive decision."

"We don't think you'd do this on purpose," my mom assured me, which wasn't reassuring at all. "We just want you to be safe."

Swallowing hard, I sat straighter, steeling my spine. "I understand what this might look like. I understand you don't quite trust me to make my own decisions when it comes to dating."

"It's not that—" Mom started.

"It is," I interjected. "And I understand. But my mistakes happened when I was sixteen. I'm twenty-four now. I've grown in my magic, and I can make the right decisions on my own. You need to trust that I know what's best for me. I'm not going to stop dating him even if you disapprove of him."

That had my dad scowling and clamping his jaw, his eyes rolling with gold. Alpha was definitely saying quite a few words in his head. Thankfully, he didn't let Alpha speak. My mom reached over and placed a calming hand on his forearm.

"If you're sure, then there's nothing we can do to stop you."

"That depends on—" Dad started, but Mom squeezed his forearm tight, and he clamped his jaw shut again.

"We'd like to meet him," she added gently.

"Of course," I agreed. "I'd like that too." Because he was going to be a part of this family one day. "When would you like to do that?"

Dad cleared his throat again and said, "Next Sunday at family dinner."

"At the Cauldron?"

"Where else do we have family dinner?" he shot back.

My tummy flipped. "Well, that's, um, that's kind of a lot."

"You just said he's your boyfriend," Dad continued, "which hurts since we didn't even know he existed until last night."

"Mateo," Mom warned.

"I'm just saying she's just told us he's obviously important in her life. If that's true, then he should meet the whole family."

Dad was smiling now. It was that devious one I knew he wore when he and his wolf were in full agreement on something.

Taking Ronan to family dinner would be a test of his character. Dad was probably hoping it would scare him away. But they didn't know my Ronan.

"Fine," I agreed with a smile. "I'll bring Ronan to family dinner next Sunday."

"Okay then." Mom clapped her hands and smiled. "That's all settled." She raised her hand to Samara. "We might as well order something and get some breakfast."

"You haven't even started yours," Dad said, gesturing to my untouched plate with that glint of challenge in his eyes.

I wasn't about to admit that I'd entirely lost my appetite, so I dug in, forcing myself to eat. I refused to show any signs of nervousness or concern that Ronan's first meeting with my family would be my *entire* family. I hoped he was as brave as I believed him to be because he sure as hell would need some courage to handle the challenge of our crazy family dinner.

CHAPTER 19

~RONAN~

"It's called PTSD. Post Traumatic Shifting Disorder," Dr. Theriot said with a completely straight face.

"Cute." I chuckled. "Is that a real diagnosis?"

"In the supernatural psychological community, it certainly is. And a traumatic one to recover from."

"But why do you think that's what I have?"

"Because your wolf went into hiding immediately after the accident with your mother, which was obviously a very traumatic event in your life. Why don't you tell me what happened that day you were in the car accident?"

In our sessions, we'd always skated around this exact question and what had happened that day. She was so direct and natural asking about it that I wasn't prepared for a way to evade it as I always did. When other people have asked about my mother's accident, I'm usually ready with a way to change the subject. I simply froze and stared at her while she sat there, tranquil and patient and waiting.

"Since our time together," she started, "it's become apparent that your wolf is in hiding. It's a defensive move. Something happened that scared him *and* you so much that he decided he'd better stay away. And you decided it was best you hold him back too."

"I never blocked my wolf."

"Maybe not consciously. But subconsciously, you have. So why don't you tell me about the accident?"

A flood of adrenaline pumped through my veins at the memory of that day. I'd never forgotten one single second of it. The nightmare haunted me often enough, but I always tried not to think about it. To push it away. Maybe like I'd pushed my wolf away.

"We'd been grocery shopping at Walmart that day." I swallowed at the thickness that had suddenly filled my throat.

"Did you often go grocery shopping with your mother?"

"Always. She was a single mother, and though I was growing up, she didn't like to leave me home alone. Plus, I was a help to her." I smiled, thinking about how at twelve I had been taller than she'd been and could reach the top shelves.

"How so?"

"I'd help get the things she wanted that were too high up for her. I helped bag and load the groceries."

"I'll bet you were a great help to her."

I nodded, my heart pumping faster as I walked through every moment of that day.

"It had been the perfect Saturday." My voice rasped with regret. "It was the first weekend of the month, and my mom got paid once a month for her secretary job at the school. She always treated me on that weekend."

"She wanted you to be happy."

"She did," I agreed. "She was always doing little things for me to give me a better life. To make me happy. So we'd gotten some burgers at this diner I loved and had a picnic in the park. Afterward, we'd gone to Walmart." I rubbed my sweaty palms on my jeans. "Like I said, it was around her payday, and she sometimes bought me a toy or something extra I wanted as a treat."

"She bought you something special that day?"

Closing my eyes, I nodded, visualizing holding what she'd bought me. "It was a new sketch pad with special multicolored art pencils. The expensive kind. I wasn't into kids' toys anymore, and she knew how much I loved art class."

"So you were an artist when you were younger. Have you ever thought about being an artist? I know that many werewolves go into the field."

"I did. But after that day, I never wanted to be one again."

"I see. Keep going, Ronan. You're doing well."

Combing both hands through my hair, I stood and walked to the window. Dr. Theriot never minded me moving around as I often did. I always got restless when our conversations got personal or difficult. This was the most difficult discussion we'd ever had, one I'd never shared with anyone. But something gave me the courage today, urging me to tell it all, to let it out. It wasn't just my subconscious, but a tingling of magic whispering in my veins.

"After we packed all of the groceries in the car, we headed home. I should mention that it was Mom's new car. Not brand new, because she could never afford that. But a newer used Nissan sedan. It had real leather seats. She was so proud of that new car." I chuckled bitterly. "It was late afternoon. The sun was just beginning to set. I'd taken the art pad and pencils with me in the front seat so I could sketch on the way home. We lived a little outside Amarillo along a country road, so I had a good amount of time to sketch."

I paused, remembering how I'd begun sketching characters from this favorite video game I liked.

"Go on, Ronan," Dr. Theriot urged gently, still seated behind me.

"I wasn't really paying attention because I was sketching my characters. But, apparently, I'd let my new pencils spill onto my seat. Mom must've looked over because then she said, 'Ronan, put those pencils away. They'll stain my leather seats.' And like I said, I wasn't paying attention. I was really into my own head. I didn't do what she said."

I licked my lips, staring out at the crape myrtle tree with puffy purple blossoms, my heart beating faster. I could hear my mother's voice in my mind. I could still smell the lemon Pledge on her hands from dusting the house that morning and the lavender shampoo in her hair.

"When she told me the second time to put them away, she reached over, and my wolf, he just reacted for me. I wasn't in control of him as I'd just hit puberty and had shifted only a few times before this."

My chest felt tight as I remembered her eyes widening when I growled and my claws came out.

"I actually slashed at her hand with my claws. She'd snatched her hand back in time, but right then, at the same exact moment, a deer ran in front of our car. My mom jerked the car suddenly to the right. Unfortunately, on this long-ass road with few trees at all, there was one big, thick oak directly in front of us. Mom swerved hard so that when we hit, it was mostly on her side."

I couldn't speak anymore, thinking about being back in that car. Mom was completely crushed by the steering wheel, her head bleeding from where it hit the top corner of the car in the crash.

"I jumped out and waved down a passing truck, who called 911."

"Were you injured?" she asked softly.

"Not badly. I'd fractured my ankle, but I didn't feel it. Once I got the man in the passing truck to call the ambulance, I returned to the car to be with Mom."

I held her hand and squeezed it while she smiled at me and shushed me.

It's okay, Ronan. Don't cry.

Her soft words as her breathing became shallow and she slowly died beside me brought all of the old fear back. I was losing the only person who truly loved me.

You're such a brave, smart boy. I love you so much, son. I'll always love you.

Then she stopped breathing, and my world as I knew it ended.

"You know what's the worst part of it?" I asked, voice hoarse.

Dr. Theriot remained quiet.

"I'm a werewolf so my senses are heightened. I could hear every fucking thing. The wet rasp of her breathing as blood filled her lungs. The slowing of her heart as it fought to beat and keep her alive. And I could hear the exact moment my mother's heart stopped beating. When she left me on this earth all alone." My voice cracked.

Dr. Theriot walked up beside me and handed me a Kleenex. I took it, not realizing that I was crying. Two cardinals alighted on the crape myrtle outside. We stood in silence, watching the birds hop from branch to branch, sort of chasing each other and singing back and forth.

"That was an awful tragedy for so young a boy." Her voice was filled with compassion. "But I am certain now that it was the inciting incident when you put your wolf away, caged him deep inside you, since he lashed out at your mother. You punished him and therefore punished yourself. Since then, you've not only been coping with survivor's guilt but also with the belief that you somehow caused your mother's death." She paused for a moment, then went on. "Please know that you lashing out at your mother did not cause the accident, Ronan. You did *not* kill your mother."

I wiped away a fresh trail of tears, having always believed it was my fault.

"It was an unfortunate series of circumstances, Ronan. Even if your wolf hadn't reacted in that moment, it is entirely believable that your mother would've reacted in the exact same way with the deer and hit the exact tree in the same way. Your distraction of her attention for a few seconds may not have had any impact at all. But even if it did, it was still an accident. You did *not* kill her. You must know that and understand that."

"I just don't understand why it had to happen at all. It's so fucking unfair." My voice broke again.

"It is unfair. So many tragedies in this world happen for no good reason at all. It is up to us to take those tragedies, mourn our lost loved ones, and do better in the life we have left to live.

To be better versions of ourselves and to live fully and completely in order to honor those who can no longer do so."

We watched the birds for a moment, sweet little things hopping around.

"One thing I noted of importance in your story," she added, "was that your mother didn't have time to avoid the tree, but she did have enough time to protect you. She made sure the brunt of the crash impacted her. She wanted the son she loved so much to be safe and whole. To go on and live a full life, even without her."

I nodded, exhaling a heavy breath, unable to say in words that I knew that was true. We stood in silence while I tried to recover.

"You know?" I whispered, having finally dried my eyes. "I read once that spirits can sometimes come back from the afterlife and visit their loved ones as cardinals. Do you think that's true? I see them a lot."

"It could be," she said. "But your mother's spirit has likely been watching over you and visiting you your whole life. The Goddess of Nature or God the Creator, whichever you believe in, or both, has guided you on your path, a path your mother would be proud of."

"How do you know that?" I asked, finally turning to her.

"First, I know, because your wolf has not left you. Even though you've kept him locked away all this time because you fear what he might do if he's uncaged, he is still there. Secondly, I know because you are striving to become better, to be better, and that means you're guided by the goodness of the mother who birthed you. But finally, and mostly, I believe it because you've left your home in Texas where you were born. It's possible you stayed there all this time only because leaving felt like leaving your mother's memory behind. But you were led here to New Orleans directly into the path of your soul mate, your supernatural mate, who was put on this earth to love you through all of life's trials and tribulations and joys and happy occasions."

Why I could never see any of this for myself, I didn't know. But it was true. I was well aware there were several states in the US that didn't outlaw wolf cage fighting. I should've moved long ago, but I never once even thought about it. Texas was my home, where I'd been born and raised, where my mom had died and was buried. It had never occurred to me to leave until Uncle Shane reached out and offered a room in his house and a job to get me on my feet after the last arrest.

"I think you're right," was all I could say.

"I probably am." She smiled. "I'm pretty smart like that."

Chuckling, I said, "Well, so what happens now? How do I get over Post Traumatic Shifting Disorder and make my wolf come out?"

"That's hard to say. Confronting your past was the first step. It might be the only step. He may come out at will or on the next full moon or on a full moon next year." She gave my arm a squeeze, filtering her Aura happy spell into me, washing away the darker feelings I'd had when recounting my mother's death. "But the good news is, you're reuniting, you and your wolf. He's recognized your mate, and he's sniffing around the surface again. He'll be coming out to play soon enough, I'm sure of it."

"So I need to keep coming to therapy to keep this progression going?"

She laughed. "That's up to you. We've gotten to the real reason your wolf is in hiding. We can continue to talk as long as
you need."

"Thank you, Dr. Theriot." I looked at the clock on the wall.
"My time's up, and I've said about all I can say today."

She walked with me around the sofa where I picked up my
keys on the end table. "You've made great progress, Ronan. All
of your feelings are valid, but it's important you understand that
none of what happened was your fault. The best thing you can
do for your mother is live the best and happiest life possible."

With another nod, I sighed. "I agree." Then I headed toward
the door but stopped and promised her, "I'll see you next week."

CHAPTER 20

~RONAN~

"It's bullshit!" Zack shouted, pacing the locker room after our last fight.

"It is," I agreed, holding the damp towel to Bowie's upper shoulder where Carter had clawed him right below the base of throat and down his back. "But, unfortunately, there's not much we can do about it besides accuse the referee of being paid off by the owners. And who would we complain to besides the NOWFC Board, who is likely also in Baron's father's pocket?"

"Ty won his fight," Zack continued to argue. "That's just a fact. And that asshole Carter got away with nearly mauling Bowie to death. Not even a penalty, and it gave him the advantage to beat Bowie."

Both of these facts were true. Ty's bout with Baron had gone to the judges since neither had achieved a TKO by the end of the final round. And Bowie had lost his fight after Carter clawed him from the corner of his shoulder and neck and down his back. It had hurt him so bad, Bowie had frozen, giving Carter a shot at an uppercut that knocked him out for a second, enough to give Carter the TKO.

It was illegal to claw the throat, but the referee deemed this one fair. It wasn't, but what could we do? Refs made calls all the time that weren't right in every kind of sport. That was just the way it was.

I'd been on edge the whole night, my own blood still pumping hard and hot after winning my fight against Nate. It wasn't as easy as the last fight, but I forced a TKO when I pinned him face down on the mat, and he couldn't get free.

Bowie winced as I pressed the towel to the upper part of the wound where it was bleeding most. "I'll be fine. If that fucking healer ever gets here."

"Yeah," Zack snapped angrily, "aren't they supposed to have a healer ready to go? Where the fuck are they?"

Right then, the locker room door burst open, but it wasn't the healer. It was Celine, looking pale and afraid. Her gaze went to Bowie as she hurried over.

"Oh my God. Should I call my aunt Isadora? She's a Conduit and can heal him quickly."

Conduit witches had the power to use surrounding energy to heal almost any wound. If the one assigned to the NOWFC ever got here, she could take care of Bowie's fairly fast.

"If the arena healer doesn't arrive soon, then I may ask you to," I told her, not liking how deep the gash was.

Suddenly, the door opened again, and this time it was their Conduit. I'd seen her taken aside by Baron's father when we hurried Bowie out of the cage. She was a willowy, blond witch, her hair in a tight braid down her back. She wore khakis and a short-sleeved shirt with the NOWFC logo on the right front shoulder.

"It's about time," Zack muttered.

"I apologize for the delay," she said, walking swiftly toward us. "Mr. Hammond requested that I treat the other fighter first."

"Bowie is worse off than him," Zack argued.

She took the towel from my hand and nudged me away from the long bench where Bowie was sitting. "Actually," she said dryly, "the other teammate had a fractured leg that needed setting and mending. He was seriously injured as well." True, Bowie had landed a hard kick after Carter had clawed him.

Then she addressed Bowie. "Lay down on your stomach, and I'll get started."

Zack walked over and crossed his arms, hovering and scowling while she started to work.

"Does anyone else need tending?" she asked, her hands taking on a pale green glow as she pressed them directly over Bowie's injury, a buzz of magic filling the room.

"Ty?" I asked him since he'd been fairly quiet this whole time.

"No, I'm fine."

"Good," said the witch, "then you may all wait outside while I work on your teammate. It helps with my concentration." Her gaze darted up at Zack, who wore a murderous glare like it was her fault.

"Come on." I patted Zack on the shoulder as I passed him, taking Celine's hand and tugging her out into the hallway.

The second I touched her, my anxiety calmed, but the restless energy from the night burned even hotter. I huffed out a sigh. Tonight had been rough. While Zack and I had won our fights, it did appear that the ref tonight had favored our opponents. A lot of questionable calls went to them. Not to mention the final judging on Ty and Baron's fight. It should've been Ty, and I wasn't being biased. He was a better fighter and had landed more punches and kicks than Baron, even if he hadn't knocked him out or gotten a TKO.

Ty was leaning against the wall opposite the door of our locker room. "Why don't you go?" he suggested to me. He seemed to sense my restlessness. "I'll wait here with these two."

"Diego, Joaquin, and Boomer are still here," Celine said. "Do you want me to send them back?"

"Yeah," said Ty. "They can come back."

She dropped my hand to send a text.

"I should stay," I told Ty, anxious as the leader of the team. I should wait with them.

"There's nothing you can do," added Zack. "Get lost with your girlfriend."

"We're good. We can handle it," added Ty with a nod to the back door.

Celine finished texting. "They're on their way," she told Ty.

"You're sure?" I asked Ty.

He nodded, so I urged Celine toward the exit with a hand at her back. We were both quiet as we made it to my Bronco. Once I wheeled out of the lot, the buzzing energy amplified. I could pretend I didn't know what it was about, but I did.

It was common to feel this rush of heated energy after a fight, but being near Celine right now wasn't calming me down. It was doing the exact opposite. My craving to pull over on the side of the road and yank her into my lap was so strong I gripped the steering wheel tighter and shifted in my seat, trying to get my raging hard-on to settle.

I was still sweaty, having pulled on my jeans and T-shirt after the fight without showering. But that wasn't what was making me so uncomfortable. It was the heady scent of desert flower next to me and the insatiable need to devour her and bury my cock inside her.

"Ronan," she said quietly.

I actually flinched and glanced her way.

"Is your wolf riding you?"

I nearly laughed because I could feel him pacing again, wanting to take charge. And I sure as fuck knew exactly what he wanted—to mount his mate.

"It's not that."

"I think I know what it is."

Stopping the car at a red light, I looked over. She had that unsmiling, sultry look she got sometimes, her pupils dilated, her mouth soft. I liked that I could identify her expressions now. The only problem was the look she was giving me was an invitation, and I wasn't sure I could be gentle if we went there.

"Don't take me home," she finally said, the red of the streetlight shining on half of her perfect face.

My gut clenched, and my dick got harder. "Are you sure?" I asked, noting the roughness of my voice.

Her gaze flicked down my body to my crotch. There was no hiding the bulge I was packing.

"Positive."

The light turned green, and I turned toward my home, hoping like hell Uncle Shane was still playing cards with his pack friends. Rihanna's "Skin" was playing on the radio, and every word intensified my need to get Celine into my bedroom and get her naked.

By the time we pulled up the gravel drive and past the shop to the house, my entire body was humming with need. I smiled at the empty spot where Uncle Shane usually parked his truck.

Once parked, I rounded the Bronco and scooped her up into my arms like a bride. She squealed but then moaned when I took her mouth in a searing kiss. My body reacted to the silky touch of her tongue, the plushness of her mouth. I couldn't imagine how good it would feel to sink inside her.

She broke the kiss suddenly. "Get me in the house, Ronan."

"Yes, ma'am."

I practically ran through the yard and up the steps. I set her down to unlock the door, then corralled her inside, my hands on her waist as I shut the door behind me with my boot.

She gripped my shoulders as I guided her backward. "Which one is yours?"

"What's wrong? You in a hurry?" I asked playfully, even when I was the one already breathing hard with anticipation.

"Yes," she said confidently. "I've been thinking about this for a long time."

"Oh, baby." I pushed her into my bedroom and shut this door, too, with my foot. "The things you say."

She grinned and stopped walking as I scooped my hands to her ass and kissed her hard, nipping at her bottom lip. She moaned and rocked her hips forward, my cock so hard it was painful.

"Fuck," I whispered. "Let me take a quick shower. I'm all sweaty."

"Okay."

I had to close my eyes. It was hard to look at her with desire painted on her pretty face and walk away. "I'll be fast," I promised.

She laughed as I turned and hurried into the bathroom, bumping the door closed partway. I stripped quickly and stepped into the shower, sliding the glass door closed. I planned to get in and out in less than two minutes. But as soon as I soaped my chest and gave my painfully erect dick a stroke, the bathroom door pushed all the way open.

Through the cloudy steam and the opaque glass door, I could see Celine standing there watching me—completely naked.

֍

~CELINE~

I DON'T KNOW WHAT IT WAS ABOUT RONAN, BUT HE MADE ME FEEL brave and bold. Or maybe it was that I felt safe enough with him to be anything and everything I wanted to be.

He slid the glass door open, revealing his incredible body. He was beautifully made, all tightly packed muscle, chiseled abdomen, wide shoulders. His wet hair was darker and slicked back, water sluicing down his body in tantalizing rivulets.

I pulled out my ponytail holder, letting my hair fall around my bare shoulders. Ronan grunted with a sort of pained look and held out his hand. I didn't hesitate, stepping into the shower with him.

He slid his hands into my hair, tilting my head back, his mouth on mine. I moaned as he pressed me into the cool tile wall with his hot, hard body, nipping up my jaw to suck and bite at my throat.

I clenched my fists in his hair as his hard cock flattened against my belly, the warm spray of water beating on us, making our skin slick. His hands were everywhere, sliding down my back, squeezing my ass, then up my hips and on my breasts, fingers lightly pinching my nipples.

"Ronan," I pleaded, pressing my hips forward.

He pressed his forehead to mine, gliding his fingers between my legs. He slid his middle finger along the slickness of my slit before pumping it inside me.

"I need to be inside you so bad, baby," he practically growled.

"Then get inside me. I'm on the pill."

On another groan, he cupped my ass and lifted me, my back sliding on the wet tiles as I wrapped my legs around his waist. He shifted his hips, his cock nudging at my entrance. We were both panting as he let me sink down onto his cock before thrusting once to bury himself deep.

I gasped at the tight intrusion, clawing my blunt nails into his scalp and shoulder where I held on.

"Fuuuck." He closed his eyes, clenching his jaw before he murmured, "So tight and perfect."

"Ronan?"

His eyes slid open, a brilliant, bright blue, predatory and feral.

"I need you to fuck me."

He was so still, his stare so intense, it sent a shiver over my body.

"I don't need you to be gentle." I made it quite clear, panting, heart pounding. "In fact, I'd prefer that you weren't."

That deep purring of his wolf vibrated in his chest, teasing my nipples to hard peaks. Then he dragged his dick out to the tip and slammed back inside me.

I moaned at the pleasurable jolt, tipped my head back to the tile, and closed my eyes.

"Like that?"

"Just like that."

He thrust in hard again, grazing his wet mouth along my jaw to my ear. "Your pussy was made for me." He pumped in and out again with a deep thrust. "You were made for me, Celine." Then he began to drive faster, harder. "You're mine," he growled, fucking me hard now. "All mine."

"Yes," I whimpered. "Yes, more."

I wrapped both arms around his neck as his hands cupped my ass. He shifted one hand on my bottom, his finger sliding to rim the tight hole of my backside.

I whimpered, the new sensation both strange and intoxicatingly arousing. His finger worked my back entrance, just a fingertip. It was blindingly pleasurable while his long, thick cock pumped inside me.

"Oh God!"

"Mmm," he hummed, the narrow blue slits of his gaze watching me with fierce intensity. "Need to feel you come while I'm inside you, baby."

His voice and his body held me completely captive. But even more, the pouring of his emotions that soaked into my skin and sang to my blood were unlike anything I'd ever known.

"Goddess above," I whispered against his lips where he hovered close so he could watch me, "what is happening to me?"

I was unraveling at the seams, as if my maker had decided He or She wasn't quite done with me, as if I'd only ever been half-made, the body and the spirit not yet complete, still moldable and raw. The threads of my being were pulled apart and resewn into the one holding me in his arms, driving so very deep inside me, willing our souls to fuse.

"You know what's happening." He breathed hard, still stroking deep but slowing his pace. "You feel it as much as I do."

Swallowing hard at the realization that he felt it, too, there was no doubt, no possible other course but to see this through, to make our bodies and souls one.

"Ah!" I cried out as my orgasm swept through me like an avalanche of sensation. "I'm coming!"

"That's right. Let it go, Celine." His canines were lengthened and sharp, his eyes ice-blue with the wolf, his voice dark and deep. "Let me feel you."

I scraped his nape with my nails as I came, my sex pulsing with pleasure. "Yes, so good."

He bent his head and sank the tips of his teeth into the crook of my shoulder. There was a prick of pain, but somehow also euphoric pleasure, sparking a second orgasm through me.

"Yes, yes." I rocked my hips, bathing in sexual bliss.

He licked the small wound he'd made, the mark he'd put on me, an animalistic growl of satisfaction vibrating from his chest. Then he kissed my mouth, grinding his cock inside me in a slow circle until he too was groaning and coming, his cock throbbing as he spent himself.

We both kissed and moaned through the ecstasy, savoring the savage sweetness of this moment. When he drew his mouth from mine, both of us panting, the shower still beating down on our bodies, he simply stared at me. Slowly, his lips curled up into a smile, his canines still sharp. He didn't move to set me down or pull out of my body.

"Are we going to stay like this forever?" I teased.

"If it were only possible, I'd be in heaven." He brushed his lips against mine in a wet, feathery kiss. "I'm pretty sure I am in heaven right now. I just don't remember dying."

"I nearly died from that orgasm."

He smirked. "The first or the second?"

Then I laughed, my sex squeezing him. He hissed in a breath, then chuckled, his gaze shifting to the shoulder he'd bitten.

"Sorry about that."

"No, you're not." I smiled. "You and your wolf are proud of that."

"Maybe a little." Then he frowned. "Does it hurt?"

I lifted my shoulder. "Feels a little tender, but it's fine. Did you break the skin?" I tried to look, unable to see it since it was at the juncture of my shoulder and neck.

"Fuck, I'm sorry. I don't know what came over me."

He lifted me by the waist, withdrawing from my body, and set me on my feet. When he started to turn toward the shower spray, his mood growing suddenly uneasy, I gripped his arms and forced him back to me.

"Ronan, that was a good thing."

He remained quiet, obviously upset, even while one of his hands trailed down one of my hips and back to my waist. His soothing brush of hands always amazed me. He was constantly touching me in tender, reassuring ways, like it was his job to make me feel cherished and protected. It was also *my* job to make him feel the same way.

"This is a sign your wolf is resurfacing even more. He's making himself known." I coasted my hands up to cup his jaw.

"He's marking his territory," I added lightly. "And I like that. Very much."

"Mmm," he hummed with that deep masculine sound while guiding me under the shower spray. "Let's get you washed."

He didn't say more, but proceeded to carefully bathe me. After lathering his hands with shower gel, he cleaned my shoulders, back, and thighs before turning me to tend to the front. He didn't crack a smile as he soaped and washed my breasts, belly, between my legs. Then he squeezed some shampoo into his palm.

"Turn around."

I did, closing my eyes as he gently massaged the shampoo into my scalp, taking a leisurely long time. It was luxurious.

After I rinsed, he was already beginning to soap himself.

"No," I told him, pressing two drops of shower gel into my palm. "My turn."

Finally, he smiled, standing perfectly still as I took my time washing his shoulders, chest, abdomen, and thighs. I didn't miss that he was half-hard again by the time I finished with his back and behind.

He rinsed, and quietly we exited and toweled off. He rubbed his hair roughly with the towel while I used his brush in my damp hair. When we returned to his bedroom, he glanced at my clothes I'd set neatly on a chair next to his dresser. While he opened a drawer and slipped on some boxer briefs, I draped a fresh towel on one pillow, climbed into his bed, and lay down there, not wanting to soak the pillow with my wet hair.

He froze and blinked at me for a second. "I thought you'd have to go."

"Do you want me to go?"

"No!" he snapped quickly, then he lifted the covers and slipped in beside me, facing me. "Won't your parents wonder where you are?"

"I told my mom not to expect me home."

"Told her you were staying at Samara's or something?" The inflection of his voice didn't change from basic curiosity, but I sensed with my empathic gift that he was nervous now. And I knew why.

"I told my mom I was going to see your fight and not to expect me home. I'm pretty sure she can figure it out."

"What if she tells your dad?"

I shrugged. "So she tells my dad."

He grinned and laced our hands together, tucking them beneath his chin. "So you decided you were staying the night before the fight?"

"Yep." I tugged our laced hands back and pressed a kiss to his knuckles, one of which was bruised and swollen.

His other hand slid around my waist, and he tugged me closer. "Thank you."

"For what? Accepting multiple orgasms with my boyfriend? You're very welcome."

He laughed. "Damn, baby. I'm so into you."

He said it easily and naturally. That was another thing about Ronan that turned me on beyond belief. There were no games or guarded niceties between us. It was real and true, and it gripped my heart in a hot iron fist.

"Me too," I whispered.

Even though I'd admitted that I was falling for him fast last week, I knew I was beyond that now. I'd well and truly fallen— hard and deep, but I was still too scared to say the words.

Still, as we curled up together in his bed, our bodies entwined, I felt his love wrapping me in its protective warmth. I never wanted to leave the safe cocoon of Ronan's arms.

CHAPTER 21

~RONAN~

"What's the occasion?" Uncle Shane asked when he walked into the kitchen the next morning.

I was at the stove, having cooked up plates of bacon, sausage, hash browns with diced peppers, and toast, and was now making scrambled eggs.

"If you're hungry, grab a plate," I told him.

He was fully dressed, his hands propped on his hips, ready to head to the shop. Then his nostrils flared, and his gaze went to my open bedroom door.

"Did you have a girl over last night?"

He had come in late, long after Celine and I were asleep.

"Yeah," was all I said as I poured some milk into my bowl of eggs and then kept whipping.

"Oh, hell, Ronan," he grumbled, then whispered, "Is that Celine Cruz?"

A REBEL WITHOUT CLAWS

I poured the whipped eggs into the pan, the butter and oil popping. Before I could answer, I heard her shuffle out into the kitchen.

"It sure is," she said.

I glanced over my shoulder, my heart plummeting into my stomach when I saw her wearing her own jeans but one of my T-shirts. A harsh grunt of appreciation huffed up my chest, followed by a low growl. Shane's wide-eyed gaze swiveled to me.

"Was that your wolf?"

Instead of answering him, I left the stove to walk over to Celine and kiss her lips, still minty from toothpaste. She obviously found the new toothbrush I'd left in the bathroom for her with a sticky note. I'd run up to the convenience store a mile away when I first woke up. Waking with her in my bed and my arms was beyond exhilarating. I'd never been so blissed out, except perhaps last night when I'd come inside her.

After snuggling for a few minutes, I couldn't get over the need to get up and do something, to be ready when she woke up. My need to make her happy had set me in motion.

"Good morning," I whispered. "Come sit and eat." I nudged her to the table.

Once she was seated, I rushed back to the eggs and stirred them, shaking some Tony Chachere's Creole Seasoning into them. When I glanced over my shoulder, Uncle Shane was still standing there, awkward and puzzled.

"Have a seat, Uncle Shane."

Then I poured the fluffy scrambled eggs into a bowl and set them on the table with everything else.

"Do you always cook breakfast like this?" Celine asked sweetly.

"No," grumbled Uncle Shane, taking a seat as he scowled at me.

I laughed. Nothing could get me down today. I scooped some eggs onto Celine's plate next to me, then passed her the plate of bacon and sausage.

"Oh, do you want some coffee?" I hopped back up, jittery and excited.

"Yes, please."

"Cream or sugar?"

"Both."

"Mmm. That fits." I winked at her.

She smiled, staring down while a pink blush flushed up her cheeks.

"Well, fucking hell, Ronan." Uncle Shane dished himself a heaping pile of eggs and then plopped the bowl down heavily on the wooden dining table. "You sure know how to get yourself into trouble wherever you go."

"How is dating Celine getting into trouble?" I stirred her coffee, unperturbed by my uncle's piss-poor attitude.

"Here, baby." I set her coffee down gently, then moved my chair closer to her before I sat across from him. Not satisfied, I tugged her chair even closer to mine.

Celine simply smiled while she sipped her coffee.

Uncle Shane's gaze flitted from me to her, then back to me. "Damn." He shook his head. "I'd have never figured that."

He just realized she was my mate. Not sure what set it off, but it was either my obvious territorial and protective behavior or that my bite could be seen from the gape of my oversize T-shirt she was wearing.

I didn't bother commenting as I dug into my breakfast. "Did you get some hash browns?" I asked her. "My aunt Sarah taught me to cook them that way."

She forked some of the crispy diced potatoes and green and red peppers, then took a bite. "Oh, they're delicious."

She smiled at me, and my entire soul lit up with joy.

We both settled into eating again while my uncle sat in his chair and stared at us both. I ignored him, realizing how hungry I was after last night.

My mind had wandered to the next time I could get her alone when Uncle Shane blurted out, "Does your father know about this?"

Celine looked up. Calm and poised, she wiped her mouth with her napkin and nodded. "Yes. He knows we're dating."

"Huh." He finally took a bite of the eggs on his plate. "But does he know it's more than that?"

"He will," she said confidently.

I'd never had the urge to howl like a wolf, but I did right then.

"He'll know tomorrow, anyway," she added, "when Ronan comes to family dinner."

I paused, setting my half-eaten sausage on my plate. "I am?"

"Sorry." She cleared her throat and sipped her coffee again. "I was going to ask you last night, but with the fight and, um, everything else, I forgot."

"What happened at the fight?" Uncle Shane asked with concern.

"Nothing. Just Bowie got a hard hit."

"Not a hit," Celine added. "He was clawed down the back, but it was close to his throat."

I cringed when Uncle Shane made that disapproving grunt. "That shit is dangerous, Ronan. You should stop messing around in the ring."

Same old speech. I was about to tell him to keep his opinions to himself when Celine piped up again.

"Oh, it isn't messing around. It's a well-recognized sport. And Ronan is amazing in the ring. He's an incredible fighter. You should come and see him." Then she dug back into her hash browns like she hadn't just rocked my world.

She had defended me to my uncle like it was nothing, telling him something I would never have been able to get him to understand on my own.

Uncle Shane didn't comment, likely out of politeness to Celine, and kept eating. We ate in silence after that. Uncle Shane shoveled his breakfast down fast, then he hopped up to put his plate in the sink.

"Well, thank you for breakfast, Ronan." Then he clapped me on the shoulder and leaned down to say, "Sure wish I was a fly on the wall when you meet the whole family." His chuckle to himself was downright sinister as he headed outside. "See you around, Celine."

"Bye."

That was a little disturbing. I knew that Celine had a big family, but I'd already met her brothers and a few cousins. I wondered what could be so ominous about the rest of them.

"Can you give me a ride home?" Celine snapped me out of my reverie as she stood and set her plate in the sink.

"Actually, I was going to let you take my Bronco."

"What will you drive?"

"They've got a bike in the garage that's sort of community property at this point."

"What?" She laughed as I followed her to get her purse from my bedroom, lamenting the fact we weren't still cuddled under the covers.

"Some rich guy left it a while back." I took her hand once she put her purse over her shoulder and guided her back through the house and outside. "He sold it to Uncle Shane for next to nothing, and he lets anybody use it when they need to."

"What if I wreck your Bronco?" she asked as we walked down the porch and the walkway to the drive.

"You won't. And if you do, she'll protect you. She's sturdy and tough."

"I see."

I turned her at the driver's side and gripped her waist, leaning into her against the car. Tucking her hair behind her ear, I said, "Thank you for last night."

"No, thank *you* for last night."

We were both grinning like smitten teenagers, and I didn't give a fuck. That's how I felt. This was new and fresh, so different than anything I'd felt before.

"So I meet the *whole* family tomorrow?"

"Yeah. About noon at the Cauldron, my aunt's pub." She exhaled a heavy breath. "Sorry I didn't tell you before. I didn't want to worry you during the week with the fight ahead of you."

"Why would it worry me?"

"My family can just be a handful, but they're going to love you. I know it."

I suppressed the feelings of doubt, not wanting to taint this perfect morning. "As long as you're there, I don't care what anyone else thinks."

"It'll be great." She brushed a lock of my hair off my forehead that had fallen over one eye.

"And thank you for telling my uncle what you did," I told her.

"I meant what I said, but I can't pretend it doesn't worry me." A line formed between her brows. "I was so worried when Bowie got hurt last night. I don't know what I would've done if it had been you."

"It's part of the job. But no one gets seriously hurt."

"Never?"

I had seen a guy mauled near to death when a fighter shifted into his werewolf form and got hold of him before they darted his ass. But I wasn't going to tell her about that.

"Don't worry, Celine."

"Did you find out if Bowie is all right?"

"He is. I texted him this morning."

"In between buying me a toothbrush and cooking me breakfast?" she asked playfully, lightening the tension.

She pulled out the sticky note from her back pocket and held it up to me. She'd folded the sticky part back, so she could slip it easily into her pocket, still revealing my messy scrawled words. *Good morning, beautiful. I bought this for you to keep here, hoping you'll be using it very often.* ♥ *Ronan*

"You gonna use that toothbrush a lot?" I squeezed her hips.

"So often I'll need a new one by next month." She kissed the note and tucked it back into her jeans pocket.

"I like the sound of that."

Then I kissed her softly, savoring the sweetness of her mouth in the early-morning light.

"Yo, Reed! Stop kissing your girl and get your ass to work!"

We both looked over at the body shop to see Zack waving me over and grinning like the Joker. Rolling my eyes, I opened the door and handed her my keys.

"Drive careful." I leaned in and gave her another kiss through the open window.

"See you tomorrow." She smiled up at me, the golden sunlight shining across her hair, the copper strands glowing. My angel's halo.

"You're so beautiful it makes my heart hurt sometimes."

"Ronan." She took my hand and kissed the center of my palm.

I don't know why I didn't just tell her I loved her, because I did. She had to know that I did. I suppose I was afraid to let those dangerous words out of my mouth because you can't take them back. And if she didn't love me like I loved her, then I'd be devastated.

The hard fact was that I was willing to take whatever affection she'd give me. Being mated with someone didn't force you to love them. Love was an action and an all-consuming emotion that made you bare your heart and soul to someone else. If she didn't return the soul-shattering love I had for her, I think I'd lose my mind.

So I kept those words inside my mouth, then smiled and waved. I pressed my palm to my sternum, trying to stifle the pain of watching her leave.

CHAPTER 22

~RONAN~

"Holy fucking hell." I stood at the entrance of the Cauldron, staring at the madhouse before me.

"Ronan!" Celine beamed as she hurried over and looped her arm through mine. "Don't worry. I know it looks scary, but it's not so bad."

"We'll see," I muttered, steeling my spine as the uncles standing near the bar turned to stare me down when I walked into the menagerie that was family dinner.

"This isn't how the pub usually looks. We rearrange the tables when we have family dinner so we can sit together."

There were several four-top tables stacked together down the center of the pub, set with silverware and napkins. There were more tables against a wall with covered dishes that smelled delicious.

But I couldn't even think about eating as Celine walked me straight toward the lion's den—her father. He was sitting next to a woman who must be Celine's mother at one end of the long table. He immediately stood as we drew closer.

My gut clenched at the imposing figure of her father. He was about my size, but that didn't diminish the alpha dominance radiating off him. There was no doubt he'd rip my throat out, or try, if I stepped one toe out of line with his daughter. Thankfully, I didn't plan to. Ever.

"Mom and Dad"—Celine blew out a nervous breath and dropped my arm—"this is Ronan Reed. Ronan, these are my parents, Evie and Mateo Cruz."

"It's nice to meet you." I extended my hand to her mother first.

"And you, Ronan," Evie said lightly, shaking my hand with a warm smile. It was obvious where Celine got her optimistic, cheerful personality.

I then held out my hand to her father. "It's good to meet you, Mr. Cruz."

His stare was so hard it almost made me laugh. He was obviously trying with great effort not to throttle me on the spot. I'd been in his house, his daughter's bedroom, without his permission, and he had to know where she'd spent last night.

But Celine was an adult, and if he didn't want his daughter to disown him, he had to play nice. I'd never met a father of a girlfriend. Perhaps because my relationships lasted all of a couple weeks before they fizzled. No woman had ever captured me but for a few moments.

Celine wasn't my girlfriend. That word was too small for what she was to me. She was my everything. My beginning and end. And no matter what her father thought of me, I would never leave her.

So I stood there, my hand extended, waiting like a jackass for him to welcome me into the fold. To shake my hand like a man. For a breathless second, I thought he might not. Both of the women in his life stood there, staring wide-eyed, waiting like me.

Fucking finally, he lifted his arm and shook my hand. Surprisingly, he didn't do that machismo bullshit of trying to squeeze my hand to death, the kind of pissing contest I expected from people like Baron Hammond. No, he shook my hand with a decent grip, then let go and said, "It's nice to meet you, Ronan. Could I talk to you for a minute?" He gestured off to the side.

"Dad," snapped Celine.

"Mateo," his wife said with a hint of warning.

He raised his palms to them with a semi-smile. "It's okay. I just want to talk to him, man to man."

Celine turned to me and whispered, even though every werewolf, vampire, and grim reaper—I'd noticed at least one at the bar—could hear everything she said. "You don't have to."

I cleared my throat so I wouldn't laugh. I definitely had to do this. She might not understand the man-to-man, especially alpha-to-alpha, dynamic. Backing down would make me a coward. And I wasn't that, especially when it came to her. I'd stand up against a thousand alphas for her.

"It's fine." I touched her back gently. "Let me chat with your dad."

Mateo's brows shot up in a semblance of respect before returning to the grave expression that had greeted me. Then he walked to the back corner of the pub with a small stage where they must have live music.

We took seats opposite each other. I clasped my hands loosely on the table, waiting for the threatening speech he planned to give me. My advantage was that I'd been given more hard speeches in my lifetime than most of the people in this entire room. From my grandfather to my aunt and uncle, my high school counselors and teachers, my juvie parole officer, past bosses at the mundane jobs I'd held, I'd been given a hundred you-better-straighten-up speeches.

I understood why they gave them to me. I was a bit of a fuck-up in my youth until I found fighting as an outlet. But even that came with shitty speeches from relatives. It had led me into a life of violence, inside and out of the ring. But, eventually, that had led me here to New Orleans—to Celine—where I belonged.

So it didn't matter what her father was about to say. I'd accept it and go about loving his daughter with all my heart regardless of whatever threats he planned to lay on me.

"I looked into you, Ronan."

Here we go. I didn't nod or offer any response. I simply waited.

"Quite an impressive streak of arrests in Texas."

Still, I sat there, not saying a word. There was nothing to say. Not yet.

"But I'm not going to judge a book by its cover." He glanced at my cheek where I knew I had a bruise from Friday's fight. "My daughter speaks very highly of you."

I had no idea why, but my heart rate sped erratically. This was unexpected.

He paused, then went on. "I don't know you. That will come in time. But I know my daughter. She's smart and strong, and I trust her. So if she cares about you the way she does, then she sees good in you."

My entire body locked up. I gulped hard, my chest rising and falling more quickly. He could detect that, of course, which I didn't much like. I didn't want anyone knowing they'd gotten to me. But this father, who didn't know me one fucking bit, giving me the benefit of the doubt, had my emotions in a tailspin. Not what I'd expected at all.

"So I suppose what I wanted to say was that"—he leaned forward, elbows on the table—"I'm not going to kill you for sneaking into my house that night. I know what it feels like to pursue your mate."

I actually startled at that. "You know?"

He scoffed. "Yeah, Ronan. I know." A heavy dose of sarcasm laced his voice.

"Then you know I'm not going anywhere."

"That's why we're having this conversation. I'm very protective when it comes to my family, especially my women."

"I get that."

"Good. Then I guess we understand each other."

Done with this uncomfortable, if surprising, conversation, I stood. So did he.

Then his voice dropped wolf-deep, his eyes flashing gold as he said, "But if you hurt her, I'll kill you."

For some reason, that made me smile. He loved her deeply. As he should.

"Sir, hurting Celine would be like cutting out my own heart. That's not going to happen."

His eyes darkened to the normal brown, and his brows shot up in surprise. "Let's introduce you to the rest of the family."

As soon as we walked back toward the circus milling around the room, Celine grabbed my hand and steered me toward the bar. "You need a drink."

"More than anything," I agreed.

She laughed, squeezing my hand to reassure me, my insides melting at her sweet affection.

Then we were approaching the bar where her many uncles stood along with Samara and a woman with blond hair and blue-dyed ends. They all turned at our approach.

"Okay, everyone. This is Ronan. He's Shane Reed's nephew. Be nice. Ronan, this is my uncle Nico."

He gave me a nod. "I know your uncle well."

"Yeah," I said. "I heard he kidnapped your mate once."

They all laughed except Nico, who rolled his eyes. "Don't remind me. She can take care of herself anyway." He wrapped his arm around the waist of the woman with partly dyed hair.

"You bet your ass I can." She held out her hand to me. "Hi, there, handsome. It's so nice to finally meet you."

When we shook hands, I felt her magic like a cool shiver rushing along my skin.

"Oh wow. Great energy, Ronan." She pursed her brow.

"This is my aunt Violet," Celine said.

Then Celine went down the line and introduced an insanely long list of family members whose names I wasn't sure I'd ever remember.

"Nice to meet you all," I said, blowing out an exhausted breath. "Can I get a beer?"

Celine pushed me around them all to the bar where a brawny bearded man, a human, was making drinks. She told me that he was her uncle JJ who wasn't a blood-related uncle but who might as well be. I was beginning to understand that Celine's family encompassed even more than the ten thousand blood relatives I'd just met. They seemed to gather others into their fold, simply because that's the way they were.

JJ slid some kind of vodka drink from the smell of it to Violet, then turned to me. "What's your poison, son?"

"Anything cold and alcoholic," I said quickly.

He grinned, and I thought in another life, he'd make a great werewolf. "How about something a little stronger than beer?"

"Yes, please."

Celine wrapped her arms around my waist and hugged me close as if her relatives weren't all around us, stressing me the fuck out. Besides the adults, there were a ton of kids everywhere, some younger ones who must be elementary age and also some loud teenagers in another corner doing some kind of TikTok dance or something. A set of blond-haired twin girls giggled at videos on one of their phones at the main table.

"My other aunts are in the kitchen. Joaquin and Diego too. Joaquin learned his love of cooking from my aunt Jules, who owns this place."

"Diego likes cooking?"

"Hell no." She laughed. "But we take turns helping in the kitchen for each meal. I got a reprieve this time since you were coming. So thank you for saving me from cooking duty."

"You don't cook?" I asked, smiling.

"Nope. So now you know my weakness."

I leaned down to her ear and whispered as low as possible. "I know your real weakness." Then I gave her hip a squeeze.

She blushed and whispered back, "Yeah, you do."

"Good thing I'm not completely useless in the kitchen."

"You can cook more than breakfast food?" she teased.

"Just wait till I cook you dinner. I can make a mean manicotti."

"Truly?" Her green eyes lit up, lifting the anxiety from meeting her family.

"I'm not a chef or anything, but I can keep us alive with some decent meals." Then I frowned, realizing what I was insinuating. "I mean, if later we would live together."

Her expression softened. "Yes, that's a good thing. We'd spend a fortune on takeout otherwise." Her little comment meant everything to me. She was thinking long term now, and that's all I needed to know.

"Here you go." JJ slid a drink my way with an orange and lemon rind. "That's a Sazerac. Sip it slowly."

"Thanks."

"Dinnertime!" yelled her aunt Violet as people carried platters and bowls of food out to the buffet table.

It was a madhouse as this giant family lined up and made their way through the line. After filling my plate with blackened redfish topped with crawfish étouffée, parmesan truffle potatoes, asparagus with buttery garlic sauce, and freshly baked french bread, my stomach was actually growling.

"This is family dinner?" I huffed a laugh as we sat down.

"Yeah," said Diego, taking the seat next to me. "We do bougie family dinners with two chefs in the family now."

"Is this your étouffée?" Celine asked Joaquin on a whisper.

He nodded, glancing down the table at their aunt Jules.

"Yessss," she hissed quietly.

"What's the secret?" I whispered.

"Joaquin's étouffée is spicier and is just a little better than Aunt Jules's."

Joaquin shushed her. "Don't say that at the table."

Morgan sat next to Joaquin. "I can hear y'all from the buffet table," he grumbled. He had the personality of most grims rather than a vampire. "Your whispering is still too loud."

"Anyway," said Celine, "taste it."

I took a bite as Samara joined our group on the other side of me.

"Damn." I shook my head. "You may have to give me some lessons," I told Joaquin. "I may need them." Then I winked at Celine.

She blushed again and settled into eating her meal. Violet and Nico sat near us, too, then Mateo and Evie on the other side of them. Everyone dug into their meals, and for a few minutes, the only sound was forks on plates.

"Hey," said Diego cheerfully, "has Celine ever told you about her most embarrassing moment?"

"Diego," warned Celine. "*Don't.*"

"Remember that, Joaquin?" He turned to their triplet.

"You mean Morgan's fourth birthday party at his house?"

"Stop, Joaquin," commanded Celine. "I'm your favorite, remember?"

Joaquin pretended he didn't hear her and added, "That was hilarious."

"What happened?" I asked, palming her thigh underneath the table and giving her a squeeze.

228

"You don't want to know," she told me.

"But I really do," I said.

"We were around five, I think," said Diego. "It was a swim party with sprinklers to jump through and slip-n-slides. Uncle Ruben had decked out their whole backyard with the works."

"They have a huge backyard," added Joaquin.

"The problem was, Celine had been raised with brothers." Diego grinned.

"I hate y'all," she said.

Diego continued. "So when we ran off into the bushes to go pee like we'd done a million times back at our house while playing in the yard—"

"I'd like to say that was only the wolf in us," interjected Joaquin, "but we all did it. Even Morgan."

"Yeah, it was no big deal at home," said Diego. "But Morgan had all these rich friends, kids from all the elite vampire families there, along with their parents, watching over us in the yard." He laughed. "And Celine didn't even try to hide herself in the bushes. She just stopped by a tree, squatted in her bikini, and peed by the tree."

"I so hate y'all." Celine's head was in her hands.

Her father was staring at his plate, obiously trying not to laugh.

Then Aunt Violet piped up. "Cici, sweetie, it's nothing to be embarrassed about."

"Says the sister who's never embarrassed by anything," added Evie. "But you were so little, Celine. No one noticed."

Morgan, Diego, and Joaquin all guffawed. "*Everyone* noticed," said Diego. "It was priceless. Perfect little princess peeing on a tree in front of all the rich vampire families of New Orleans."

Celine shot a murderous look at Diego, and I noted the stress lines around the tightness of her mouth. I didn't like that.

I squeezed her thigh under the table, catching her gaze. "Good thing none of that shit matters. Who cares what the rich vampires think? You're not mated to any of them."

The table went silent, and I didn't give a shit. All I cared about was the way Celine looked at me, her eyes glassy with adoration, though she still wasn't smiling.

Then I said low, only for her, "Isn't that right, baby? And I think you're the most amazing woman I've ever met."

The whole family was watching this display, and I honestly didn't care. I just wanted her smile. Then she gave it to me.

"Yeah," she said a little hoarsely. "That's right."

I leaned in and kissed her cheek. "You can pee on my trees anytime you want."

That broke the silence, and everyone laughed. Even Celine, her joy making my world right again.

We all dove back into the delicious food, but I didn't miss the glance from Mateo and the approving nod he gave me before he returned to his meal.

CHAPTER 23

~CELINE~

I FINISHED TYPING UP MY LAST FEW NOTES ON MY NEW CLIENT AND shut my laptop on my desk. Smiling, I reached over to the teacup and turned it a little so the dragon faced me, thinking about the family dinner a few days ago. Ronan was such a good sport. And brave as hell to meet the whole damn family like that.

I wished he didn't live on the Westbank. It wasn't terribly far away, but too far for my liking. The truth was, I wanted to be with him every second I wasn't working.

Wondering if that was an unhealthy state of mind or simply the normal effect of falling in love, I locked up my office, knowing Dr. Theriot and Michael were long gone. Then I set the alarm and locked the front door as I left. Before I was down the front walkway, someone whistled at me.

Frowning, I glanced to my right, my pulse leaping with instant joy. Ronan sat astride a motorcycle with a helmet propped on one thigh under his arm.

"What in the world?" I asked, walking straight for him.

"Come take a ride with me, beautiful."

"Is this the community bike from the shop?"

"Yeah. I wanted to see my girl and take her for a ride with me."

My entire soul puddled into mush. I glanced down. "Good thing I wore pants today."

He swung off the motorcycle and gestured for me to come closer. When I closed the distance, looping the thin strap of my small bag over my neck and across my chest so the purse sat on my hip, he lifted the helmet gently over my head.

He took his time adjusting the strap, his gaze intense and serious until he was done.

"How do I look?" I giggled.

"Perfect." He leaned in and swept a brief kiss over my lips. "As always."

I rolled my eyes, but then he took my hand and tugged me to the bike. After he put his helmet on and swung his leg over, I took a minute to slide in behind him. The seat was long and wide, and seemed to be made for more than one person.

"Where do I put my feet?" I asked.

"Right here." He reached down and lifted one foot to the little rest.

I found the one on the other side, then wiggled closer and wrapped my arms around his waist. He grunted as he rubbed a hand along one arm and gave me a squeeze. Then he started her up and slowly pulled out onto the street.

It was late afternoon—evening really since it was nearly seven—but there was still sunlight this time of summer. The press of the wind and the sensation of spooning Ronan's strong body while we cruised through the Lower Garden District was heavenly.

I wasn't surprised when he headed into City Park, turning toward the area where towering, century-old oak trees created an ethereal canopy for visitors. Pale sunlight dappled through the leaves onto the street and onto us. It was lovely.

Ronan slowed and pulled the bike to a stop in a parking spot along the street. Reluctantly, I slid off and unbuckled my helmet. Ronan stowed them both on hooks attached to the back of the bike.

"Come on. I want to show you something."

He took my hand and led me along the walkway that wound deeper into the park, away from the street. We walked hand in hand, content simply to *be* together.

We came to a small pond and a walking bridge. He pulled us to a stop in the middle and leaned on the banister.

"Look right over there." He pointed to a weeping willow, its leaves draping into the pond.

"What am I looking for?"

"You'll see. Just keep watching."

He shifted behind me and wrapped his arms around my waist. The wispy leaves of the weeping willow moved. Or rather, something moved behind them. Then three little ducklings swam out of the leaves and into the open pond, the mother duck right behind them.

"Oh my goodness. Look at them," I gushed on a laugh.

He squeezed my waist tighter and pressed a kiss to my temple. "I thought you'd like seeing them."

"Since when do you wander in the park looking for little ducklings to woo your girlfriend?"

He chuckled. "I wasn't. I actually had to run an errand for Uncle Shane. Had to pick up a small part he needed in the city. He told me to take the bike, so I did. Then I decided since I was here, I might as well wait until you got off. So I wandered over here this afternoon and waited around."

"When was that?"

"About three hours ago?"

"Ronan." I turned in his arms. "Won't your uncle get pissed he sent you on an errand and you ditched for the day?"

"Nah." He nuzzled me closer, hands at my waist. "He didn't need it back today. And I needed to see you."

Nervous, I asked, "What about?"

He laughed, the deep, rich sound finding its way directly to my heart. "Nothing bad. I always need to see you."

"We're both ridiculous," I admitted. "I've barely been able to concentrate at work. My poor clients aren't getting their full hour's worth, because my brain sidetracks to you every couple minutes."

"Maybe we should just both quit work and run away to a cabin in the mountains and live off the land together."

"Could we?" I asked excitedly.

He grinned, then pressed a soft kiss to my lips. "You say the word, and I'll make it happen."

Then I was distracted by his mouth, his lips, and his tongue, sweetly coaxing me to open up and let him in. I did. He slid his hands to my backside and pulled me tightly against him while we kissed in the twilight, the sound of chirping ducklings behind us.

When we came up for air, he whispered, "Maybe we can just take a trip like that together. Whenever we both get the time."

That daring girl inside me, the one who'd been making herself known since the day I met Ronan, said, "Maybe we can do that for our honeymoon one day."

His eyes flared a bright, pale blue, his wolf liking what I said. "Oh, baby," he growled against my lips, "I'll make that happen, don't you worry."

He angled his mouth over mine and stole my breath, delving deep and pressing me back into the banister of the bridge. I whimpered, taking whatever he was giving me, and still wanted more. I always wanted more when it came to Ronan.

After a languorously long kiss, he eased back, sliding his hands to my waist and giving me a squeeze. His expression became pensive as he stared at me.

"What?" I asked.

"I did have a thought today."

"I hope you have thoughts every day."

He reached behind me and pinched my ass. "Ow!" I squirmed, laughing, but he kept me corralled to the bridge between his arms.

"What I meant was, while I was waiting for you, I wished I could check on you at the office to make sure you were still there and hadn't gone home early. When I went to your office, I saw your car so I just waited."

"You could've texted."

"Yeah, but I didn't want to bother you if you were with a client. And sometimes I want to check on you. Make sure you're home safe. I was thinking we could follow each other on the Life360 app."

I knew the app, because I was connected to my family for safety reasons. But the thought of giving it to Ronan suddenly sent a spike of panic through my body, my heart racing faster.

"Hey, hey. What's going on?" He eased back, concern pinching his brow.

"I don't know." But sweat began to break out all over.

"You're scared," he said. "I can hear your heart racing."

"Um, I don't know why, but—"

"I do. Fuck, I'm sorry." He cupped my face. "You're getting anxiety because I want to be able to know where you are. Forget I asked." He pulled me close and hugged me. "I'm sorry I asked."

"Why am I reacting this way?" Now I was angry at myself. "I completely trust you."

Didn't I? If so, then why was my body suddenly in panic mode at the thought of us following each other on a tracking app?

"Don't worry about it. It was just a thought. I'm a little obsessive about checking on you and making sure you're safe. I guess it's a wolf thing, I don't know."

I huffed a little laugh into his chest. "No, it's a protective instinct, I think. It's normal. It's my overreaction that isn't normal." I heard my voice crack, but I refused to cry over something so stupid. "What is wrong with me?"

He eased back and smiled down at me. "*Nothing* is wrong with you. It's fine. Forget I said anything at all. Let's just watch some cute baby ducks together."

That finally made me smile and eased the tension stiffening my spine. Biting my lip, I simply nodded.

So we did. We stayed and watched the mother duck and her babies swim in and out of the weeping willow leaves until it started to get dark. By then, my near panic attack had subsided, and I was calm again.

We walked back to the motorcycle. Ronan leisurely drove me back to my car at the office. When he helped me with my helmet, he asked, "Are you okay?"

"Of course I am." I gave him one more kiss before I said, "Thank you for ditching work and taking me for a ride."

"Anytime." His smile was soft and tender. "Text me when you get home."

"I will."

He made sure I got into my car safely before he pulled away from the curb.

All the way home, I sensed this agitation building inside me. It took me a few minutes, but by the time I pulled my car into my driveway, I figured it out.

I think I expected Ronan to react with anger when I rejected the idea of following each other on the app. I seemed to be waiting for him to blow up at me for not trusting him. But he didn't do that. He did the opposite.

Because he was Ronan, my soul mate. He wanted only the best for me, to make sure I was happy and whole. Which meant if following each other on an app scared me, then he certainly wasn't going to push me.

When I went inside, I texted Ronan that I'd made it home safely. I seemed to go through the rest of the night in robotic motions. I ate dinner with my parents, not contributing much to the conversation and excusing myself early with a headache, then headed to bed.

But I didn't have a headache. I was anxious, but not for the reasons I was at the park. After a hot shower, I crawled into bed. Then I tossed and turned and sighed, frustrated with myself.

After trying to go to sleep for over an hour, I shot up in bed and flipped on my bedside lamp. Huffing in frustration, I took my phone off the charger and opened the Life360 app. Without hesitation, I punched in Ronan's cell number to add him to my circle to connect with. It was only ten thirty, so I figured he'd be up. I stared at the app, waiting for him to accept the connection.

Then my phone buzzed in my hand with a text.

Ronan: You don't have to link with me on the app.

Me: Just accept my damn invitation.

There was a pause where I could swear he was laughing at me in his house on the Westbank.

Ronan: Damn. I think I like bossy witch. Can you do that next time we're alone?

I snuggled down into the covers, grinning.

Me: I'll do whatever you want if you accept my invitation on the app.

There was another brief pause, then a notification from Life360 informed me that I had a new connection in my family circle—Ronan Reed.

Ronan: Just remember. You said whatever I want.

I sent him a kiss emoji and told him good night.

Ronan: Goodnight, baby. Sleep tight.

I put my phone back on the charger and switched off my light, then sank down into my covers. Sighing deeply, all the tension simply vanished. Gone in an instant. And I knew, right then, that I was truly healed from the old anxiety as I so often called it. The one that gripped me sometimes when I was afraid I was being followed or watched.

Ronan didn't heal me, but he allowed me to heal myself. I don't think he could ever understand how important that was or how much I appreciated him in this moment.

He told me to sleep tight, and I did. That night, I don't think I had ever slept so good.

CHAPTER 24

~RONAN~

ZACK AND TY HAD WON THEIR MATCHES WITH TKOS. NEITHER WENT TO the judges, which was exactly what we needed. But then Bowie's match with Baron had, and just like we'd figured it would, the judges declared Baron the winner.

We'd trained all fucking week. My uncle had even given us time off from work to train since business was slow right now. It paid off. The guys were looking fantastic, which was why Bowie's loss irked me so much, especially after the last match where he'd been illegally clawed and the refs didn't call it. This time, Bowie didn't actually lose again. But the judges said otherwise. The likely *paid* judges.

Now, the pressure was on me. If I won against that big fucker Carter, our team won this round. If not, it was another draw, which meant the Iron Claws had another chance to defeat us and keep their championship title. And they could be moving on to the state round, not us.

"You've got this," said Zack, massaging my back.

I was plenty loose and ready to go. I wasn't concerned about beating this big asshole.

"Remember," said Ty, "wear him down and get him winded, then give it to him hard in the third."

Nodding, I hopped up from our bench outside the cage as the referee opened the door. My gaze drifted to the spot where Celine sat with Diego, Joaquin, and my uncle. I could hardly believe he'd actually shown.

Celine smiled as I made the circuit of the ring and bounced in place to keep loose as Carter entered the ring. This dude was big, bigger than me. But he was slow and relied too much on his size and weight to defeat his opponent.

It was a no-brainer before it even started. Baron and his teammates whispered to Carter through the cage, likely last-minute tips on how to beat me. It only made me smile.

When Baron looked my way, his expression was brutally serious. Ty had beaten him by TKO, his first loss in the last two years from what I read online. He wasn't happy. Nor was his father from what I could observe. He was sitting next to a bunch of other rich assholes in the front row seats.

The ref said his spiel about the rules while Carter and I faced off. He wore a cocky expression. I had no idea why. He had nothing to be cocky about, especially since I was about to wipe that grin off his face with my fist.

As soon as the bell rang, I dodged to his left side, ducked under his first swing, and jabbed him in the ribs. He swung again and clipped my shoulder, then we were circling each other.

I couldn't let him land one of his early blows full-force. We'd talked about this fighter extensively in training. In his first two rounds, if he landed a punch to the face or ribs, it would result in a knockout or, at the very least, broken bones. But by round three, he slowed down, and his swings would lose force of impact.

"Baron had a question for you," he mumbled as he circled closer.

I didn't bother to respond because his shit-eating grin told me he was going to say it anyway.

"He wants to know if that redheaded pussy is as good as it looks."

I flinched but kept circling. Trash talk wasn't unusual or unexpected, but it was the first time anyone had said anything that actually had an impact on me. And, of course, he went on when he caught my reaction.

"He wants to know if you don't mind sharing your witch. Says he'd like to give her a good ride."

My entire body went white-hot. "You keep your fucking eyes and hands away from her unless you want to lose them both."

He chuckled. "I told him you'd say something like that." He nodded toward the bleachers. "He's going to give it a go anyway."

My wolf growled a low warning in my chest. Instantly, my gaze shot to the bleachers, fearing I'd find that dick Baron harassing my girl. But he wasn't there, and I realized my mistake too late. That's all it had taken, two seconds of my attention off the fight. It had never happened before. And I'd never been caught unawares.

All I remember was Carter coming fast and hard in my peripheral vision, then it was lights-out.

When I woke, it was to the roar of the crowd and my team's worried faces hovering over me. The ref was there, too, concern in his brow until he saw me trying to sit up. He turned and took Carter's arm and lifted it into the air, announcing him the winner.

It was the second tied match between our teams, but the crowd was on its feet, most of them cheering for the Iron Claws. Even though it was a tie, it was still a win for them. I'd been undefeated until a few seconds ago when I let this fucking douchebag's trash talk actually distract me.

It had never happened before. I was actually stunned as Ty and Bowie lifted me to my feet and walked me toward the exit of the cage.

"Get used to the feeling, Reed," shouted Baron as we passed him. "You're up against me next."

I didn't even bother to respond. Actually, I couldn't. I thought I might be in shock or something because I could barely comprehend what had happened as the guys ushered me back down the walk way through the bleachers and to our locker room.

When the guys sat me down on the cushioned bench where Bowie had nursed his wound from the last fight, I stared at the ground.

"He may be concussed," said Ty.

"Or going into shock or something," added Zack.

They could be right because I felt disassociated from myself. Leaning forward, elbows on knees, I combed my hands through my sweaty hair.

"What the fuck?" I whispered in utter disbelief.

A minute later, Celine and my uncle rushed into the locker room. Not what I wanted right now. I needed a fucking second to process that I'd lost my first match to that piece of shit fighter with one of the oldest tricks in the book. Trash-talk distraction.

Most good fighters didn't even try that shit. It was low and common, unprofessional. I'd dealt with that kind of shit in alley fights back in Texas, but there was never anything anyone could say that could possibly get its hooks into me.

Except when they talked about *her*. About Celine. The second he'd said one single filthy thing about my girl, I was gone. My sole concern was for her, even though logically I should've known Baron wouldn't and technically couldn't leave his team's bench before the final fight was done, or he'd be disqualified. Team rules.

But the second Carter mentioned her, my mind went blank, and I wasn't thinking straight. It wasn't her fault. I was fucking furious, but it was all directed toward myself.

"Ronan, are you okay?" Celine's voice trembled as she approached, placing her hands on my shoulders.

I eased her back and stood from the bench, needing some space. I walked three steps to the line of lockers and punched my fist into one with a roaring, "Fuck!"

All the while, the celebratory cheers in the arena echoed down the hall.

On top of all of that, it was the first fight my uncle Shane had actually shown up to watch. The first time he shows, and I fail miserably in the first round.

"What did he say to you?" Uncle Shane asked. "I could tell from our seats he'd pissed you off. Your wolf flashed in your eyes."

I'd felt him too. I almost wondered for a split second if he'd decided to finally show himself. I would've been disqualified. It didn't matter. I lost all by myself anyway.

"It doesn't matter." I remained facing the lockers, mortified that I'd allowed this to happen.

So fucking stupid.

The healer, that blond witch, pushed into the locker room and froze when she surveyed the room, finding me now leaning back against the lockers, arms crossed.

"Are you in need of a healer?"

"No," I snapped.

She obviously caught the mood of the room. To her credit, she didn't balk or slink away. "Why don't we clear the room so I can determine that?"

Zack rolled his eyes and nudged Bowie toward the door.

"You good?" Ty asked.

I nodded, remaining fixed with my back to the lockers.

He left behind Uncle Shane, but Celine stayed. Nausea swarmed in my belly, both at the monumentally disappointing loss and at the fact that she didn't run from the room. From me. I was a boiling mess of emotions, and I couldn't calm down to be nice or ease her distress. I was fucking royally pissed off.

The Conduit witch walked straight to me. "I'm going to touch your arm to read your health. Do not move."

She must've been expecting me to snarl and lash out like a rabid animal. I was still pissed but somewhat in control now. I was just in a fucking awful mood. I wasn't going to hurt her.

When I didn't respond, she slowly reached out her hand and pressed it to my forearm. Closing her eyes, she obviously used her Conduit magic to see if I was internally injured, fucked up in the brain, or something. Her magic felt like a cool brush of wind that I could feel on the inside.

After about ten seconds, she stopped and stepped away. "You're fine. No internal damage."

Behind her, Celine let out a soft breath of relief. My gaze finally found her. I was too embarrassed to even look at her when she first stepped into the locker room, wanting everyone to just leave me the fuck alone.

But as the healer left without another word, I knew I didn't want her to leave. I wanted to lay my head in her lap and let her take this awful feeling away from me.

"I'm sorry," she said softly.

"You have nothing to be sorry for." I still hadn't moved, my arms still crossed defensively.

She walked closer, slowly. "I'm sorry you lost. I don't know what happened."

Like I'd fucking tell her.

Standing close now, she eased her palms up my biceps to my shoulders, drenching me with her soothing magic. She pushed her calming spell into me. It felt the exact opposite of the Conduit's magic. It was a humming balm, warming me down to my bones.

"I'm sorry you're upset," she said.

Upset didn't begin to cover it. I was beyond that. It was humiliating to lose in the first round by knockout because of a stupid fucking mistake. Not because I wasn't as good a fighter as him, but because I didn't keep my head in the game.

Celine slid her hands down and tugged at my crossed arms. I let them fall to my sides as she eased her arms around my waist and pressed her cheek to my chest.

"I'm sorry you're feeling so awful." She squeezed my waist, and I couldn't help but wrap my arms around her on a heavy sigh. "I feel awful too."

And even so, she was using her magic to ease my anger.

Finally, I said, "I'll be fine. I'll get over it eventually." Because I knew I would.

With every setback in life, I'd managed to move past it and forward. I was used to life's setbacks, except it was usually because of something fate had done to me. I was rarely disappointed in myself.

"I was terrified," she whispered into my bare skin since I was still shirtless from the fight.

"Why?" I asked.

She scoffed and leaned back to look up at me. "Are you kidding? I watched you get knocked unconscious, Ronan."

That was when I saw the fear on her face, tears pooling in her eyes.

"I'm okay," I reassured her, cupping her face with one hand and wiping the tear that slipped down her cheek. "Please don't cry."

"I can't help it. I almost had a heart attack watching you get knocked out."

She had no idea how badly it hurt to hear her say that.

"I'm fine," I said with more force than I intended.

"You don't seem fine."

Gently, I pushed her back so I could remove myself from her arms. I needed space.

"Look, I'm fine. This happens. Can you go wait with the guys or something? I need to get a shower."

She nodded but didn't move as I grabbed my bag off the floor and headed into the showers.

The whole time I was cleaning up, I tried to wipe away the overwhelming feeling of embarrassment and disappointment of the loss, but it wouldn't go away. Celine's magic had calmed me down. I wasn't raging with anger now, but it hadn't removed my true feelings.

Still, after a long hot shower, I managed to at least see with some clarity that even though I let that asshole beat me, it wouldn't happen again. Baron was in for a rude awakening if he thought to pull the same shit in our next fight.

That's when I started to finally feel better. I managed to push it out of my head and look forward to the next fight when I'd kick Baron's ass. Grabbing my phone, I read the text from Celine telling me she was waiting with Ty in the parking lot. I quickly headed out of the locker room and down the hallway to the back door, not wanting a run-in with the Iron Claws.

Bowie and Zack were sitting in Bowie's SUV, next to Ty's.

"You good?" Zack shouted from the open window.

"Fine." I gave them a wave. "We'll catch up tomorrow."

"Sounds good," said Bowie, rolling up his window, then driving off.

When I got to Ty's car, Celine sitting next to him, they were chatting softly. Probably about me. Heaving a sigh, I opened the passenger door and leaned down. "Thanks, Ty."

"No problem. We'll talk tomorrow at the body shop."

That's what I liked about Ty. He thought like me. No need to dwell on the loss. We needed to look forward to the next fight.

To strategize and train and prepare for any more bullshit they might throw at us.

After we were belted in my Bronco, I felt her gaze on me when I turned in the direction of the city rather than heading toward the Westbank to my place. We hadn't talked about her coming home with me tonight, but I needed to be alone.

The streets teemed with people. It was a Saturday night in New Orleans, crowds milling in and out of the bars and restaurants. But inside my truck, it was painfully quiet. We were nearly to her house when she finally said something.

"I was thinking about the teacup today."

Surprised, I glanced at her as I took the next turn onto Magazine Street.

"You're not just good at painting," she added. "Your skill level is exceptional."

Clearing my throat, I said, "Thank you."

This seemed out of nowhere, and I had no idea why she was bringing it up. Until she went on.

"I was just wondering why you never pursued something in the arts."

Her father was a successful sculpture artist. Her mother was a graphic novelist who'd hit bestselling lists. It wasn't an unusual question seeing as she was surrounded by artists who made good livings at their craft. Nor was it strange since werewolves had an affinity for creativity.

"I was never interested in that," I told her as I pulled to a stop at a red light. "Not as a career."

An edgy sort of tension pulled my stomach tight.

"It would be much less dangerous than fighting," she said softly.

Then again, everything about Celine was soft—her temper-
ament, her body, her walk, her smile. Even as she expressed her
hatred for my chosen career path, she did so softly, with kind
eyes and a small smile.

I drummed my fingers on the steering wheel. "I like fighting, Celine." I kept my voice steady as a sourness spread in
my gut.

"I understand. I just wondered if you'd ever considered something else. Something that didn't lead to you being knocked
unconscious. Or worse."

Clamping my jaw tight for a second, I said, "You didn't have
a problem with it before."

"It didn't seem my place to say anything before, but I've never
liked it, Ronan."

The light turned green, and I drove on.

"It's because I lost tonight." Acid churned in my belly. "But
that won't fucking happen again."

"It's because I care about *you*, not who won the stupid fight."

I turned off Magazine onto her street.

"I don't know what to tell you, Celine." I pulled to a stop in
front of her house and shoved it into park a little roughly. "I'm
not going to quit fighting. Especially after tonight."

"Just because you lost?"

"I've never lost before." I stared out the driver's side window,
needing to get away from this conversation and from the jagged
disappointment that the woman I loved wanted me to quit the
only thing that had ever given me confidence and purpose.

"I just think there's so much more you could do," she said into
the silence.

"I get that." I turned to look at her, worry lining her pretty face. "But I like fighting. Being a champion is all I've ever wanted."

"Maybe I'm just not the competitive type so I don't get the need to win or this drive to fight."

"Can we not talk about this tonight?" I snapped. "It's been a rough one already."

She blinked at my tone and paused. Without waiting for an answer, I hopped out of the truck and walked around. She was already on the sidewalk when I reached her.

"I'll be training a lot this week," I told her, my tone harsh, but I couldn't help it. "I may not get time to come and see you." I stuffed my hands in my pockets. "If you want to see me, that is."

"Of course I do." She reached for me, then dropped her arm at her side. "I'm sorry if I upset you even more tonight."

"Don't be sorry about telling me the truth. At least now I know."

Not that I knew how to handle this truth. Because all it did was fuck up my life.

"Ronan, I—" She paused, her expression pinched with concern and regret.

I'd seen that expression on every single person who meant something to me, whenever they wished they had the words to make me change my ways or who I was.

"I'll text you," I promised, then leaned in and kissed her cheek, willing her to leave me so I could go home and be done with this awful fucking night. "Good night."

She stared at me for another moment, then smiled. "You're sure you're okay?"

I nodded stiffly and lied, "I'm fine."

I wasn't about to tell her that she crushed me worse than losing to that asshole in the ring. I swore to her father that I wouldn't hurt her, and I didn't plan to.

"Well, good night. I'll text you tomorrow," she said, seeming to force a cheery voice.

She hesitated before finally turning away. I watched to make sure she made it safely inside, then I hauled ass out of there.

By the time I was back on the interstate nearing the Mississippi Bridge, my head was pounding, and I couldn't seem to catch my breath. I rolled down the window, letting the warm wind off the river rush into the cab. My hands were shaking, so I gripped the steering wheel tight and breathed deep.

I'd never had a panic attack before, but right now, it felt like I was having one. For the first time, I wished my wolf would come out, and not just to the surface. I wanted him to take over the man so I could disappear for a while.

This aching pain wouldn't subside, the one telling me I was yet again a disappointment to someone. But this time, it was the most important person in the world to me who I'd let down. It swallowed me whole, leaving me in a muffled, muted place.

"Come on, you fucking wolf."

I pulled into my gravel drive, parked, and stepped out, staring up at the humped moon. Feeling like a fool, I tried to summon him. When I felt no response, I closed my eyes, hoping he'd hear me.

But . . . nothing.

Yet another failure.

Giving up, I turned for the house. At least I knew there was a bottle of whiskey in Uncle Shane's kitchen that might help me find the peace of oblivion I needed.

CHAPTER 25

~CELINE~

Samara poured me a second glass of red wine with her telekinetic power. Her TK touch was so refined that the bottle barely touched the lip of the glass as it seemed to pour itself. She swished a finger and the bottle set itself back down on the coffee table.

That was one gift I never harnessed at all, the telekinetic power most witches had. Funnily, it was the only witchy gift Samara inherited from her mother. But otherwise, she was all vampire like her father.

"I totally get that you're worried about him," she said, "but think of every job where the spouse has to worry. Police officers, firefighters, the military, rodeo clowns."

I let out a small laugh, which was exactly what she was trying to do. Then just as quickly, my tummy rolled with nausea yet again. Ever since the fight three nights ago, I'd been sick with worry.

"Seriously, though." I took a big sip then set my glass on her kitchen table. "When he was punched unconscious, I almost vomited, then nearly fainted. It made me physically sick to watch. I could hardly stand it. I don't know if I can ever watch that happen again."

"Then don't go to his fights," she said simply as a loud hammering sound echoed through her living room wall. "Dammit. I wish they'd hurry the hell up."

"What's going on?"

"New neighbor. I saw the moving van yesterday and, apparently, they're hanging art on every single wall in their damn apartment." She topped her glass again with a wave of her hand, the bottle floating over and back to sit on the table. "Anyway, back to the hot werewolf boyfriend who makes you faint."

"It's not funny, Samara. Since the fight a few days ago, his texts are so, so . . ."

"Mean?"

"No."

"Cold?"

"No."

"What, is he ghosting you?"

"No."

"Then what's the problem?"

"I can just tell he's upset. He's not his usual self."

"Well, I guess not. You basically told him to give up on his dreams."

"I didn't say that," I protested. "I just told him he was talented and could do something else that didn't require getting beaten unconscious."

"Exactly. You told a fighter he shouldn't fight. Like I said, you told him to give up on his dreams."

My blood ran cold. "Did I do that?"

I prided myself on my ability to use words and therapy to get to the heart of a problem, and I hadn't seen that I was the one causing this problem.

"I'm afraid you did."

Samara's expression was sympathetic, but I loved that she was always the person who didn't judge and gave me direct, sound advice.

I pulled at a loose thread fraying at the hem of my pink cut-offs. "So what should I do now?"

"That's obvious. What do you normally do when you're in the wrong and you've hurt someone you love?"

"You can tell?"

"That you love him?" She laughed. "Of course. I've known you your whole life, and I've never seen you this happy with anyone. Well, except right now you're pretty fucking miserable. But that's because you know you're wrong and you hurt him, and you need to fix it."

I sat up straight on the sofa. "Samara, I *am* wrong."

"Yes, I know."

I jumped to my feet. "And I've got to go fix it."

"As I said."

I pulled up the Life360 app on my phone. He was home. Of course he was home. Sometimes he watched film footage at Ty's place pretty late some nights, but not this late.

"Where's my purse?"

"You're not driving. You've had too much wine. I'll drive."

"You've been drinking too," I pointed out, finding my purse on the kitchen table.

"You know my tolerance is higher than yours." A hammer started pounding next door again. "Besides, I need to get out of here before my new neighbor drives me insane."

I always seemed to forget that vampires rarely got drunk. They metabolized alcohol faster. They could become more intoxicated by drinking from a potent blood-host than from drinking a bottle of vodka.

"What time is it?" I checked my phone as we headed out the door. "Hell, it's almost midnight."

"Something tells me he won't care," she said as we hopped in her Jeep Wrangler.

"Where am I going?" she asked, pulling out of the small lot.

"The Westbank."

As she zoomed toward the interstate, my heart began to race as well.

"It's only that I've never felt like this for someone," I started babbling.

She laughed. "Yes, I know."

"It scared the bejeezus out of me to see him get hurt."

"All of that's understandable, but didn't you tell me he's basically jumped around a lot since his mother died? Don't you think he may not have had a ton of support, and it might've hurt him quite a lot that his new girlfriend doesn't support him?"

"Goddess above. I'm a terrible person."

"No, Celine. You're just in love."

I pointed her the rest of the way there, nervous and desperate to see him.

"Oh no." We pulled up the drive, all the windows dark. "They're asleep."

Instantly, a light snapped on in a back window, right about where Ronan's bedroom was. Then another.

"Not anymore," said Samara, pulling the car to a stop.

"Thank you." I jumped out and slammed the door, hurrying up the front steps to the wooden porch.

Right as I reached the door, it swung open, and everything I was about to say left my brain. Ronan stood in the open door in boxer briefs, and that was all. It had been only a few days, but good heavens, I nearly melted in a puddle on his porch.

"What's wrong?" he growled, scanning over my shoulder, then sweeping the area, obviously looking for danger.

"I am," I blurted, dragging my gaze off his thick thighs, chiseled abs, and all the loveliness in between. "*I'm* wrong, Ronan."

There was the sound of footsteps behind him as my brain caught up.

"If you want to be a fighter, then I have no right to stop you. Actually, I should be giving you my full support. Even if watching you get hurt gives me high anxiety and makes me want to throw up, that's no excuse. I'll sit at every match because that's what you do when you're in love with someone." His eyes widened as I licked my lips, trembling now. "And that's me. I'm in love. With you." I stammered a little before getting it out ineloquently. "I love you."

That's when Ronan's uncle appeared next to him in the doorway—also only in his underwear. Obviously, the fine-body gene ran in the family.

Uncle Shane blinked at me once, then pivoted. "You've got this," he mumbled, padding back down the hallway.

Vaguely, I noted Samara's Jeep reversing and crunching on the gravel as she drove away.

I stood there, looking up at him, shaking in my tennis shoes, waiting for him to say something.

His aura was a vibrant hot pink. That shouldn't have been sexy, but it so was. It dawned on me that while he was an obviously attractive man, that wasn't the real reason I was soul-stirringly magnetized to him. My longing for him came from a much deeper well.

His eyes—midnight-blue and entrancing—examined me for one more second.

"Come here." But he didn't wait for me to comply. He reached out and pulled me into his arms.

I instantly burst into tears. "I'm so sorry I hurt you. I didn't mean it. I was so selfish. I was so scared. I've never felt this way."

"Shh. You're breaking my heart, baby."

He pulled me tighter against him, engulfing me in his warmth. He rocked me gently, soothing a palm up and down my back, pressing his mouth to the crown of my head while I cried it out.

After a few minutes, he eased his hold but only a little. "I want you to listen to me."

I sniffed and nodded, my cheek still pressed to his chest.

"First, thank you. I can't pretend I haven't been on a downward spiral since the other night. I needed to hear that apology from you. Second, I'm sorry I didn't hear you out more or consider how hard that was for you to watch. If it were the other way around, I'd have lost my mind if I saw someone hurt you."

"I would never fight for a living, though. You don't have to worry about that."

He cupped my face and smiled, wiping my tears away with his thumbs.

"And third," he said gently, tenderly, "I love you, baby. More than anything or anyone on this earth. If I had to give up fighting to keep you, I would. It was just taking me some time to process."

"No. I don't want you to do that. That's selfish of me and unfair to you."

He brushed his mouth against mine, tasting my lips and tongue.

"Can we have make-up sex now?" I whispered.

He smiled. "You've been drinking a bit."

"I'm not that drunk." I coasted my hand to the growing bulge in his briefs.

He grunted. "You sure?"

"Ronan, don't make me beg." I rubbed my palm down the hard length of him. "I need you inside me."

He made a gruff sound in his throat, then lifted me off the ground. I wrapped my legs around his waist and kissed the strong column of his throat. He squeezed my butt cheeks and carried me toward his bedroom.

"This seems familiar," I teased.

"I've been thinking about these pink shorts since the first day I met you in them."

He set me on my feet next to his bed and shut his bedroom door. "Really?"

My trembling hadn't gone away, but now it was about anticipation instead of nerves. He returned to me in three long strides, holding my gaze in the dim light of his bedside lamp as he unsnapped and unzipped my shorts, shoving them over my hips. When they dropped to the floor, he glanced down and gripped my hips.

"They look good around your ankles."

I smiled as he nudged me to the bed where I fell willingly onto my back. He grazed his long fingers up my thighs, then slid one finger under my panties.

"Unh." I rocked up, seeking his touch.

He hissed in a breath, sliding one finger inside me.

"So wet."

"Ronan," I moaned. "Stop teasing. I need you."

He made that low grunting sound and pulled his finger out of me. While he shoved off his boxer briefs, I wasted no time lifting my top over my head, then unsnapped my bra and tossed it onto the floor.

He shook his head, raking my body with his gaze as he crawled over me onto the bed. I slid my body up and my head onto a pillow. He stopped halfway and opened his mouth over my nipple. When I rocked my hips on a groan, he grazed the peak with his teeth and circled my clit with two fingers.

"Please," I begged, wanting him to ease the ache.

On a low growl, he shifted up onto his knees and gripped the bottom of my thighs, pushing them up and wide, his dark gaze fixed down below.

He rocked forward, his cock sliding against my clit, up and down my folds before he pushed slowly inside me.

"Mmm," he hummed. "So fucking perfect."

I gasped as he filled me up, fisting my hands into the sheets. He pumped in and out, the glide slick from my excessive arousal.

He let my thighs go and lowered onto his forearms, scooping his palms beneath my head. He cradled me gently, nipping at my lips while he rolled his hips, grinding with deep thrusts.

"Yes, like that." I curled my fingers into his back, loving the way he rubbed my clit with each downward stroke.

That purring growl vibrated from his chest to mine, sending a tantalizing shiver over my skin. I coasted my palms down to his muscular buttocks, getting more turned on at feeling his muscles tighten as he thrusted inside me.

"Yes, baby," he murmured against my mouth. "So tight and sweet. You take me so well."

Moaning, I scraped my blunt nails down his back. "I'm about to come."

"That's right." He pumped faster. "Come for me, baby."

Suddenly, I was, screaming his name, not even caring if his uncle heard. Or the neighbors down the street.

He kissed me hard, swallowing my moans as if he wanted them all to himself, while my orgasm quaked through me.

As it slowly subsided, he broke the kiss and hovered over me. He then traced my bottom lip with his tongue as I whimpered at the ecstasy coursing through my body and soul.

Suddenly, he pulled out and flipped me over onto my stomach, sinking his fingers into my skin and lifting my hips higher. Then he drove inside me with a single stroke.

"Fuck," he growled.

Even while the spasms of pleasure lingered, I longed for more, curving my spine to take him deeper.

"Yes, baby. Let me have you."

Where he gripped my flesh hard would definitely leave bruises, but I didn't care. The overwhelming sensation of pleasure—what he'd given me and I was giving him—overrode any slight pain I felt at all. Our flesh slapping as he drove deep and hard, his rhythmic grunts filling the room, the cool sheets beneath my breasts and cheek, my fists curled into the bedding to hang on as he pounded into my body. It was all utter bliss—a level of joyful euphoria I'd never experienced. And all I wanted was—

"More," I murmured, "more."

He growled, thrusting harder, faster, sliding his thick cock so deep inside me until I felt it swell bigger. He was about to come.

He fell forward, pressing me into the mattress as he planted deep and ground his hips into my ass. He covered my hands with his, lacing his fingers through mine as he emptied inside me, his cock pulsing hard.

He didn't bite me this time but nipped and licked softly along the base of my neck while I panted, bathing in the greatest high I'd ever had.

He nuzzled up my throat to my ear where he whispered, "I love you so fucking much it scares me."

"Why are you scared?"

"Because I can't lose you. I'd die if I lost you."

"You won't lose me." I pressed a kiss to the back of his hand still curled around the back of mine. "I love you too, Ronan."

He lifted and pulled out of me and rolled me over quickly before settling back on top of me, pressing skin to skin so wonderfully.

"Say it again," he demanded, all serious and grave.

Threading my fingers into his hair, I held his gaze. "I love you, Ronan Reed." Then I frowned. "What's your middle name? I don't even know it."

"Michael, after Saint Michael. My mom was Catholic."

"Then I love you, Ronan Michael Reed."

He smiled. So did I, both of us staring and absorbing this lovely feeling growing even bigger between us.

"You know," I noted, "Saint Michael was an archangel. A warrior."

"That's right." He leaned his weight on one elbow and pushed my hair behind one ear. Then the pads of his fingers glided softly down my throat.

"Maybe your mom had a feeling about you even then. You've had to fight for everything. And then you became an actual fighter."

"Maybe so." He let out a sigh. "I sometimes worry what she'd think of me. How I've fucked up so many times. Like you said, always fighting. And not necessarily in a good way."

"But now you are." I swallowed the regret of having hurt him before, still upset with myself. "I know I reacted poorly after the other night, but Ronan, you're an amazing fighter. You're so talented. Even if I hate the idea of you getting punched and kicked, I can see that."

"Thank you. What happened the other night was a fluke, I can promise you. It won't happen again."

"What did happen?" I recalled that night, how he was on his game, but then he looked up into the stands, and that was when his opponent punched him so hard it knocked him out.

"He said something to anger me, to distract me." He was toying with a lock of my hair. "It's never happened to me before. I'm always laser-focused in the ring."

"How did he do it, then?"

"He was talking about you." He met my gaze steadily. "But now that I'm aware they plan to play dirty, I'll be ready for Baron in my last fight."

"This next one is the last?"

"For the NOWFC, then it goes to the state championship in Baton Rouge in the fall. Then finally to the international league. But all of that is only if we win in each tournament."

"So for the NOLA league, your team has won one, tied, and lost one. Which means the next fight determines everything."

I nodded. "That's right."

"So you'll need to be training a lot."

"Yes. But I don't mind midnight visits." He swept a soft kiss over my lips. "Or anytime visits, if I'm honest."

We subsided into kissing each other for several minutes before he rolled to the side to face me. "Let's get some sleep."

I rolled to face the window. "Come curl up behind me."

"My pleasure." He scooped me around the waist and pulled me into the curve of his big body.

Giggling, I nuzzled into the pillow and wrapped my arm over his. Even while I lapsed into a contented silence, I could feel the anxiety radiating off him, my magic poking at me. I could never rest whenever someone was upset near me.

"What's still worrying you? The fight?"

"Mm-hmm."

"Go to sleep. Rest." I poured my empathic magic into him, sending him a spell to ease his mind.

After a few minutes, his body went heavy around me, and I knew he was asleep. I fell not long after, finally content myself. Not just because he was tranquil, but because I was being the mate he needed. We were a perfect match.

CHAPTER 26

~RONAN~

We were ready, all of us. Including myself. I leaned against the tree in our sparring area behind the paint barn, watching Ty grapple with Zack. My uncle Shane had excused us all at noon every day for the past two and a half weeks before this final fight.

We'd gone over the footage online of every single fight the Iron Claws had been in. We painstakingly practiced every maneuver to outfight them in both defensive and offensive modes. It was important to know your opponent, not just to outfight them but to outsmart them.

Now that we knew they played dirty at any cost—trash talk being a minor offense, using claws illegally and getting away with it being a major one—we were ready for tonight. On top of sparring, we'd trained in the gym down the road from the body shop—increasing our cardio endurance and strengthening with weight lifting.

There was nothing else we could've done to prepare for tonight. I felt confident and strong, and yet there was still this niggling doubt circling my mind. I wasn't sure why or what it was.

My relationship with Celine was perfect. Since I'd been training so hard, she'd come to my house at least every other night and stayed with me, winding me down with her luxurious body and calming me to sleep with her serene presence.

"Just never let him get a hold of your wrist like this." Ty was showing Zack another maneuver he'd noticed Carter using. Zack was up against him tomorrow night. His match was first.

Uncle Shane sauntered through the back open door. "Hey, Ronan!" he called. "You mind having a visitor?"

Assuming he meant Celine, I said, "Of course not."

He nodded, then headed past me toward the guys, someone following him out of the shadows of the barn. I stood and walked toward the open door, expecting her to walk into the sunlight. But it wasn't Celine. It was her father, Mateo.

I stopped in my tracks, a little shocked to see him. What the hell was he doing here?

He glanced over at Ty and Zack, who'd stopped sparring, "Y'all training for that wolf fight club thing?"

"First rule is you don't talk about wolf fight club," said Zack seriously.

Bowie chuckled from where he was sitting in the grass with a half-empty water bottle in his hand.

"We can talk over here," I told him, leading him back into the barn.

Uncle Shane had walked over to talk to the guys, something about a new bike job coming in next week.

"Is Celine okay?" I asked since that was the only reason I could imagine why he'd come to see me.

"She's great," he said, following me back into the paint barn. "I just wanted to chat a minute."

I stopped and turned, crossing my arms to face him, waiting for whatever the fuck this was.

"I'm sure you're wondering why I'm here."

"Yes," I stated emphatically and possibly a little too aggressively.

He laughed, and I realized it was the first time I'd ever seen him laugh. He was much more relaxed than in our past meetings. Of course, the first time, it was his wolf shifting on the other side of his daughter's bedroom door before he burst through it, and the second time was our first official meeting where I got the don't-hurt-my-daughter lecture.

"I hope you don't mind, but Celine told us you've been on your own most of your life."

I didn't comment because what the fuck was I supposed to say? *Yes, I've been all alone in this world for most of my life.* That wasn't an admission I planned to give him. I was only willing to be that vulnerable with one person. Celine.

"It's come to my attention from my daughter that you haven't shifted in a long time."

Okay, not what I was expecting. And that was an understatement. I'd shifted a handful of times when I was twelve, but then he vanished altogether until recently. And even now, he was still quiet, not ready to come out.

When I still didn't comment, he went on.

"I'm not sure if Celine told you, but I once had that issue."

"She mentioned it."

"Not the same as yours," he clarified, "but I know what it's like to feel the frustration of not shifting. Of course, I'm not sure if Celine told you or not, but my wolf speaks to me."

"She told me."

"Thought she did. For those months, it had been difficult for me, feeling a little out of control."

"I don't have that problem," I stated easily and truthfully. Mostly. "I haven't shifted since I was twelve, so he's never really been a part of me. I've taken care of myself all by myself."

He went quiet, assessing me with dark, shrewd eyes. "I see that."

This conversation was beginning to irk me. What was this all about? "I know it may seem strange to you, being an alpha, but I don't need my wolf."

His eyes rolled bright gold, his beast likely saying some shitty words about me. Whatever. Bring it on, Alpha.

"Well, that's all a load of bullshit," said Mateo.

I huffed out a laugh at his frankness.

"Every werewolf needs his wolf. And you saying you don't need yours is a lie too. Because he sure as hell realized before you did who your mate was, didn't he?" He paused, arching a superior brow. "My daughter?"

Well . . . fuck.

Clearing my throat, I said, "Yes."

Heaving a sigh, I dropped my arms, propping them low on my hips. "Look, I'm not saying my wolf hasn't recently been, I don't know, lingering at the surface. I know he helped me see Celine was my mate. But it wasn't the wolf who realized she was the love of my life. And she is," I told him. "I figured that out all on my own."

His expression shifted to shock, possibly because I was being so honest. But I'd never been a liar. Ever. So I'd better come completely clean.

"But I don't need him the way most werewolves need theirs. If he decides to never come out and take over my skin, then I'm fine with that. I've been doing just fine all on my own my whole life."

Mateo didn't say anything for a moment before finally adding, "You may believe that's true, but we all need others. A mate. A family." He glanced out the open barn door where I could hear the guys sparring again. "I was a loner too once, thinking that was enough, but I discovered quickly that wasn't true—the minute I met Celine's mother and discovered who she was to me." He turned back to me. "She showed me there was more to life than trying to survive all on your own."

I had no idea what he was saying or why he was really here until he said, "I'm just here to let you know that you have Celine. You know that. But you have us too. Our family takes care of our own. So don't think you have to survive this world all alone anymore." He gestured toward the open barn door. "It looks like you've got some good friends, and I know Shane is very happy to have you here. But we're here too. If you're Celine's family, and that's what it means to be her mate, then you're ours too."

I truly had no words. No one had ever welcomed me so openly, so personally. I'd thought Celine's dad was this overbearing, overprotective prick. She'd told me he cherished family, and I thought I understood that. But I truly hadn't until this moment.

I'd also never experienced the wave of intimate emotion that rocked me at the thought that I had more than Celine to depend on. I had an entire family unit who saw me as their own.

Staring down at my feet, I simply nodded, still so unsure what to say to that, a little afraid he might suddenly take it back or something.

"That's all I came to say. I'll let you get back to training." He clapped me on the shoulder as he walked past me. "See you at the fight tomorrow night."

That had my head jerking up as I turned. "You're coming?"

He laughed. "The whole family is coming. So you better win," he added lightly, then he continued out the other barn door.

Dumbfounded, I walked to the open door where Uncle Shane chatted with Bowie in the shade of the tree as they watched Ty and Zack going at it.

Something stirred and awakened, rising with a sudden realization. I had thought it a simple act of fate that I was drawn to this place in the Deep South where I'd rekindled my bond with my uncle—my blood. Then I'd also forged true friendships with the men out there in the yard. I'd also delved deep into my psyche with the help of Dr. Theriot to discover the root cause of my deeper anxieties, the trauma I'd been holding on to like a boy in a raft, clinging to an anchor that was slowly sinking him.

Finally, I'd met Celine—my person, my true love, my meaning for being. For there was no future for me without her in it. And now, her father—a man I truly expected to hate me for life—welcomed me into his family as his own.

It wasn't simply fate or the divine Creator. It was someone else. A strange, cool wind rushed through me, a floral scent wafting past.

"Thanks, Mom," I whispered, then I went back out into the yard.

We had a fight to win.

CHAPTER 27

~RONAN~

"I'm so nervous," said Celine, pressing her palms to her cheeks in the cutest way, her eyes lit with excitement.

"Don't be nervous, baby." I held her close, pressing my forehead to hers. "We're going to win every match tonight. I promise you that."

"I know you are." She hugged me tight. "You're the best fighter in the whole world."

I laughed because I knew she was telling me the most supportive things possible to make up for last time. I wasn't the best fighter in the whole world. But hearing her say it boosted my confidence even higher.

"Let's not go crazy yet." I lowered my mouth to her ear. "But I'm your fighter, and I can't lose tonight. Not with my girl here rooting me on."

"I'm here." She beamed up at me. "I'll always be here."

"Ronan!" Ty called from across the locker room near the door to the hallway where Bowie and Zack were walking through. "Time to go!"

"You hurry and get to your seat." I pecked her lips and swatted her ass.

She laughed and took off in front of me. Diego was in the hall.

"Good luck, guys. Go kill 'em." Then he and Celine hurried ahead of us.

Zack was bouncing on his toes, left to right, like always. "I noticed our Instagram following passed the Iron Claws this weekend." He grinned.

"No shit," I said, liking that a whole fucking lot.

Bowie and Ty laughed. We were loose and warmed up, fists wrapped, and ready to go, wearing the trunks and the new short robes Uncle Shane had bought for us, making the Blood Moon Body Shop our official sponsor. They were the same deep red as the trunks with our logo, the howling wolf, finely stitched on the backs.

Eminem's "Lose Yourself" blared in the arena as we marched out, and thousands of fans jumped to their feet, roaring and cheering to the rafters. Zack slid a grin sideways to me as we strode out together toward our bench. The Iron Claws had already made their grand entrance, now mean-mugging us from their bench on the other side of the cage.

I actually laughed. They were obviously so fucking pissed the crowd they'd once owned seemed to be on their feet for us more than them. We raised our hands, waving and riling the throng up even louder. The place was wild and roaring.

When we made our way to our bench, the music subsided and the referee blew a whistle to call up the first fighters. The roster had Zack against Carter first, that fucker who'd knocked me out last match. He called over to me as he stepped into the cage with Zack. "How's that jaw feeling, Reed?"

I didn't respond, entirely unaffected. They had no idea the strength that was in me tonight. Nothing they could say or do would penetrate the shield I'd formed around myself. I was stronger than I'd ever been and tough as fuck.

"Come on, Zack!" yelled Bowie.

None of us were sitting, all standing on our side of the cage as the ref went over the rules as required. I glanced to the sponsor's bench, finding the healer sitting there as well as the judges at their table, and the handler with the tranquilizer should things get out of control. Uncle Shane was also there too, now that he was our official sponsor, alongside Rhett. And Baron's father, a hard-looking man with a barrel chest and a head of gray-speckled black hair. His beady eyes glared daggers at me. It didn't bother me one bit.

As soon as the referee whistled for the fight to begin, all eyes swiveled to the ring, and Carter immediately started his shit. "So are you a top or bottom? I bet Bowie is the top. You seem like a bottom." He'd resorted to slinging bigoted slurs about gays at Zack, thinking that would bother him.

Ty growled next to me. When I glanced at him, his eyes were wolf-green. I'd never seen his wolf come out.

"Don't let that bother you. Fuck him, Ty."

"Are you kidding me? I'd never fuck that dirty bastard."

275

I laughed as he played it off.

Then we were both watching as Zack swung and caught Carter in the jaw, then quickly dodged under his retaliating swing.

"Nah, man." Zack grinned. "I'm more into juicy cougars. Your mom said I was a good fuck last night."

Carter's face flushed red as he charged Zack, swinging wildly and landing only a glance off his shoulder. Zack was fast, dodging and laughing. He jogged around the ring, smiling at us as he passed. "He's too easy."

We clapped and hollered like the rest of the fans. I wished I hadn't let Carter get me off balance that last fight. But if anything, it only taught me a lesson I wouldn't ever let happen again. I always learned from my mistakes.

Zack's bout went three rounds before Carter became winded chasing Zack around the ring. We should've known Zack would be a perfect match for the giant werewolf. Zack had stamina well beyond the big fighter.

By the fifth round, Zack was ready to make his move. He swept Carter to the floor and pummeled him in the face until the ref called him off.

"TKO!" we yelled on the sidelines in unison, laughing at Zack's fantastic first win.

Zack knocking their biggest fighter to the ground and coming out unscathed was a serious improvement for him.

Next up was Ty with that dick, Nate. The match didn't make it more than thirty seconds before Ty grappled him to the ground.

Again, the three of us on the sidelines yelled together, "TKOOOOOOO!"

We were high on life by the time Bowie went into the cage with Adam. It was in the third round that Bowie knocked him out cold.

The arena went insane as Bowie stood over him and stared down Baron, Nate, and Carter like a warrior. It was the coolest fucking thing I'd ever seen.

Finally, it was my turn. I was well aware what was riding on this last match between me and Baron. Technically, we'd already won. But Baron was undefeated, and I wasn't. There was a chance the WFC wouldn't let me move up at the state level if I didn't beat him. My entire career seemed to be leading up to this moment. Me fighting in a legal ring for the chance to prove I was the best.

But now I was ready to prove to myself and to the world that I was the real deal. I belonged here and was ready to go to the next level. I was a champion.

Glancing up at the stands, I saw Celine sitting next to her brothers, her mother and father, my uncle as well as Violet and her husband, Nico. They were all screaming and cheering, but it was Celine on her feet, smiling directly at me and yelling, "Go, Ronan!" that put fire in my belly as I launched into the cage.

I also didn't miss Baron's father and his cronies in the front row, glaring and fuming at me. Like I gave a fuck.

Baron stood, sneering, while the referee went through the rules as required.

"Just about over," I told Baron lightly. "Don't worry. I'll make it quick."

He scoffed. "You can't beat me. We're still the champs."

Technically, he was right. Baron was undefeated in the cage. If I didn't beat him now, then the state decided and they might still choose his team to go to the next level. The only way to ensure our spot at state was for me to beat Baron. Right here, right now.

Then the fight was on. Baron and I circled each other. He liked to wait for his opponent to make the first move. He was best at defensive maneuvers that helped him grapple his opponent into submission and then get him locked into a TKO position.

So I didn't give him the opportunity. I waited him out, knowing he'd get frustrated first. We kept circling, neither of us going after the other.

The crowd didn't like it. Hecklers started yelling. "Come on!" and "Fight, you fuckers!" and "Stop dancing around!"

None of that had ever bothered me, but I could tell it was irritating Baron. He shot a death glare at one guy in the front row when he yelled, "Give me what I paid for!"

Knowing his father ran the operation and, ultimately, was responsible for keeping the customers happy, seemed to get to him like I knew it would.

That's when Baron launched at me. He swung, but I dodged and planted a hard punch to his jaw. He turned and came again. I let him land a blow so I could get him in close and sweep him to the floor.

His eyes went wide since I was the one who fought best on my feet. My game wasn't on the floor. That's why I trained hard as hell the past few weeks to find the best way to get him on the ground. He wouldn't be expecting it. By the look on his face as he tried to quickly roll over, he hadn't been.

He never made it the full rotation. I was on him and had his right arm locked in an armbar, slowly putting the pressure to hyperextend it if he tried to get out of my hold.

"Fuck," he muttered, twisting and writhing, trying to shake me.

"Not gonna happen," I muttered. "Better tap out or I'm going to fuck up your arm bad."

I didn't want to, and I wouldn't break it, but he had to tap out for this to be a TKO.

He growled, his eyes flashing bright gold, his fangs elongating as he tried to shake me. He wasn't going anywhere. I only locked on harder, my legs around his waist and thighs, keeping him from maneuvering much at all.

Even when he realized it was useless, he gnashed his teeth, trying to bite me. The referee would've blown the whistle, disqualifying him if he was able to reach me with his jaws, but he couldn't. And I didn't want to win by a ref call. I put a little more pressure on that elbow. I wanted Baron tapping out, surrendering.

He reached back with his one free hand, able to claw at my outer thigh, only managing to tear through my trunks. I laughed at his useless flailing. He was panicking, trying anything to get out of my hold.

"I'll break it, Baron," I whispered as I put on more pressure, my wolf present and strong, growling deep inside my chest.

The crowd yelled and cheered as it was obvious I was about to win. When I thought the ref was about to blow the whistle, Baron tapped his claws on the cage floor.

Rolling away, I launched to my feet, both arms in the air as the entire arena roared to its feet. The ref held my arm and announced, "The winner is Ronan Reeeeeed!"

I could barely breathe as I gulped down air and the reality that I'd done it.

"The new champions of the New Orleans Wolf Fighting Championship are the Blood Moon Crew!"

Ty, Bowie, and Zack were in the ring lifting me in the air onto Bowie's and Ty's shoulders. Everything was a blur as I laughed and yelled, "Yes!"

Immediately, I found Celine on her feet, tears running down her face, cheering loud and hard for me. My heart couldn't handle the joy. It was too much.

Then the guys were setting me on my feet and the ref was wrapping the giant belt with the NOWFC gold buckle around my waist. The team wrapped our arms around each other's shoulders, huddled, heads together.

"You did it!" screamed Zack.

"We did it!" I yelled. "Thank you," I added more quietly as the sound of applause and whistles and cheers roared even louder. "I couldn't be happier or prouder than to have done this with you, brothers."

There was a moment while we shared that intimate emotion of brotherhood for something we'd done together against all odds. Then familiar voices broke through the roaring cheers.

"Ronan!"

I turned to see Celine and Diego running into the ring. She launched herself into my arms, and I swung her off her feet, kissing the hell out of her in front of everyone. My mate. My beautiful, sweet mate.

She laughed and held me tight, tears streaming down her pink cheeks as she cupped my face. "I'm so proud of you."

"Thank you, baby." I pressed my forehead to hers. "Thank you."

"I love you," she whispered low. But I heard her even though the noise was deafening.

And my world was so extraordinarily perfect. It didn't matter to me if my wolf ever showed up for real. With her in my arms and my life, I was complete and whole.

CHAPTER 28

~CELINE~

Elijah waved as he walked down the walkway with his mother to their car.

"See you next week," I called before hurrying back inside to clean and lock up.

We'd painted using watercolors today, so I rushed to empty the cup of water and put the drawing of his home and a tree with a tire swing out front on the back counter.

Lauren had called me screaming with excitement about an hour ago, right before my last client, that she'd passed the bar. She then begged me to join her for a celebratory drink at our favorite spot from college since it was where we celebrated all our big events back in the day. As spontaneous and wild as she was, she was also extremely superstitious, which was kind of cute.

I agreed but only for a drink or two before I had to hurry to the party for Ronan and his team at Howler's. Lauren was heading back to Baton Rouge tomorrow to officially close out her apartment there and pick up the last of her things to move back home. Otherwise, I would've tried to reschedule. Eventhough it was playing it close with the party for Ronan, I agreed to meet for an hour right after work.

I texted her that I was on my way, then headed toward Mid-City. It wasn't a regular college bar, which is why we liked it.

When I parked along the street, I sent Ronan a quick text that I was at the bar and would let him know when I was on my way to Howler's. The bar, which was a popular drinking spot for supernaturals and humans, had a decent crowd for happy hour. Lauren was sitting on the right side of the bar that wrapped in a big rectangle.

"Ciciiiiiiiii," she squealed and jumped up to give me a big hug. She was one of the few friends who used the nickname my family gave me. She squeezed me super tight. "It's so good to see you, girl."

Laughing, I hugged her back. Lauren's aura was always so effervescent. She was the outgoing, charismatic one of the two of us. It was likely the reason we got along so well in college. I was always the shy but levelheaded one.

She had her brunette hair up in a big clip, her blue eyes sparkling with joy as she pulled me to our little spot in the back where we always sat. Although Lauren wasn't a witch, she had the alluring persona of a supernatural. She always seemed to draw people into her orbit.

"Can you believe it?" she asked excitedly. "I'm going to be a lawyer. My daddy never believed in me, but you always did."

"He always underestimated you, and of course I knew you would. Lauren, you're the one person in this world who can manifest the hell out of anything and make it happen."

She burst out laughing. "Or manifest a disaster and make that happen."

I settled next to her. "You were good at that too. But hey, college was never boring."

She waved the bartender over, her sangria half gone. That was always her favorite drink. "You want a sangria?"

"Sure thing."

"Can we get two more?"

The bartender nodded and then took another order from some guys next to us. Happy hour was hopping, the bar already pretty crowded.

"So what now?" I angled toward her on my stool. "Will you work for your dad?"

She heaved a dramatic sigh. "I don't know."

Her father was a well-known and successful attorney in the city.

"But I'll bet he's already clearing out a corner office for you at his firm."

"He's said as much. I just want to make it on my own first."

I totally understood that.

"So how are things going with Ronan?" she asked excitedly.

Instantly, I beamed, and she laughed.

"That good, huh? Let's go. Give me the details."

So I did. By the time I finished my first drink, I'd confessed how I'd fallen hard and was positively in love with him.

"I'm so happy for you," she gushed with that overflow of joy in her aura beaming out of her. "You deserve all the happiness, Cici."

"And so do you. Any new prospects for you? What about that guy you were telling me about in your study group for the bar?"

She snorted, then sipped the last of her second drink. "No way. Total douche. Still a single Pringle."

"You'll find the right one."

"No worries." She scanned the bar. "Lots of pretties in here to play with."

I glanced at my phone to check the time.

"Oh no," she whined. "Please stay for one more. I think those hot guys are coming over, and I don't want to hang alone."

"You know I hate playing wingman."

"Please, please, please. Just ten more minutes. That'll be long enough to see which one I want."

Sighing, I hopped off the stool, glancing toward the restrooms. "I need to go to the bathroom, then ten minutes and I have to go."

"You're an angel. Hey, two more sangrias, please," she called to the bartender as I zigzagged through the thickening crowd of after-work drinkers.

After using the bathroom and washing my hands, I felt my phone buzz.

Ronan: I see you're still at the bar. Coming soon? I miss you.

Smiling, I texted back quickly.

Me: Leaving in 10! Promise. I miss you too ♥

Ronan: ♥ ♥ ♥

I tucked my phone back into the pocket of the new pink dress I'd bought for Ronan's celebration party. I wanted to surprise Ronan with something new and pretty. It had a sweetheart bodice and a billowy skirt with lots of waving folds, the hem stopping a few inches above my knees. He would love this dress.

Hiking my purse back on my shoulder, I left the bathroom and returned to Lauren to find a group of guys gathered around her. No surprise there. When one of them stepped back to make room for me, I instantly felt the buzz of supernatural energy. When I sat down and turned to get a look at them, my stomach flipped sickeningly.

They were the Iron Claws team.

"Cici, these handsome gentlemen wanted to join us."

Baron, the one I recognized first, stood closer to me. "We know each other already, actually. Don't we, *Cici?*"

Lauren instantly picked up on the anxious vibes I must've been projecting.

"You know them?" she asked, her brow pinching with a slight frown.

"We do. Her boyfriend's team just won the wolf cage championship." Baron smiled, but my radar was on full alert, even as he reached over with his bottled beer and clinked it with the sangria I held carelessly in both my hands, needing to hold on to something. "No hard feelings, though." He didn't mean it. I could read him too well, but I was trying to figure out how to extricate ourselves without making a scene.

"Lauren, I think we should go." I glanced around nervously. The bar was packed, and I didn't want to be dramatic, but my instincts were telling me to get the hell out of there. *Now.*

"Aww, not yet," protested Baron with a smile. "How about a toast, guys? To the new champions of the NOWFC."

They tapped beer bottles and drank while my heart raced wildly. Automatically, I took a sip while Lauren knocked the rest of hers back.

"I think that's enough for us, guys," she said with a bang of her empty glass on the bar.

She jumped up from her stool and instantly stumbled forward. I leaped to my feet and lunged for her, as did that big guy on their team, Carter.

"Lauren!" I reached for her, but Carter held her up, her body sagging against him. She was completely knocked out.

"What happened?" I asked, realizing my speech slurred.

"One more sip, sweetheart." Baron gripped me around the waist and shoved my drink up to my mouth.

"No." I tried to push it away, but my arms were weak, my limbs feeling heavy. Some of the drink slid into my mouth before I jerked my head away.

"What a stroke of luck, eh, Baron?" one of his teammates said as my knees buckled beneath me.

Baron caught me as I fell. "For us, it sure as fuck is. But not for her."

Then all went dark as their laughter echoed around me.

CHAPTER 29

~RONAN~

"WE'VE GOT A LOT MORE TRAINING TO DO TO COMPETE AT STATE," I told the guys, specifically Zack who had just recounted our easy wins three days ago.

"Yeah, yeah." Zack waved me off. "Let me just enjoy the victory a while longer." He turned to the bartender. "How about another round of those old-fashioneds? Those were fire."

Diego was at the bar, laughing something Boomer said under his breath while he drummed his sticks on the bar, chatting with Elizabeth while she worked.

The owner of Howler's, one of Uncle Shane's buddies, had closed the bar just for our friends and the guys at Blood Moon Body Shop. Rhett had even bought my first drink, finally coming around since he knew—like everybody else—that Celine wasn't just my girlfriend but my mate.

I had a speech prepared, mostly a thank-you to the guys for joining my team and working their hearts out, but also to Celine for supporting me. But I couldn't make the speech without my girl here.

"Have you looked at the top teams headed to the state championship?" asked Ty.

We'd moved to one of the tall tables near the dance floor. No one was dancing, but I had a good view of the door from here.

"Of course I have."

He chuckled. "And do we have a shot?"

"Oh yeah. More than a shot. But we'll be putting in more time at the gym."

"Not a problem. I enjoy the workouts."

We both looked at the door when it opened. Joaquin strode directly to us and said "Congratulations" rather stiffly, which was kind of his usual demeanor, then walked to the bar to join Diego and Boomer. Ty's gaze followed him.

"Hey, Ronan!" shouted Zack, carrying a large white bakery box from the back room toward us. "When's your girl getting here? We need to cut the cake."

"You got a cake?" Ty asked as Bowie sauntered over.

"Of course I did. Check it out." He set it on the tall table next to us.

When he flipped open the top, Bowie peered over Zack's shoulder and laughed.

"Righteous, huh?"

The cake was a monstrosity. Covered in red icing, there was a howling gray wolf's head coming out of the center. Beneath the wolf was a giant number one badge and written in script was *The Blood Moon Crew will make you black and blue.*

"Wow," said Ty dryly. "Don't quit your day job to become a poet."

"What's wrong with my poetry? It rhymes."

We laughed as my phone buzzed in my pocket.

I tuned them out to step away, expecting Celine to be texting that she was on her way or almost here. But it was a video sent from a blocked number. The frozen image on the video with the play symbol on the top sent an icy chill through my blood.

I stepped farther away and clicked play.

"Hey there, Reed," said Baron in a friendly manner, his eyes glassy with drink. He had his arm around *Celine's* shoulders.

Her eyes were closed, and she was slumped against him. She was unconscious. My entire body went cold, my heart rate tripling as my brain tried to make sense of what I was seeing. I was so paralyzed I missed whatever the fuck Baron was saying. I quickly dragged my thumb across the bottom to start the video over.

"Hey there, Reed. Look who we found at one of our favorite bars." He squeezed her closer, and her head rolled to the side on his shoulder. "Such a great coincidence. She was partying with a friend, but we decided they'd have more fun partying with us."

The person holding the phone panned the screen to the right where a brunette was passed out on her back on another sofa. That must be her friend Lauren.

In the background of what looked like some sort of small cabin—the walls were all wood with two deer heads mounted on one—I saw Nate and Adam shooting drinks at a card table. That meant Carter was recording with the phone.

The screen panned back to where Baron was lifting Celine's legs to drape over his lap.

A REBEL WITHOUT CLAWS

I was going to vomit. No, I was going to *kill* him.

His smile fell, and I saw the cold asshole I was used to.

"You and your team lost me a lot of fucking money. Lost my father even more."

He wasn't just talking about the winner's pot of money, our take of the door. His father likely bet far too much that his son's team would win.

"But no worries, Reed. I'm going to let your girl pay me back."

Acid burned a hole in my stomach.

He leaned his face toward her hair and inhaled. "Damn. She smells pretty good," he said so fucking casually it gutted me.

Carter laughed at that while Celine's eyelids fluttered.

"That's enough," Baron told Carter, pushing to a stand. Celine slumped over on her side. "Time to get this party started."

Then the video went blank.

"Ronan?" It was Ty. "What's wrong?"

I realized then that I was growling—a low, menacing sound vibrating in my chest.

"What's going on?" Bowie walked closer.

I opened the Life360 app. Her phone was on a highway outside the city near a wooded, swampy area. But it wasn't moving at all. They probably found it on her and tossed it out the window. But at least that gave me a direction.

My wolf growled again, pacing madly in my mind. We'd find her as soon as were close enough to catch her scent. That's all I needed. A small whiff of her within a couple of miles and I could track her. But she could be fifty or a hundred miles from her phone. Still, that was my starting point. I had to get there *now*.

291

Ignoring the guys, frowning and wondering what the hell was up, I replayed the video to check for any clues I might have missed. I didn't care they were watching over my shoulder.

Blocking out Baron and the helpless sight of Celine before I went fucking feral, I focused on the background, noting a rifle cabinet on a wall and fishing rods leaning in a corner. It was a hunting camp.

"What the fuck?" Zack muttered.

My chest was heaving as I turned, tucked my phone in my pocket, and started for the door.

"Wait, Ronan!" Ty was on my heels, grabbing my shoulder.

I spun and snarled. "Get the fuck off me!"

He flinched and put up his palms while I panted through the panic taking hold of me.

"We just want to help, man."

"That looked like a hunting cabin," said Bowie.

"Help with what?" asked Diego. He, Boomer, and Joaquin had wandered over. So had Uncle Shane, Rhett, and a few of their friends who worked at the body shop.

I stared at Diego, so distraught I couldn't even say it. Zack was the one who did.

"Those assholes we fought in the cage have your sister."

"*My* sister?" Diego's eyes instantly flared wolf-gold, and his canines extended.

"They sent him a video," added Bowie.

"What's on the fucking video?" demanded Joaquin.

"We don't have time!" I roared, my voice dropping several decibels. "I know where her phone is."

I checked the app to see if her phone had moved. It hadn't, and there was no store or house even close to where it was surrounded by woods.

Bowie looked over my shoulder at the phone. "That's close to Bayou Segnette, the state park. There are several hunting camps near there. My uncle owns one. Lots of werewolves use them for the full moon."

"Take me there," I demanded, noting my wolf had taken over my voice completely.

Bowie and I were running out the door and so was everyone else. After piling into trucks and SUVs, we took off with Bowie in the lead.

I was in the front passenger seat while Ty, Zack, and Diego were in back.

"I'm starting directions to her phone," I told Bowie. "We can find her from there."

I slammed my phone on his console, my entire body trembling.

"Easy, Ronan," said Ty from the back seat. "Let's hold it together until we get there."

He seemed nervous that I was close to shifting, and that wouldn't go well in the confines of this SUV, especially in the fierce rage that filled me and had my body trembling.

I gripped my knees, grunting when my nails transformed into claws. That was the first physical sign I'd seen of my wolf in decades. And I welcomed him. I needed him. *She* needed him.

I felt like I was going into shock, but I was fully aware of every sight and sound around me. Actually, even more so than usual. Magic hummed under my skin. I felt like . . .

"Fuck," I muttered in a guttural voice, "I'm about to shift. He's coming."

"Hang on." Diego's voice had gone deep, too, as he reached forward and planted his hand on my shoulder, his claws curling into my shirt. "Not yet."

Strangely, his touch grounded me, kept me calm despite the terror and rage trying to split me open and release the wolf. Perhaps it was his shared DNA with Celine, I wasn't sure. But it worked.

I closed my eyes, trying to control the fury spiraling through me, like a whip lashing my spine, urging me to let go. Breathing through the expanding pressure, I watched the icon on my GPS as we drew closer to her phone.

Then my mind went to her—my sweet Celine. Was she afraid? Were they hurting her right now?

I was going to rip them apart limb from limb. Literally. Deep down, a voice I'd heard only a handful of times whispered, "*Yes.*"

"It's up ahead on the right." Bowie snapped me to full alertness.

We were on a country road leading into swampy woods. Bowie veered onto the shoulder where my GPS showed we were right next to Celine.

My heart twisted because I knew she wasn't here. Only her phone they'd tossed out the fucking window as they took her somewhere against her will.

Jumping out before Bowie had come to a full stop, I instantly found it, her scent heavy on the cell phone. It had landed in a weeded area, suffering only a small crack in the corner. But I smelled another scent I knew quite well on the phone—Baron.

A dark, rumbling growl rolled up my throat. A flash of heat swept through my body, flaring to a bright, sharp pain.

It's happening.

A pop, then another and another as pain seared me, my bones breaking and realigning, my chest and limbs stretching and growing, ripping through my clothes. The transformation was agony for a few seconds until I finally felt him take full control.

Mate. I inhale. *She is near. Her sweet scent is on the wind.*

"Goddamn." **My packmate speaks. I turn. It is the one who behaves like a pup.** "What the fuck, Ronan?"

He is shocked at my size. And afraid.

He should be. All should fear me and submit before me.

Their eyes are bright with their wolves as they shift into beasts—my brethren. Yet, I still tower over them all. I accept their presence for they will help their alpha hunt and draw blood.

Snapping my head toward the woods, I breathe deep. I smell her. She is near. And so are the enemies.

CHAPTER 30

~CELINE~

THEIR VOICES WERE MUFFLED AT FIRST AND THEN SO LOUD, LAUGHING close by. I was lying on my side on a couch in some place I'd never been.

I didn't sit up, knowing I was in danger. Though my mind was foggy, I remembered what happened at the bar and realized they'd taken us somewhere else.

They were at a table, two sitting, two standing, doing shots of something.

"Dude, he's probably crying right now. Freaking the fuck out."

That was the big one's voice. Carter.

"Wait till we send him the next video." That was Baron.

"Wish I could see his face for that," said another I didn't recognize. They all laughed louder.

Without moving my head so I didn't draw their attention, I looked around the room.

Lauren. She was on the sofa adjacent to the one I was on. There was a back door in the corner of the room opposite the table where the men were.

"Come on. One more," said one of them.

They were loud and cheering, "Go, go, go" as someone funneled a beer.

Taking a chance, I slid off my sofa and crawled behind the sofa where Lauren was passed out. I bit my lip to keep from making a sound as a tear slid down my cheek. I'd get help and come back for Lauren. I had to.

My limbs were still heavy and my head fuzzy from the roofie, but I kept my focus on the door and made my way silently across the thin carpet. I counted myself lucky they were obviously drunk, or they would've heard me already. Slowly, hand trembling and heart pounding, I reached for the knob, still on all fours, and opened the door, then crept out.

It was dark as I pushed to my feet, swaying. A nearly full moon glowed in the clear night sky, shining on my surroundings. Trucks, a small shack, and beyond that, woods.

Stumbling, I ran, only to realize I had bare feet. My shoes either fell off or were taken off at some point, but I didn't care. I ran as fast as I could, straight into the line of trees across the gravel road leading to this place.

I whimpered when I stepped on a jagged piece of gravel, but still I ran, quickly disappearing into the shadow of trees.

"Celine!" one of my captors yelled from the direction of their cabin behind me.

Panting, I didn't even look back, tearing through the brush. Then I stepped into shallow, murky water.

"Shit," I muttered, knowing I must be in the wetlands somewhere outside the city.

"Where are youuuuuu?" one of them called in a singsong voice. It echoed creepily around me. Their laughter floated closer. They were chasing after me.

I sloshed through the water, not even stopping when something big splashed in the water to my left. Turning right, I waded into the calf-deep water, stepping on a sharp stick, but didn't stop.

Then the swampy water ended, and I was back on dry land, hoping the water masked my scent. I could hear them somewhere behind me, laughing and crashing through the underbrush.

"That's okay, sweetheart!" Baron called. "We like a good chase!"

"You better ruuuuuun, Celiiiiine!" one of them hooted.

"Run, fast!" called another.

More laughter, but then it changed to growls. A sharp wave of magic sparked the air, an aggressive energy flowing at my back. They were shifting.

"No, no, no," I whimpered.

I flew through the woods, keeping to the strip of land that wound through the swamp, but I knew it was hopeless. I couldn't outrun werewolves. I'd seen the beasts that my father and brothers became. I was going to die out here.

Moonlight beamed down through the trees, guiding my way. I sprinted on, my foot aching, likely bleeding, but I didn't care as I fled into a clearing. Panting and out of breath, my entire body shaking with adrenaline and terror, I started again toward the other side of the clearing, knowing wherever I ran, I was in danger.

Then a deep growl stopped me in my tracks halfway across the small meadow. Heaving deep breaths, I backed away from the sound as a gray werewolf stepped from the shadows. It was Baron. He had the same hazy gray aura as he did in human form. Then another leaped from the right, a larger, brawny werewolf. He was that big guy of their group, Carter. The other two surrounded me from behind, their jaws slack, tongues lolling between rows of sharp fangs.

Never in my life would I have imagined a death like this. I'd never feared werewolves. Even as the terrifying killing machines they were, the men I loved most in my life were these same ferocious creatures. And they would never hurt me.

They gray one—Baron—fell to all fours, his head still a foot taller than me, and then he circled closer. He panted in a way that made his wide, sharp-fanged mouth look as if he were smiling maliciously.

"Please, don't." I raised my palms, wishing I could touch his fur long enough to give him a calming spell. But that wouldn't be enough. There was hatred in his eyes. He planned to make me suffer because of Ronan; that was certain.

Ronan. I sobbed, wishing I could see him one last time, wishing I could tell him that I loved him and see the love shine back in his eyes.

Baron's wolf growled, his eyes narrowing. I didn't want to feel fear at my death, so I tilted my head back and stared up at the moon. I prayed to the heavens for peace and no pain, for it to be quick. I prayed for my family and friends, that they would have beautiful, blessed lives—even without me.

And I prayed for Ronan hardest of all. I prayed he would not mourn forever, that this would not break him, and he would know I'd always love him, even when I moved on to the afterworld.

As I felt Baron's hot breath on my throat, his growl vibrating the air, I thought only of peace and—

A sudden crash of noise barreled through the woods— branches breaking, water splashing, and a wolf growling. Then a quick flash of fur as a werewolf leaped into the clearing and pushed me roughly to the side. I fell as he whipped around to face the others.

The creature was *huge*. With silvery-white fur, he reared up onto two legs and roared at Baron's beast. He was the biggest wolf I had ever seen, towering over me at least sixteen feet above the ground. He was bigger than my brothers, even my dad.

I only had a few seconds to take him in before he attacked the burly werewolf, Carter, his entire jaw engulfing his shoulder with a sharp snap and a crack of bones. Carter yipped and clawed. The white werewolf tossed him into a tree where he fell and lay still. The white wolf looked at the two smaller werewolves and snarled, baring finger-long fangs. Quickly, the two smaller ones turned and fled back into the woods.

Without warning, the white wolf leaped for Baron, who dodged to the left, but not fast enough. The giant werewolf swiped out with one arm and clawed deep gashes across Baron's chest. He yelped and snapped back, his jaws clacking on air.

My defender—up on hind legs planted wide, his arms with claw-tipped hands opened, poised to attack—bared his teeth and growled. It was a spine-tingling sound that brushed gooseflesh along my skin. He moved to put his body between me and Baron.

I gasped. How could I not know him at once?

"Ronan!"

He swiveled his enormous head to look at me, his snarl dying. His eyes were glacial blue—piercing, burning. I'd seen that shade before. He stared at me, blinked once, then huffed a breath. With a swift jerk, he turned and pounced on Baron in one leap. Baron screeched a high-pitched yelp as Ronan tore into him with his teeth.

They rolled in a tangle of guttural snarls and gruesome biting sounds. I scrambled onto my feet and pushed back to the trunk of a tree.

Suddenly, one, then two, then three, four, five werewolves lunged into the clearing. I recognized my brothers before they shot off with Diego in the lead after the other two captors who'd fled into the swamp. Joaquin stopped at the edge of the clearing, his russet-haired wolf form almost regal.

I nodded to him to assure him that I was okay, then he raced into the shadows. There were snarls and gnashing of teeth when three wolves I didn't recognize attacked Ronan.

"Stop!"

They kept on, shoving and clawing at him. Ronan turned on them with a ferocious growl. Then I realized why they were trying to stop him. His muzzle was stained red with blood. He was killing Baron, if he hadn't already. Baron lay unmoving beneath him.

Kidnapping wouldn't justify murder. And while Baron and his friends may have planned worse for me and Lauren, they hadn't been able to go through with it. I didn't want this burden on Ronan, nor did I want his life—or our life together—to be tarnished or sidetracked with him suffering in the supernatural court system.

Even though my aunt Jules was the Enforcer of our laws here, she couldn't simply look the other way. Not even for me.

"Ronan!" I shouted.

The white werewolf instantly looked at me.

"No, Ronan." I pushed off the tree, wincing at the pain in my foot as I limped toward him.

He lowered to all fours and strode between them, snapping his teeth at a big black werewolf who I suspected was Bowie. He backed away as Ronan made his way to me, a constant growl rumbling deep and low.

"Oh, Ronan." His aura was flame-red, vibrating with rage. "I'm okay," I assured him.

Stepping closer, I buried my face in his fur and wrapped my arms around his neck as far as they would go. "I'm okay. Shhhh."

I managed to summon my serenity spell and poured it into him. His growl transformed slowly into that soothing purr.

"I'm so glad you came," I said, wanting to laugh at such an understatement, but I was too exhausted by both fear and relief.

He eased back and lowered until his belly was on the ground, then he nudged me to his side. It took me a second to realize what he wanted.

Slowly, I stepped to his side and climbed onto his back, digging my fingers into his fur to hold on. When he stood, he stared at the three other wolves in the circle of moonlight. They were his teammates. I recognized their auras, which were all the same hue as when they were in human form. Only Ronan's was currently darker and angrier than normal.

His muscles tensed beneath me, and then he arched his neck toward the moon and howled. It was a long, sonorous, lovely sound, a well of emotion I'd never quite felt in such a powerful rush. The howl lingered until it faded to a sad, hoarse cry.

When it ended, there was a brief moment of silence before the other three—Bowie, Zack, and Ty—lifted their heads to the starry night sky and let their voices be heard too. All three howled in return, an answer to their friend who'd become more and who needed to feel their kinship in this moment of reckoning.

For this was a reckoning for Ronan—the moment where he and his wolf were one, where his past loss and pain and shame of regret were washed away when he became all that he could be . . . to save me.

He snuffed the air and walked across the clearing. As we passed the others, I told them, "Please go get my friend in the cabin. They left her there."

Bowie growled and left first, the other two disappearing after him.

Ronan looked back over his shoulder at me. Those pale-blue eyes held nothing but warmth, and I marveled that for someone who'd never truly known his wolf this way, he had full control of both man and beast. How could I expect anything less of him?

"I'm fine," I assured him. "I can hold on."

When I smiled, he blinked and snuffed the air, and then he ran.

Curling my fingers into his fur and digging my heels into his flank, I held on tight. I couldn't see hardly anything at all as the woods whizzed by, snatches of moonlight illuminating between the trees. Occasionally, I'd hear a werewolf howl in the far distance. I hoped that meant they found Lauren and the other two who'd fled.

Diego and Joaquin would know what to do. They'd immediately contact my aunt and get them to healers. I hoped they weren't dead. Not because I cared so much about their lives, but because I cared too much about Ronan's. He didn't need another trial to suffer through.

While he was loud before when he crashed through the trees to my rescue, now he was silent as he slipped through the swampy woods. Ten minutes later, he came out onto a road. He turned left and trotted along the blacktop, his claws clicking on the cement as the moon guided our way.

When I saw the outline of trucks and SUVs up ahead, I instantly recognized Bowie's and my brother's. I sat up straight when Ronan slowed to a stop, then I slid off his side. He turned and snuffed again, then nuzzled me with his snout, nudging me toward Bowie's vehicle. I backed up to the hood.

Werewolves weren't entirely wolves or men, somewhere in between, but there was a beauty about Ronan as he stood on all fours, staring at me with those clear, blue eyes.

He looked at me so intently, and I stared right back.

"You're quite beautiful, Ronan. As a man and a wolf."

I swear he arched a brow at me. Then he rose up onto his hind legs, showing his magnificence fully to me. I almost thought he was showing off until I heard the splintering of bones. He shifted back quickly and immediately gripped my upper arms, leaning into me and sniffing like he was still in wolf form.

"I smell blood." His eyes were still the color of ice.

"You're covered in it," I told him, noting his jaw, neck, and chest bore the signs of the violence with Baron.

He huffed a breath, his mannerisms still more like the wolf than himself. "He's lucky to be alive."

"And is he?" I asked gently. "Still alive?"

"For now."

I didn't question any more because then he was sniffing me again along my shoulder and down to my ribs.

"It's my foot." I lifted the injured one. "I stepped on a rock when I ran away."

That menacing growl vibrated again in his chest as he swept me into his arms and carried me to Bowie's SUV. Once he belted me into the passenger's seat and ran around to the driver's seat, still completely naked, he cranked it up with the key fob sitting in the console and tore it around to head the other direction.

"What about Bowie and them?" My voice was shaking now. The shock of what I'd escaped and witnessed had just caught up to me.

"They'll find a way. Don't worry."

I nodded, a tear sliding down my cheek at the memory of waking in that haze and finding Lauren unconscious and both of us in dire danger.

Ronan swerved over to the side of the road, jerked it into park, and hauled me sideways into his lap. He hugged me close, tucking my head beneath his chin. "You're all right. You're okay."

I sank my fingers into his shoulder and let the tears come, knowing it was the release that would set me straight.

Then his voice quivered. "Aren't you? Okay?"

I realized what he must've thought, what they might've done before he arrived. Looking up at him, I nodded. "Yes, Ronan. I'm all right, thanks to you. How did you find us?"

"Your phone."

"What?"

"They threw your phone out the window. But the fucking idiots didn't do it far enough away."

"Oh." I smiled, thanking the Goddess that I'd taken that step to connect on Life360 with him. "That was lucky." But not really. It was more than luck.

He held me close while I let the tears go and took solace in his arms. His labored breathing finally slowed until we were both simply quiet and content, basking in the safety of being in each other's arms.

Then he spoke softly. "My mom had corrected me in the car. She told me to put something away. I lashed out at her with claws. I didn't mean to, but my wolf was aggressive and defensive then."

It took me only a few seconds to realize he was confessing his most tragic moment, that he needed to tell me this. "In the accident, you mean? When she died?"

"Yes." He continued to soothe a hand up and down my spine, petting me, but it was he who needed the soothing now. "Right at the moment I swiped at her, a deer ran into the road. She swerved, and we hit a tree." He swallowed audibly. "I thought I'd killed her. So my wolf went away, or I sent him away. Or both."

"You didn't kill her." I lifted my head to look at him. "You know that, don't you?"

His smile was sad. "I do now, after quite a few sessions in therapy."

He cupped my cheek, and I leaned into it.

"But he finally came back to you tonight," I noted softly. "That's remarkable, isn't it?"

He stroked his thumb along my cheek, his eyes now a deeper shade, a somber expression engulfing his face. "He had to. His mate needed him."

"I'll always need you, Ronan. I promise."

He nuzzled into my hair, which was a horrid mess, but he didn't seem to care, taking gulping breaths of me.

"And I'll always be here." He hugged me tighter against him, his hand cradling the back of my head. "I promise." He heaved out a shaky sigh. "I was scared too."

"I know. But I'm okay. We're both okay."

We remained there for some time, holding one another while I spread my aura magic, wrapping it around us both in a blanket of safety and serenity. It was more apparent than ever in that moment that this was how our life would go. One might fall or be afraid or sad, and the other would pick them up and reassure them with love and tenderness.

In a million years, I'd have never thought that the sexy, bruised-up werewolf I met in the body shop garage that morning would be my perfect equal and partner.

My magic hummed as it swirled around us, a golden-orange glow filling the small cab of the car. And warming both of us with the promises of love made between us.

EPILOGUE

~RONAN~

I watched her expression transform from confusion to complete delight, and that's all it took for my heart to trip faster. I wasn't sure how long it would take for my body to calm down in her presence or to stop reacting when she entered a room, but I hoped it never did.

"It's the same flower on my teacup, isn't it?" she guessed correctly as she leaned over to sniff the blooming pink flowers.

"Yes. It's called the desert rose." I watched her, sitting on our new sofa in our new house on Camp Street, admiring the potted plant I'd given her. "It grows in Amarillo where I lived and in the cemetery where my mom is buried."

She looked up with those wide, enchanting eyes.

"And the scent has always reminded me of you," I added.

She blinked away the glassiness of tears before they fell. "Well, I'm not like my aunt Isadora. I don't have a green thumb, but I will take precious care of this one." She picked it up and set it in the window, then walked over to me and wrapped her arms around my waist. "Thank you for such a sweet gift."

I kissed her, soft at first, but then she touched her tongue to my lips, and that was all it took for me to bury my fingers in her hair and kiss her hard, delving deep.

Knock, knock, knock.

We both jumped.

"My parents," she said.

"Your parents?"

"They wanted to wish us well on our first night in our new house."

But when I opened the door, it wasn't just her parents. Diego, Joaquin, Zack, Bowie, and Samara stepped in before them.

"Hey, man." Diego clapped me on the shoulder, a twelve-pack of bottled Abita Amber in the other hand.

"Damn, Ronan! This place is *nice*," said Zack with a grin, also carrying beer.

"Sweet," said Bowie behind him. "Nice place for parties."

"There will be no parties," said Celine in her matter-of-fact tone that made me want to shoo them all out of our house so I could get her naked in our bedroom. I'd been planning to tonight, but now we had all these people here.

Samara squealed and hugged Celine, whispering to her, "Have you two christened every room yet?"

"*Samara.*" Celine swatted her away.

She giggled as she walked off with some kind of chocolate dessert.

Joaquin carried a platter of what looked like his famous brisket sandwiches. He simply nodded and said, "I'll put these in the kitchen."

"I thought we were keeping it just us for the housewarming," I whispered down to Celine, who curled an arm around my waist.

She shrugged. "You're a part of a much larger family now, babe. This is what they do. Invade your space. With food and love." She smiled brightly, and I wasn't sure if it was that or the words she'd said that made my heart flutter.

"*Babe?* Awww. Y'all are so cute," said her mom, Evie, as she gave me a kiss on the cheek, carrying in another covered dish. "Aunt Jules sent over her crawfish macaroni and cheese." Then she gasped. "Oh, Celine! It's gorgeous. Come and give me the tour."

I closed the door behind Mateo, who was last to enter. "Hello, Ronan."

He'd become much more accepting of my presence, especially after what had happened with Baron and his teammates. I was afraid he would blame me for getting her into that mess, like I did myself for a while until Dr. Theriot set me straight, informing me over and over that I wasn't responsible for other people's actions. That had taken several months, but I was finally starting to believe it.

"Hi, Mateo." I shook his hand. "Want the tour?"

"Might as well."

We followed Celine as she went from room to room, showing off the house we'd bought together. My winnings in the final fight for the regional championship with NOWFC, along with the state championship we'd won last month, had given me a sizable amount to invest. Celine and I didn't want to wait until we were married, and Uncle Shane was sick of our sleepovers. He said he couldn't handle one more night bunking somewhere else since he always left when she came over.

Celine and I had talked about marriage many times now, but we decided to wait until after the nationals. Besides, I was still looking for the perfect ring. Celine was so unique and precious that I wanted the ring to be the same.

When Celine led her mother and Samara upstairs, Mateo motioned for me to stay behind. All the guys stayed as well. We'd been waiting on final news about Baron and his teammates.

That night of the incident with Celine, they'd been turned over to the supernatural authorities, who'd kept them jailed to await trial. Baron and Carter had needed extensive time and numerous healing sessions from Conduit witches before that could happen. If anyone thought I was sorry about that, they'd be wrong.

The other two, Adam and Nate, had been roughed up as well, but no one on the Supernatural Police Force had batted an eye. What the four of them had done was unforgivable, and what they might have done if we hadn't arrived in time would've put them away for life, if not given the death penalty. As it was, they'd had their trial in Baton Rouge since it was decided Celine's aunt couldn't be impartial here in New Orleans—a closed trial as all SPF court hearings were—and we'd been awaiting sentencing.

"Fifteen years," said Celine's father, "for Hammond's team-mates and twenty for Hammond since he was apparently the one proven to be in possession of the drugs that were used."

"Where will they serve the sentence?" I asked, somehow managing to keep my voice civil.

"At the SPF prison in Texas."

I smiled, somehow finding that appropriate. I'd never done real time in prison when I lived in Texas—only overnight stays in the local human jails—but I knew the SPF prison there was a rough, scary place. It somehow felt like justice that they'd serve their sentences in my home state where life was about to get very unpleasant for the lot of them. They'd need their fighting skills, that's for damn sure.

"I'll tell Celine," I said, "later. Not tonight."

He nodded. "I don't know if I officially thanked you for that night."

"Thanked me?"

"For saving her. Diego told me that you managed to get to her first. That you were the fastest. In those situations, every second counts."

"Not just the fastest," added Diego with a sly smile. "He's the biggest werewolf I've ever seen. Bigger than you, Dad."

Mateo frowned, his eyes flashing gold. "I doubt that."

"It's true," said Zack, nudging me with his elbow. "I've never seen a fucker that big."

I tried not to grin too big.

Mateo's voice dropped rough and deep with his wolf. **"I can still kick your ass if you hurt my daughter."**

I laughed at that before adding sincerely, "You know that won't happen."

He eyed me with admiration and gave me an approving nod as the women came back down the stairs, chatting animatedly about color schemes for the bedroom.

Speaking of the bedroom, when were all of these people going to leave? I wanted her to myself.

But that wasn't to be for several more hours. As we ate and drank in our new dining area, Celine's smile brightened the room and my heart. It wasn't simply her joy that filled me that night as everyone laughed and talked around our dining room table. It was my own at finally finding somewhere I belonged.

Little did I know when I left Texas that my fresh start in a new place would lead to finding this—my mate, a family, and my home.

When the meal was over, Evie said, "Well, I think we all best be leaving so these two can have some peace and quiet in their new home."

Uncle Shane quirked a brow at me. I bit my lip as I stifled a laugh. He knew damn well that we weren't about to be peaceful or quiet.

We walked them all to the door and stood on the porch as they left through the wrought iron gate to their cars parked on the street in front of our house. I hugged Celine to my side with a hand around her waist. She had both of her arms around mine.

"That was nice," she said softly.

"It was," I agreed as the last sliver of light dimmed beyond the houses across the street.

"Oh, look," she said, pointing to our single elm tree in the front yard. "I've never seen cardinals this late at night."

When I looked, there was a red cardinal sitting on a branch, seeming to watch us. My heart expanded at the sight. The little bird hopped on another branch, chirped, then flew away, and I knew Mom had come to wish us well.

"You know," she said, "my cousin, who's a grim, often says that cardinals carry the souls of past loved ones when they want to say hello."

I hugged her closer and looked down at her. "I've heard that too."

We stared at each other for a moment, both of us feeling the presence of a visitor from the afterworld, but neither of us saying any more.

She smiled. "Let's go into the house. I've got dessert for you."

"As long as that dessert is being served on those fancy, expensive sheets in our bed, I'm fine with that."

She laughed as she took my hand and tugged me into our new home.

About the Author

JULIETTE CROSS IS A MULTI-PUBLISHED AUTHOR OF FANTASY AND paranormal romance. She's a mood reader as well as a mood writer if that wasn't obvious by her eclectic book list. She loves lazy nights with her husband, old-fashioneds, and family gatherings. Co-hosting the podcast *Smart Women Read Romance* with her niece Jessen is her favorite way to connect with the romance community and find her latest book obsession.